Return to Grace

Mandi Grace

Chapter 1

MARK

Mark crossed his arms, leaning against the rough wood of the stern of the ship, watching the shore of Calais draw closer and closer. Sailors were moving about the ship in a hurried but controlled manner as they drew closer to the wharf. Robin and Lucy were standing against the railing off to his left, farther up the ship. They both seemed annoyingly calm.

Sure, they'd made it to Calais alright, but Sir Hugh was still coming for them. They weren't safe. He was at Dover! More than likely he'd already boarded a boat and was following them across the channel. They were still in danger.

But they wouldn't have been in that position if Lucy had done as Mark had begged her to do; just kill Sir Hugh and be done with it. She'd had the shot, she just had to take it.

Watching her lean into Robin's embrace, a smile on her face, and peace in every movement of her body language, Mark dug his nails into his forearms. The anger surging through his veins was white with heat.

She let Sir Hugh live.

Mark shoved off the wooden rail and moved toward the ladder leading below deck. As he walked, the captain of *The Rose* moved past him.

"We'll be letting you and your companions off the boat first," he said, giving Mark a glance. "I'm going to tell Robin Hood."

Mark didn't respond. He made his way down the ladder quickly and then along the open room beneath the deck where all the cargo was stored.

Mark finally reached the end of the storage and found the room filled with hanging hammocks where the rest of the gang were still hiding.

"How is everything above deck?" Dusty asked as he entered the room.

"We're coming into the wharf," Mark replied. "We'll be disembarking soon."

Mark leaned against the wall, crossing his arms again. They were in Calais, but they would never be safe until Sir Hugh was dead.

Lucy had had the chance to kill him back in Dover and she'd chosen to let him live. It wasn't entirely out of character for Lucy to show such mercy; in fact, it was exactly what Lucy was always going to do. That didn't make her actions any less frustrating to Mark.

Mark clenched his hands at his sides, trying to temper the overwhelming feeling of anger that surged in his breast with more congenial feelings. He failed.

What Lucy had done could very well cost them all their lives.

Mark glanced around the small room, trying to think of something else. Dusty and Will were sitting in one corner with their son and daughter, John and Daniyah. They were all four of them calm and peaceful-looking. Mark turned away from them, disgusted with his own emotions, so contrary to the contentment he could see in their faces.

Mark should have taken the bow out of her hands, and made the shot himself. Maybe he wasn't as great a marksman as she was, but he could shoot just fine. He would have killed Sir Hugh and this nightmare would be over.

"We should all prepare to get off this boat," Little John said quietly. Mark glanced toward him, standing beside the hammock where his wife Elinor with her new baby Rachel were laying. Mark lingered on little Rachel for a moment, wishing she would never have to grow up. The world was a cruel place.

"It isn't as though we have much to gather or pack up," Allen said. He was sitting on the floor not too far from where Mark was standing, his hands full with his rambunctious twins— Edward and William—climbing all over him. The sight made Mark smile, despite the frustration pounding in his head. The two boys were as crazy as any child Mark had ever seen, other than perhaps little Marian.

Marian was feisty, just like her namesake. Mark sighed, missing once again the sister that had filled his life for so many years before her untimely death.

Lucy had chosen not to take a shot then, too, and it had cost him his sister. And now she refused to kill Sir Hugh, and it might cost him everyone he loved.

Mark took another glance around the room as his frustration mounted.

Jane stood by a hammock in which she'd placed Marian and Richard to keep them contained. Marian was talking animatedly and waving her hands all about, making the hammock rock violently beneath her. Jane caught hold of the thick fabric to keep it from tossing the two small children onto the floor.

Hearing the sound of a baby crying, Mark turned to see Much and Mary in the far corner trying to soothe their little girl.

Nearly everyone he loved was on this boat, and Sir Hugh was coming to kill them all.

The wooden door to their small room creaked open and Mark glanced over in time to see Lucy enter. He felt a hot wave of anger wash over him at the sight of her and stiffened, glaring at Robin's wife as she stepped into the room.

"We've landed. The horses are being unloaded. Robin wants to leave immediately."

As soon as Lucy had spoken, everyone moved to get up, scooping up their children and heading out of the room. Lucy caught Marian in her arms as the little girl threw herself out of the hammock she'd been in, in her eagerness to reach her mother.

Mark turned away from them all and raced up on deck. For a moment, Mark was struck with the icy wind that whipped about him and took his breath away. Then he gathered himself and took a deep breath. Their escape was far from over. He could see Robin on the wharf, surrounded by their horses, waiting.

Mark made his way over to the gangplank and down onto the dock. He swung himself up into the saddle of Jack, one of Robin's many horses. He was brown and calm and had served Mark well so far on this desperate escape from England and Sir Hugh. Mark knew he could count on Jack. Jack would probably be more likely to kill Sir Hugh than Lucy was, that was for certain.

The rest of the gang soon joined them on the wharf, and Mark reached down to pull Jane up behind him. They didn't have enough horses to go around, so Andrew's wife rode with Mark, carrying her son Richard in her arms. Andrew had been missing for months, ever since the initial ambush in Sherwood that had sent the gang fleeing England in the first place.

Robin mounted his own horse Hero, pulled his wife and daughter up behind him, and then surveyed the group. "Are we ready?"

Mark leaned forward to pat Jack's neck, trying to ignore Robin. Not because Robin was at all offensive, but because Mark couldn't bear to look at Robin's wife right now.

"Where are we going?" Little John asked from atop Ember whom he rode with his wife and baby.

"Paris," Robin replied. "I hope to be able to hide among the dense population there."

"We'll follow you anywhere, Robin," Will said. "Just lead the way."

Robin took a moment to count heads and assure himself everyone was there, and then lifted his hand in farewell to the captain of *The Rose* who was standing at the top of the gangplank, watching them.

Robin urged his mount forward and trotted down the dock toward the city of Calais and Mark followed on Jack, the rest of the gang falling in line behind them.

IDA

Ida watched her breath materialize in front of her face and then dissipate. Taking another deep breath, she rolled her shoulders, trying to ease the ache that was growing at the base of her neck. The sounds of metal striking metal and men grunting in exertion echoed across the front lawn of Gisbourne manor.

Guy had gathered a number of the villagers and farmers who worked the land of the Gisbourne estate in order to train them. Some of them had used weapons before, some of them had not. All of them needed to be prepared. It was possible that Sir Hugh, a mercenary from Scotland commissioned by King John, was coming to kill them. It was equally likely the King himself would come calling, though it might take him longer considering he was currently abroad disputing with his nephew Arthur over

6

his rights to the English throne, as well as his possession of certain lands on the continent.

Guy, Andrew, and Ida had been training these serfs for a number of hours and so far it wasn't promising. Ida had to keep reminding herself that this was only day one. Give them a week and they'd look less pathetic; a month, and maybe they'd be ready for a fight. If Sir Hugh or King John took a good long while to come and find them at Gisbourne estate, then maybe they'd be well trained before the enemy arrived. How likely that would be, though, Ida wasn't sure.

She didn't know anything for certain. Where was her husband? Nobody knew. Where were her sons? Nobody knew. What had happened to Robin and the rest of the gang? Nobody knew.

Ida wasn't alone, of course. Guy, Andrew, and Guy's wife Faith and daughter Lucy had all come to the Gisbourne estate when they'd run from that first attack in Sherwood four months before. They'd had no news of the others since that day.

Four months since she'd seen her husband, her sons, her friends.

It was hard not to be discouraged.

Ida hadn't wanted to come to Gisbourne estate at all. The plan had been to go to Scotland if the camp in Sherwood was ever discovered. Yet they hadn't gone to Scotland, they'd come here because Guy had insisted it would be safer. And so far, it had been safer. No one had followed them; no army, no mercenary, nothing.

But she had no idea what had become of her family, and they would have no idea where she was either. It was that not knowing that ate at her insides.

Guy was lucky. His wife and daughter had come with him. Ida wanted to despise him for that, among many other reasons. Some days the ache of missing her family was unbearable.

"Andrew!"

Ida pulled herself out of her reveries and turned toward the voice. Guy was walking toward Andrew some yards away from Ida. They had both been overseeing the serfs training with swords while Ida trained them with the bow. In some ways, Ida felt she was better equipped to teach them swordplay than Andrew was, but she was a far better shot than either Guy or Andrew so she absolutely had to be the one to take on that role in training.

Guy's booming voice carried easily over the cold December wind. "Keep training these men, Andrew. I'm going to go see how the fortifying of the walls and gate is going."

"Okay."

"In another fifteen minutes let the men go inside for some warmth. Faith is creating a feast for us, I've been told."

Guy turned and walked off in the direction of the gate at the front of the manor.

Ida surveyed the men scattered about Andrew, training in hand-to-hand combat. They were practicing a specific strike that Guy had demonstrated a few minutes before. Some of them seemed to be getting the hang of it, but most of them were not.

Their movements were stiff and awkward and it was painfully obvious to Ida that none of them knew how to fight. None of them would help stave off Sir Hugh's army.

Ida turned back to her own men and her make-shift archery field where targets had been hastily thrown up that morning. She had thirty or so of Guy's serfs under her instruction, and was attempting to teach them in the use of the bow. Very few arrows seemed to be hitting the targets.

They were doomed.

Ida strode forward and grabbed a man's elbow firmly, pulling it into the proper position. "Here, Matthew," Ida guided him, pulling back his arrow, "Like so." Ida watched with satisfaction as the arrow hit the target.

"Now I just have to do that on my own," Matthew grunted, smiling slightly. Ida didn't return the smile.

War was coming for them, and she knew they weren't ready for it. Yet they had no choice. There was nowhere else for them to go; they had to fortify Gisbourne estate and hope for the best.

WILL

As the sun began to set, the already freezing temperatures dropped even lower. Will transferred Fiddle's reins to one hand and wrapped his other arm tightly around his one-year-old daughter Daniyah. She was curled in a tight ball against his chest, his cloak pulled around her small frame to shield her from the unforgiving environment. Dusty's arms were wrapped around his waist from behind and he could feel his four-year-old son John's body pressed between his back and his wife. Hopefully, he was staying fairly warm sheltered between them in that manner.

"Robin, when will we find shelter for the night?" Will asked, bringing Fiddle alongside Robin's mount Hero. Little Marian was huddled between her parents in a manner similar to John.

"Soon. The next village or town that comes our way." Robin glanced over his shoulder at the rest of the gang riding behind them. "Everyone is too cold to make camp out in the wilds tonight. We need warmth and we need to regroup. There's been no sign of Sir Hugh or any other adversary yet."

They rode on in silence as darkness stole over the world. The pitiful cries of young Rachel soon broke the silence, however. The child was only two weeks old and already her life consisted of more danger and intrigue than most could boast.

On into the stillness and cold they plodded, not a word spoken between them. Everything had happened so quickly. Their reprieve in Scotland had been refreshing. That sense of peace and safety had left them all in a state of happiness. Rachel's birth had only added to their joy. Will had begun to actually picture raising his family in Scotland and letting the past go—England, Nottingham, King John, all of it. But then Sir Hugh had appeared at their doorstep with an army and the race to Dover had begun.

The tense search for a ship and the desperate escape as Sir Hugh closed in on them as they boarded—everything from the moment they left the abbey in Edinburgh until now had been one desperate escape after another. Running, always running. Will wanted to find that sense of peace again, the feeling that he could raise his children in safety.

A few lights soon became visible in the distance.

"That looks like a small village," Robin said, to no one in particular.

The group made their shivering way toward the lights. Soon Will could make out the homes from which the lights shone. Forty or so small buildings thrown together in no particular order were before them. Most of them appeared to be made of nothing more than straw and sticks. The cluster of homes was surrounded on all sides by fields where crops would be growing in warmer seasons along with a smattering of small barns set some distance from the tiny houses.

"Looks like nothing more than a farming village," Little John commented from his horse. Rachel was still crying softly in her mother's arms behind him.

"There won't be an inn," Jane said. "What do we do?"

"We seek the hospitality of a farmer," Robin said simply. He continued forward and the gang followed silently.

Robin stopped at the first home they came to and dismounted. Lucy remained on Hero's back, with Marian wrapped in her arms.

Robin went to the door and knocked. For a moment, nothing happened, but then the door slowly opened and a man stood before Robin, frowning. He was tall, muscular, with a raggedy mass of grey hair atop his head.

He eyed the group mounted on their horses suspiciously and then addressed Robin in French. "What can I do for you, sir?"

Robin replied in kind, and Will listened with interest. "We are simply travelers looking for a place to stay for the night. I know you don't have a lot of space, and I would not wish to impose on your home. If you could point us to one of your barns, that would work just as well as your house."

"What are they saying?" Dusty whispered in his ear. Will, being the son of a merchant who dealt with people from around the world, had learned rudimentary French at a young age. In more recent years Robin, the son of an Earl and early subjected to a higher education that included reading and writing English, French, and Latin had been teaching him more.

Will began to translate the conversation for his wife as Robin and the farmer discussed where they might sleep for the night and also the possibility of getting some food in their bellies.

Dusty had been raised in Palestine with Arabic as her native tongue, and she'd learned English during the Crusades, along with a smattering of French though her understanding of the latter was not enough for her to easily follow the conversation.

The farmer left the warmth of his home and led Robin on foot to a nearby building made of wood with a thatched roof while the others followed on their horses. He promised to bring something for them to eat and then headed back to his small home.

Robin pushed open the door of the small barn and leaned inside. "It will be a tight fit, but I suppose that will help with the warmth factor."

Will slid off of Fiddle's back, Daniyah still wrapped in his cloak. He caught hold of Fiddle's bridle as Dusty dismounted with John in her arms.

"Cold, Papa," Daniyah whimpered.

"I know, little one. We'll be inside soon." Will turned to Robin, "Robin, where are we keeping the horses?"

"The farmer's got one horse and a handful of goats in here," Robin replied, disappearing inside the dark building for a moment. He came back out a moment later and shrugged, which was barely noticeable in the dark. "We can fit our six horses on one side of the barn, and then huddle up on the other side to sleep."

Before long, the horses were stowed to one side with the goats, none of whom seemed particularly happy with this arrangement, and the gang huddled on the other side of the barn.

Will was in the back corner with Dusty leaning against one of his sides and Mark the other. John was in his lap, and Daniyah in Dusty's and directly before them, Allen lay stretched out on the small strip of earth that made up the floor between Will's feet and Little John's large frame. William and Edward were both huddled close to their father. On the other side of Little John were the horses and goats.

It was indeed a tight fit. Though he couldn't see in the dark, Will knew Little John's wife Elinor was next to him, Rachel —still whimpering—in her arms. Then it was Jane with little Richard in her arms, Much, Mary with her daughter, and Robin and Lucy near the door with their little Marian.

The farmer returned with a small lantern and a platter of bread and cheese.

"It's simple fare," he said in his native tongue. "And you can keep the light for the night."

"*Merci,*" Robin replied.

Robin sat in front of the door with the small lantern while Lucy distributed the bread and cheese.

"I'll take the first watch," Robin said. "Will, I'll wake you in two hours."

"Sounds good to me, Robin," Will agreed.

"Give it two hours and then wake Little John," Robin said. "Another two hours and then we'll likely be on the road again."

Will bit into his bread and shifted slightly to get comfortable, wondering if he would actually sleep at all during the two hours before his turn to keep watch. His son John, however, was already snoring against his shoulder.

MARK

Mark shifted uncomfortably, trying to stretch out his back without moving too much. His left leg had gone numb and there was a spasm in his neck that wouldn't stop bothering him. The darkness of the barn, along with the smell of horse and goat droppings made this sleeping arrangement unpleasant enough, but the limited space was worse. Mark couldn't adjust his legs without kicking Allen or Little John. He couldn't shift to the side without disturbing Will.

He'd slept for a couple of hours, as evidenced by the fact he could hear Robin snoring. That meant Will was probably awake beside him on watch, but Mark couldn't tell. It was too dark to see anyone and Will's breathing was even and calm.

Mark sighed. This was their life now. Hiding, cramped, in barns, in the middle of the continent, heading straight for the heart of France to escape the mercenary who ought to be dead.

As another spasm attacked his neck, Mark reached a hand up to massage his neck, trying not to curse Lucy aloud. His thoughts were screaming though.

If she'd killed him, this nightmare would be over.

"Can't sleep?" Will spoke softly through the darkness.

"Far too uncomfortable for that."

"Indeed. They appear to be sleeping now, but I expect everyone to be waking up from cramped muscles throughout the night," Will said. He kept his voice low, and Mark followed suit.

There was no need to wake everyone; as Will said, they'd probably get little enough sleep as it was.

"What's keeping you up?" Will asked.

"Too little space, cramped muscles; I'm uncomfortable."

"I've known you a long time, my friend," Will replied. "Longer than I've known the rest of the gang, save Little John. I know when you're upset. Your sighing just now was not about your cramped muscles."

Mark shifted, trying not to bump Allen or Little John. He didn't need an audience for this discussion. The possibility that someone was awake in that cramped, dark barn nearly kept him from responding at all, but Will's firm nudge with an elbow urged him on.

"When you were all below deck at Dover, just before we set sail . . .Sir Hugh was on the dock just below us and Lucy had a shot. She had her arrow trained on him and he was wide open. She could have killed him right then and there, and then we'd be free. But she didn't."

Will was quiet for a moment, and Mark let his anger boil in silence. Lucy was going to get them all killed.

"Killing isn't what we do, Mark. Any of us, not just Lucy. We fight because we have to, not because we enjoy it. We only kill when necessary."

"You don't think it was necessary?" Mark asked sharply. He hadn't meant to say that as loud as he did, and he found himself holding his breath afterward, waiting to see if he'd woken anyone up.

"I don't know," Will finally said. "But even if she had killed the mercenary, King John would simply hire another. It wouldn't have truly solved this issue, Mark. It would have stalled it, but not stopped it."

"Maybe."

"Regardless, it's done now. You can't blame Lucy for adhering to her beliefs, Mark. Life is precious, and Scripture tells us not to kill others. The fact that she won't deny her values even to keep us, her family, safe is admirable."

"Admirable," Mark scoffed. "Sir Hugh is going to follow us, and kill us all. There's nothing admirable in that."

Mark felt Will's hand press into his shoulder and tried to ignore the guilty feeling that flooded his mind.

"Don't let this fester, Mark."

Mark didn't respond. It was just too easy to be angry with Lucy. When his sister had died, he'd buried himself in blaming everyone involved, and in his mind that had always included Lucy. Of course, he'd later learned to forgive her but that didn't mean it wasn't an easy thing to slip back into that well of anger.

KING JOHN

King John leaned against the stone wall, watching the light from the fire in the hearth behind him cast dancing shadows on the wall beside him. Dawn was fast approaching. John was rather hoping it would stay away for once, or at the very least for a few more hours.

He was tired. Tired of this fight with Arthur and Philip. His nephew's claim to the throne of England wasn't entirely without basis; he was, after all, the son of John's elder brother. John had no inclination to give him the throne, however, which is why he'd come to France in the first place. That, and the fact that Arthur and Philip were taking the lands that belonged to him. He was here to take back his lands and to make sure his nephew understood he wasn't going to get the throne of England under any circumstances.

Both of those projects were taking more effort than John would have liked, which was why he was currently so tired he wished the sun would never rise.

There was also the matter of his current wife, and his desire to make a political marriage more to his advantage.

And then on top of all else, there was Robin Hood. He'd hired the most renown mercenary he could find to finally put an end to the outlaw who'd thwarted so many of his plans in the past, and thus far it wasn't working.

There was a sharp knock on his door, and John turned wearily toward the sound. "Come in!"

His guard, David, opened the door and let in a young man hardly more than a boy. He was shifting his feet nervously, his eyes darting all about the room.

18

"Well?"

"I have a letter for you, Sire."

"Hand it here then."

The boy seemed surprised for a moment, and then recollected himself and pulled the sealed letter from his pocket and handed it to the King.

"Now get out," John said, waving his hand lazily.

The boy darted from the room and David shut the door. John was alone again.

He sat down heavily on a nearby wooden chair which creaked beneath his weight and studied the seal on the letter he'd been given. The seal was that of William des Roches, a man who had originally sided with Arthur and Philip, both in Arthur's claim for England and in the stealing of John's lands on the continent. A man who'd been on the crusade with his brother Richard the Lion-Heart and had aided Richard in many ways. A man John despised, but a man with power and influence. A man who, three months before, John had finally convinced to join his side instead of supporting Arthur.

John wanted his supposedly 'French' lands back under his control—ignoring, for the moment, the fact that he owed feudal homage to Philip for the possession of said lands—and he wanted Arthur to no longer be a threat to his throne. More than anything else, he wanted very much to return to England. He also wanted a nap. A very long one, without fear of interruption.

Even the news that Sir Hugh had lost Robin Hood and his gang when he attacked Sherwood was hardly important anymore; John was far too exhausted to care at the moment.

John broke the seal and opened the letter. The message was simple enough:

Your Majesty, King John of England, etc.

I will most gratefully accept your offer of the lordship of Anjou. You have my full support, as you already know, in your wars with Arthur and Philip. My sources tell me that Arthur has fled to Angers, the capital of Anjou; I would suggest heading that way yourself and forcing a treaty to be signed in your favor.

William des Roches

The letter was to the point, as John had come to expect from William.

So Arthur had gone to Angers. The city of John's youth, the place where his father Henry had held court. John sighed. Of course, Arthur would flee there.

John would pursue him. He would take Arthur and he would take back his lands, and he would make sure Arthur understood once and for all who the rightful King of England was.

His long winter's nap would have to wait. Angers was now his destination.

John sighed again, tossing aside the letter. He'd have to get his army prepared and on the march again if they were going to catch Arthur.

And catch Arthur they most definitely would.

And once that was dealt with, John was going back to England and he wasn't going to be bothered again.

Chapter 2

GILBERT

Gilbert used one hand and his teeth to tighten the strip of cloth wrapped around his broken wrist and grimaced. The bones in his wrist had been shattered by a horse's hoof when he'd played dead nearly a week ago in order to escape being genuinely killed by that imbecile Sir Hugh. William, an acquaintance he'd made in Edinburgh while protecting Robin Hood and his family, had taken him to a skilled physician but what he truly needed was the healers in Robin Hood's gang. Dusty or Lucy; either would be acceptable. They both had healing abilities beyond mortal men, as far as Gilbert could tell. They would say it came from their God, but as far as Gilbert knew it could just as easily have come from fairies. He didn't care. What mattered was that they could fix his wrist.

The physician, along with William and their friend Marcus —a refugee from Nottingham also escaping Sir Hugh—had all insisted Gilbert stop using his hand at all and let his wrist bones heal. It was possible, under the right conditions, for them to fuse back together as they ought to and his wrist to be as it once was.

The physician wasn't too hopeful of that outcome, however, and expected Gilbert's hand to be relatively useless in the future.

Gilbert didn't care about letting his bones heal properly; he'd make his wrist work either way. All he had to do was find those two women in Robin Hood's gang. But in the meantime, it was impossible not to use his hand at all—he was, after all, a dual-wielding sword-for-hire.

William and Marcus had seen him off with many warnings about not overdoing it, all of which Gilbert had ignored. He was on his way to Dover. That was where Robin Hood's gang had fled after Sir Hugh found them in Edinburgh.

Gilbert's only real friend had died just outside of Edinburgh as he and Gilbert had distracted Sir Hugh's entire army in order to give Robin Hood and the others time to escape. Up until that point, none of his adventures with Robin Hood had been personal. He helped because Henry helped—and because he was bored of their mundane life before Robin Hood waltzed into their town. But now?

Now he was going to kill Sir Hugh to avenge Henry, and he was going to protect Robin Hood and his family until the day he died because that's what Henry would have wanted.

Thinking about Sir Hugh and Henry sent a sharp pain sizzling through him. The idea of lopping off the head of that knave the way Henry's head had been chopped off made him lightheaded with eagerness.

Gilbert rolled his neck and stretched out his arm, testing to see if the cloth tightly wrapped around his wrist would hold his hand in place enough to use it effectively.

It hurt, that much he couldn't deny, but he could manage it. His range of motion was limited, but he enjoyed a good challenge.

Gilbert stood, throwing his small satchel over his shoulder. When the bag slapped against the small cut on his back, he grimaced. It was the least of his wounds from that fateful day, to be sure, but it wasn't any less annoying than the others.

The worst of it, apart from the shattered wrist bones, were the two gashes in his torso. One on his chest, right side, two ribs up from the start of his rib cage. The other on his back, left side, just above his waist. The physician William had taken him to had insisted Gilbert ought to be bedridden for a month just to let those gashes heal, but Gilbert had been on the move the very next day. He didn't have time to heal in a bed. He needed to catch Sir Hugh and Robin Hood.

Those two wounds, however, never stopped throbbing. Gilbert couldn't move at all without sending flashes of heat and pain surging through his chest and back. His only other real wound, aside from simple scratches that would heal in a matter of days, was a deep cut on his right thigh that made walking less than enjoyable.

Gilbert surveyed himself, running through a mental checklist. Two swords swinging at his hips, a knife in each boot, dagger tucked into each vambrace, and a large knife at his waist, his bag of provisions slung over his shoulder.

With a slight nod to himself, Gilbert left the room and trudged down the stairs of the inn, every step sending painful vibrations through his injured thigh and pangs of vicious heat through his chest and back. Ignoring everyone gathered in the common room, he slipped outside of the tavern into the cold morning mist.

Just a few more days and he would reach Dover. From there he would pick up the trail and find Robin Hood and Sir Hugh and finally get justice for Henry.

SIR HUGH

Sir Hugh surveyed the army in front of him, column upon column of soldiers marching toward Gisbourne estate. Some had full-plated metal suits of armor, some were in more simple leather garb. His army was made up of knights and serfs and the younger sons of nobles with no lands of their own. Most of them weren't truly his men at all, but rather Torin's—his right hand and friend of many years. He'd killed the majority of his own men in Nottingham for their incompetence in catching Robin Hood and the other outlaws. Torin had helped replenish his troops for the trek to Scotland, the chase to Dover, and now the long march to Gisbourne estate.

They were still a few days away from that estate and the outlaws holed up there. Just a few more days and Sir Hugh could cross off a few more outlaws' names from the very long list.

He didn't actually have a list of names, of course. He did, however, have a vow to kill every outlaw he knew of for his sister's sake—murdered at the tender age of twelve by a truly vile man—and for his own enjoyment.

These particular outlaws were of interest to Sir Hugh for several reasons. The first simply being that King John of England had hired him specifically for the purpose of killing Robin Hood and his men. They had caused a great deal of trouble for the present king back when Richard the Lion-Heart was still alive and on his Crusade, and King John was apparently one to hold a grudge. The handful of outlaws hiding on the Gisbourne estate were part of Robin Hood's gang and therefore Sir Hugh was under obligation to kill them.

The second reason he wished to kill the outlaws at Gisbourne estate was more personal. They were friends of Robin Hood. Robin Hood had crossed him, had kidnapped his own daughter—if only for a day—, and therefore anyone connected to him must die.

The third, and no less important, reason Sir Hugh desired to kill these outlaws was because he had a reputation to uphold and they were sorely testing it.

He'd never had this much trouble chasing down the outlaws he was hired to kill. He always got the job done and got it done swiftly. It was why he was famous and why people hired him at all. But Robin Hood and his motley crew had somehow turned this simple task into a wild chase across England and Scotland, and now the coward had fled to France.

Well, never mind that. Sir Hugh would kill the few outlaws at Gisbourne estate and then be on his way to France himself. He was willing to travel a lot farther than France if it meant he could kill Robin Hood in the end. Slowly. Oh so very slowly.

The coward was going to pay dearly for kidnapping his daughter Isla. Even if said kidnapping had only lasted twenty-four hours. And ignoring the fact that Sir Hugh had, at that time, been in possession of Robin's own daughter Marian, which was hardly a relevant fact.

Robin Hood deserved to die in the most excruciating manner possible, whatever that turned out to be.

Sir Hugh had more than a few ideas for that wonderfully painful death.

At the moment, however, he had to content himself with riding through freezing weather to Gisbourne estate to kill a few outlaws connected with the man he wanted. Robin Hood could wait a few weeks.

Sir Hugh watched a few more columns of soldiers march by before urging his horse, Night, forward to the front of the army. He would be the first one through the gate of the Gisbourne estate, and he would personally kill as many of the few outlaws there as possible; his army could deal with whatever pitiful resistance in the form of serfs or hired knights that the outlaws may or may not have gathered in preparation.

At least he hoped they were preparing. It would be rather a disappointment to surprise them at Gisbourne estate and kill them with no resistance at all. Resistance made it more fun—assuming that resistance didn't lead to wild chases across multiple countries.

Sir Hugh sighed. It might be better if he did surprise them after all.

IDA

Ida leaned against Midnight's warm back, meticulously sharpening one of her daggers while the other dagger lay nonchalantly across her lap. Her breath materialized in front of her every few seconds, and her fingers were stiffening, which made her task all the more difficult. But for the most part, she was kept warm by her horse's body pressed against her back.

Training hadn't gone much better on the second day than on the first. Guy's lands were filled with farms and tiny villages, but none of his tenants had seen combat. Most had grown up on this large estate which had been home to one of the cruelest men in England, Guy's father. Simple miscreants feared crossing him and therefore left his villagers and farmers alone, and nobles feared him just as much and never sent knights or armies of any kind to bother him. The estate was then inherited by Guy, who at the time was also feared and cruel. The result was that the villagers and farmers, while not always happy were certainly always living in a state of peacefulness. They had never needed to know how to use a sword or a bow.

And now that they needed to know, it was likely too late.

Ida sighed and then watched in mild fascination as more air in front of her face froze than before.

If anyone came for them, they were doomed. But as of yet, there was no news suggesting either Sir Hugh or King John was coming their way, so she was trying to hold off on despondency for now.

Midnight shifted behind her, and Ida glanced in his direction. He seemed content enough, so she returned her focus to sharpening her dagger.

If someone had told Ida that she would be living at Gisbourne estate, spending every day in the company of the two men she disliked the most in all the world, she would have punched that person in the face for suggesting such a dismal future. A future filled with Sir Guy of Gisbourne and his lackey Andrew, but without her husband Allen and her twin boys? It was hell.

She was trying, genuinely trying, to be less bitter towards Guy. The realization she had come to not too many weeks ago that he had been tortured as a child certainly gave some explanation for the man he had been when she first met him. And the man he was now was arguably a good one.

But still.

He had tortured innocent people, he had killed Lady Marian, and he had probably been involved in the deaths of her own mother and brother. The latter being what led her father to run away from his life; Ida hadn't seen or heard from him in years. All of that felt like enough reason to continue to hate Guy, despite his tortured childhood or his current good behavior.

Ida heard the crunching of the frozen grass under a pair of boots and glanced up to see Faith coming towards her.

Ida turned her gaze back to her dagger and whetstone as Faith approached.

Faith lowered herself to the ground, giving Midnight a pat —which he rewarded with a soft nicker. "It's a bit cold to be sitting out here all alone."

Ida didn't think that comment warranted a response.

"Are you still thinking about Allen and the boys?"

"Sometimes." Ida's heart squeezed within her chest. "I miss them."

"I know." Faith placed her hand on Ida's knee. "I truly believe that they are alright, Ida. And someday God will lead them back to you."

Most of the gang carried the same calm assurance and confidence in God that Faith professed, but Ida didn't share Faith's comfort in a higher power. She had confidence in herself, and in what she could see. But that confidence wasn't as strong as it once had been. She couldn't protect her family; she didn't even know where they were. And she was breaking internally.

Ida sighed, and leaned further back against Midnight, lowering her dagger and whetstone to her lap. She could feel the annoying prick behind her eyes as tears formed. Being around Faith always made her emotional and she knew exactly why. She wanted that comfort and confidence she saw in Guy's wife. She wanted it desperately. Maybe then she wouldn't feel like dying every time she thought about her husband and sons.

"You just have to trust Him, Ida."

Ida rolled her eyes. "I'll trust Him when I have my sons in my arms again."

MARK

Mark listened to one-year-old Richard whining in his mother's arms directly behind him and knew why he'd never pursued the idea of having a family of his own. He loved all the children in the gang, and he enjoyed being an uncle for them, but he was immensely glad he didn't have to be responsible for any of them every hour of the day. Especially when they were crying as Richard was now.

Mark surveyed the landscape around him, the unfamiliar green and brown fields spreading for miles in every direction. They were still within King John's possessions, not technically within the confines of France yet, but still, Mark felt he was on foreign lands. He had rarely traveled so far from home. When Robin, Much, Allen, and Dusty had been fighting in the crusade with Richard the Lion-Heart, Mark had been forced to stay at home despite his desire to go. Everyone told him he was far too young for the war. And when they'd all come home from the war, the rebellion against the sheriff and Prince John was underway and he had no reason to go anywhere. The one adventure outside of England he had ever been on was when the gang had raced to Austria to save King Richard from the sheriff and Guy's attempt to assassinate him. His sister Marian had died instead.

And it was Lucy's fault.

If she had only taken the shot and killed Guy before he could strike Marian down!

If she had only killed Sir Hugh . . .

Of course, King John still wanted them dead, but he was busy fighting with Philip and Arthur. They would be safe in England, at least for a while until the King came back. They could be home, but instead, they were wandering through unknown territories, isolated, cold, without supplies or provisions. They were dependent on strangers and they were still running for their lives because of the threat of Sir Hugh.

Why couldn't Lucy have made just one exception to her rule, and simply killed him?

The sound of a cough carrying across the cool winter's air had Mark turning in his saddle to find the source of the sound. Richard was still whining behind his shoulder, so it wasn't him.

Directly behind Mark's horse was Allen on his own horse Outlaw, both his sons squirming in his lap. Behind Allen, Little John, Elinor, and baby Rachel were riding the mare Ember. It was Rachel who had coughed, Mark realized, as the small girl coughed again.

Little John tried to look over his shoulder to see his wife and child, to no avail. He couldn't turn his head that far around.

Mark turned to face the road ahead of him again, wishing Richard would stop crying just behind his ear so he could hear himself think. It was hard to fume about Lucy with the distraction of a crying babe so near.

"That doesn't sound good," Much said to his left as Rachel coughed again.

Mark glared ahead to where Lucy was riding behind Robin. If Rachel was getting sick due to running around Normandy with no shelter in the bitter cold, it was Lucy's fault. They could be home by now if she'd had the guts to simply kill Sir Hugh.

Lucy not killing people when she ought to was the bane of Mark's existence. First, she hadn't killed Guy when she had the chance and Mark's sister had died because of it, and now she wouldn't kill Sir Hugh and they were all suffering for it.

Mark felt a twinge of guilt at that thought. He'd learned to forgive Guy, Lucy, and himself as well, for Marian's death years before. He shouldn't be trudging up that old anger. Lucy not taking the shot had not been the deciding factor in Marian's death.

Mark had been right beside his sister, his hand on her arm, and she'd still died.

He could still remember it so clearly. Holding her arm and staring down Guy, watching in horror as his sword plunged through her, the feeling of her arm slipping out of his grasp as she fell to the ground . . .

Mark sighed, wishing he wasn't thinking about Marian like this. He didn't mind remembering her—in life, that is. It was recounting her death that made him ache.

Mark tried to turn his mind to happier thoughts, but when Rachel coughed again he couldn't stop the surge of anger toward Lucy that festered in his heart.

Mark noticed Will was dropping back from the front of the group where he'd been riding near Robin; he slowed Fiddle to a walk until he was riding beside Little John and Elinor. It only took half a second for Mark to realize this was because his wife, Dusty, riding behind him was the healer of the group.

Dusty had her hands full with her son John, but she awkwardly passed him forward to Will. For a moment there was a bit of a struggle as Will tried to both balance Daniyah and take John from Dusty without dropping either child. Once Will had ahold of both his children, Dusty reached for Rachel.

"Let me see, Elinor. I may be able to fix this before it goes any further."

Mark watched the exchange of the baby from the corner of his eye. It was far less entertaining than the shuffling of Dusty's children a moment before. Elinor leaned over and easily passed Rachel into Dusty's outstretched arms.

"What do you think it is?" Elinor's voice wavered as she questioned Dusty.

"Too much cold air, probably," Dusty replied, running her hands gently over Rachel's small frame. "Even an adult can get a cough from the thin, dry, air of winter. I'm not worried about her cough, Elinor. I just don't want her to develop something like pneumonia."

Elinor shuddered.

"And she won't," Dusty added, looking up. "I'll make sure of it."

LUCY

Night had fallen, and the gang had stopped to rest in the small town of Hesdin. It was, at last, an actual town and they had found an inn at which to stay. This meant two things: a real, warm, and filling meal before bed and also rooms with fires, beds, and an abundance of blankets.

Lucy held little Marian in her arms, humming softly as she rocked her daughter to sleep. Marian's head rested against her shoulder, and Lucy's heart swelled with love. She could hear Mark and Robin talking softly behind her.

Robin had procured three rooms for them which meant they had to share. Jane with her son, along with Allen and his twins, were staying with Elinor and Little John in one room. Lucy was mildly concerned about Elinor's baby, but Dusty—staying in the third room with Will, their two children, and Much and Mary, with their baby—was looking after baby Rachel, and Dusty was truly gifted in healing.

Lucy glanced out of the window as she rocked Marian. The handful of wooden homes she could see from the window all looked unremarkable. Simple homes with thatched roofs. There were some more elaborate homes in the city which she'd seen on their way to the inn. The most reassuring thing about this little town was that it was fortified; with a large stone wall surrounding the entirety of it and a fortress at one end of the town. They were within French territory now, as Hesdin was inside the territory of Artois. Whether Sir Hugh would be more or less likely to be welcomed in France as he was in Scotland and England remained to be seen. As of yet, there had been no sign of him following them.

Marian snored softly, so Lucy moved toward the bed to lay her down. Along with the bed in the center of the room, the innkeeper had also found a few straw mattresses and had them hauled into the gang's rooms. It was to one of these that Lucy carried Marian.

After laying Marian down, Lucy tucked the thick wool blanket up to her daughter's chin and kissed her forehead. Marian smiled dreamily, still half asleep.

Lucy sat on the edge of the straw mattress where she'd put Marian to sleep, and looked about the room. Robin had shaken off his boots and was sitting cross-legged in the center of the bed in the middle of the room, still looking far more pensive and exhausted than Lucy would like. Mark was pacing before the fire to her right.

Lucy watched for a moment as he marched first one way and then the other, clenching and unclenching his fists.

"Mark?"

"What?" he snapped, swinging around to face her, eyes flashing.

"Are you okay? You seem quite upset."

"Yeah, well, I don't know if you've noticed, but we're kind of in a bit of a bind here!"

"We're alright," Robin interjected. "Sir Hugh doesn't appear to be following us yet, we may have lost him when we started traveling through France."

"We're running for our lives, with no destination, no provisions, and now Rachel is dying!"

"That's a bit melodramatic," Lucy chuckled. "Rachel has a simple cough that Dusty can easily deal with."

"What if she can't?"

"She said it wasn't anything to worry about—"

"What if she's wrong?" Mark interrupted. "What if Rachel does die? What if the rest of us catch some disease and die?"

"Now that's just borrowing trouble," Lucy said. "No one has a disease and is dying."

"What if we did?" Mark insisted. "What if coming to France kills us? What if Sir Hugh catches up to us and kills every last one of us."

"I'm not sure I follow your reasoning," Lucy said softly. "How could France kill us? And Sir Hugh hasn't followed our trail; we've lost him."

"You don't know that!" Mark's outburst caused Marian to startle awake.

Lucy turned to her daughter and stroked her hair. "There, there, Marian. Go back to sleep, little one."

It took a minute or two, but Marian did eventually drift back to sleep.

Lucy turned back to her friend to see that Mark had moved to stand by the window overlooking the city of Hesdin.

"Mark?"

He turned toward her, his arms crossed, his expression guarded. Lucy stood and moved away from Marian's bed in the hopes of not waking her with their conversation.

"You are more worried than you need to be. Our fates are safely in the hands of our Lord—"

"But they would have been safer if you'd killed him!"

"Killed who?" Lucy asked, surprised.

"Sir Hugh!" Mark snapped.

Robin, still sitting calmly and cross-legged on the bed between Mark and Lucy, shook his head in response to Mark's pronouncement but he said nothing.

"I couldn't kill Sir Hugh anymore than I could kill you," Lucy said. "You know perfectly well that—"

"I don't need a lecture on Scripture right now, Lucy! Under ordinary circumstances, yes, I agree with you, but right now, we're running for our lives. Sir Hugh would as soon kill us as look at us and all the trouble we're in could have been over and done with back in Dover if you had just killed him." Mark took a threatening step forward. "That's all you had to do! Just kill him!"

"Mark." Robin's voice, though calm, held a note of warning.

"I'm serious!" Mark threw his hands in the air. "All this running around without purpose, constantly looking over our shoulders—Rachel's illness, whatever it turns out to be—it could have been so easily avoided!"

"Killing, unless absolutely necessary, is not our way," Robin said firmly.

"I think it *was* necessary!" Mark's hands curled to fists once again. "And besides, you're hardly one to give me a lecture on morals after kidnapping that little girl back in Nottingham!"

"Mark!" Lucy shook her head. "That's not fair."

"What happens if we all die because of what you did, or rather did *not* do, Lucy?" Mark challenged, every limb of his body seeming to vibrate with anger.

"What happens?" Lucy asked, standing beside Robin's bed now. "What happens if we all die? We go to heaven, that's what."

Mark sighed. "That's not what I meant . . .that's . . ."

"However much you may think our troubles would be over if Sir Hugh were dead," Robin spoke up, "they wouldn't be. King John is still out for our heads. And in any case, we can't change what Lucy did back in Dover. She chose not to kill him, end of story. Let's look forward, not backward now."

Mark didn't respond but spun back toward the window.

"Let it go, Mark," Robin said.

"We can't fight each other," Lucy added. "You're right; we are running for our lives. We need each other."

"Marian would have killed him."

Mark spoke softly, and at first, Lucy didn't quite register his words. Marian? Would her almost-three-year-old daughter kill a mercenary?

Lucy was still staring at Mark's back confused when she noticed her husband's hand slowly curling around the blanket it rested on. And then it dawned on her.

Marian.

Not the toddler sleeping behind her on a straw mattress, but Mark's sister. Robin's first wife.

Mark was right, of course; Marian absolutely would have killed Sir Hugh back in Dover without a second thought. But Lucy wasn't Marian.

The tension in the air was palpable. No one broke the silence.

Mark stared out the window, his shoulders tense, his arms crossed. Robin sat calm and cross-legged on the bed, his restless hands the only evidence of his inner turmoil. Lucy just stared at them, first one, and then the other.

"You don't think I should have killed him, Robin?" Lucy finally asked.

Robin shook his head. "Your strictness about following Scripture is something to be admired, not scorned."

Mark huffed at that, and Robin finally got up from the bed and walked to the window.

"Mark."

Mark ignored him.

Robin placed a hand on his friend's shoulder, but still Mark ignored him.

"You need to let this go, my friend. Lucy is not to blame for King John's hatred of us. Lucy is not to blame for Sir Hugh chasing us. Lucy is not to blame for Rachel's cough." Robin paused, and then said softly, "Lucy is not to blame for Marian's death."

"I know all that, Robin," Mark sighed. "I'm just frustrated."

"I know. Yet you can't take it out on Lucy. I won't have you talking to my wife in that manner, for one thing, and for another Lucy is right—we need each other. We can't alienate one another when we are all that we have in the world."

Mark sighed.

ROBIN

For a moment, Robin wasn't sure what Mark would do next, but then he turned and met Robin's eyes. Those eyes, so like his sister's . . .

Mark didn't say anything to Robin, but rather turned to slowly walk over to Lucy. Robin watched as Mark hesitantly offered his hand in apology.

"I shouldn't have said those things. Sorry."

Lucy smiled and, instead of taking Mark's offered hand, she threw her arms around his neck. "You're absolutely forgiven!"

The two of them settled on the bed Robin had recently vacated and spoke softly together, Mark offering more apologies for blaming Lucy for their troubles, and explaining his feelings while Lucy listened and reassured him.

Robin turned toward the window, staring out at the dark city.

He didn't often think of Marian these days. One might find that surprising, considering he heard her name nearly every waking hour due to his daughter sharing it. Yet he really didn't think of her all that much.

He might remember her smile at times, especially when Mark's expression would resemble hers in some way. And his daughter's feisty nature certainly brought his first wife to mind now and again. Yet she wasn't constantly on his mind and he'd certainly never compared Lucy's actions to what Marian might have done in her stead. Robin wished Mark hadn't done it, because now the thought was stuck in his mind.

Mark was right; Sir Hugh would have died in Dover if it had been Marian at his side and not Lucy. For that matter, Marian would have insisted on staying in Nottingham to begin with, and finding a way to defeat Sir Hugh there. And she would have; she always found a way.

So much would be different if Marian had lived. Though perhaps not for the better.

It was true that their current predicament might have been altered if it were Marian and not Lucy who was his guiding light. And yet, if Marian had lived, Robin might never have come to have a personal relationship with Jesus as it had been Lucy who had led him to that place.

Robin wasn't glad that his Marian had died, not by any means. He missed her dearly. But he believed good had come of even the dark circumstance surrounding her death. And it wasn't just him; Guy himself had found peace that he likely never would have had Marian's death not been a chapter in his story, too.

Chapter 3

IDA

Ida swung her quiver from her back and tossed it beside the wooden chair in her room before plopping into said chair. The arrows rattled around as the quiver hit the stone floor and bounced for half a second before settling, but none of the arrows came all the way out of the quiver, so Ida ignored them.

Another day of training the serfs of Gisbourne estate had come to a close. They were all gathered in the front hall where a number of tables had been lined up and piled with food for them. They would eat and then return to their homes, only to return to the manor in the morning to train again. Andrew and Sir Guy were with them now, partaking of the same meal. Ida had taken refuge in her own room rather than remain surrounded by the simple villagers and farmers.

She was hungry, and had asked a servant to bring food to her chamber, because she was in no mood to sit with the serfs in the front hall. She spent every waking hour with them, trying— mostly unsuccessfully—to teach them to use a bow, a sword, a dagger, even their own fists, and she needed some space. She couldn't talk about how wonderful the food was or what dreadful weather they were having or what their crop yields might look like a year from now when all she wanted to do was knock their heads together until they magically learned how to fight.

Ida was beginning to agree with Andrew's assessment of the situation. They were all going to die.

Seeing as Guy was usually the pessimist of their group and Andrew the cheerful eternal optimist, Ida thought it said a lot about how dire things were that Andrew was the first to say it.

They were doomed.

They'd certainly been in dire circumstances before, during the days in Sherwood during John's rebellion. But whenever things were overwhelming they could retreat to their camp, hidden away from the world and safe. There was nowhere safe now.

The estate felt safe and isolated when she first arrived, and the fact that no one came for them strengthened that idea. But now that they were preparing for the day that they were eventually found, it was becoming increasingly obvious that this was a terrible place to hide.

She was going to die here, when Sir Hugh and his army came calling. Or King John himself, if that's who arrived first. They hadn't been pestered by Sir Hugh or King John yet, but there were rumblings that an army was marching through England, and where else would an army be going? She was going to die on Gisbourne estate far from the people she loved.

Guy, Faith, and Andrew were the three members of their unconventional family that she liked the least. Guy and Andrew because of the obvious reason—they had been on the opposite side during the conflicts in Nottingham while King Richard was on his Crusade. Guy had been responsible for so much of the death and destruction in England during that time, and Andrew had simply followed his childhood friend without question, even though he didn't always agree with him. Ida wasn't sure which of them had been more at fault, but she had hated them equally for a long time. It was only since coming to Gisbourne estate that she had learned to think more kindly towards them both, after learning of their truly wretched upbringing under the abusive hand of the previous Lord Gisbourne. Even so, she liked them far less than others in the gang whom she loved dearly.

And as for Faith, despite their blossoming friendship since coming to Gisbourne estate, she was still the one person in the gang Ida found it hardest to respect. Even in her hatred of Guy, she had always been able to respect his prowess with a sword, his confidence, his authority. Faith had none of that. Faith was rather pathetic when it came down to it.

So here she was, surrounded by the three members of the gang whom she was the least fond of.

She was going to die without her closest friends nearby. Without her husband. Her sons.

Ida ached to see Allen again, to hold William and Edward one last time. She hadn't the least idea what had become of them in the months since their separation, and they wouldn't know about her whereabouts either. How long would it be before news of her death, or theirs—whichever came first—reached the ears of the other? Would Allen know she'd been killed on Gisbourne estate? Or was he even now laying dead somewhere himself?

Ida felt the first tear sliding down her cheek and she let it be. She didn't often allow herself to express her feelings, as it seemed foolish at times to be so emotional. But Faith was teaching her to let it go. And when she did cry, it would relieve her pain—if only a little.

Faith.

Ida didn't know what she was going to do about that girl. She didn't have time to think about it either, because a knock sounded at her door. When Ida answered it she found a servant girl bearing a tray of steaming food outside her chamber. Ida gratefully took the food and settled down at the table near her fireplace.

Somehow since coming to Gisbourne estate she and Faith had developed an understanding. Ida had always, since meeting the poor girl, despised Faith on some level. She was always so sweet and gentle and kind—and she never used a weapon or raised her voice. All those years living in Sherwood in the middle of a war and Faith refused to take part in any of the raids or the rescues and simply remained in the camp and prayed. It had irked Ida on some deep level that she couldn't get over.

Until now. Living here at Gisbourne estate, she and Faith had somehow managed to get on level footing. Ida couldn't explain it, but she rather liked Faith these days.

And then there was Faith's confidence in the future.
Whatever happened, they'd be alright in the end. Ida didn't
believe that, but she wished she could. Faith wasn't even bothered
by the idea that they were all about to die here. Ida wished she
could have that sort of comfort and assurance.

But she didn't have it.

They would die. Allen might never know what happened.
She'd never see him again. She'd never see her babies again.

Ida dropped the bread that she'd been holding, and it fell
to the plate. Her head sank to her chest and her shoulders shook as
large, hot tears splashed from her eyes down onto her lap. This
wasn't how her life was meant to be. She should be on her farm
with Allen and her boys, living in peace.

She didn't want to die.

GILBERT

Gilbert stood still and eyed his surroundings carefully. The
sounds of the surf crashing against the docks was only
outweighed by the shouting of sailors that echoed through the
morning air. Four ships currently lined the wharf and were being
loaded. Others were anchored a little further out in the harbor,
swaying gently with the waves. Beneath the voices of the sailors,
the whipping of sails and the creaking of wooden crates and
barrels being carried, stacked, and tossed about could be heard.

Gilbert could find nothing threatening in the appearance of

a normal day on the docks. All about him were simple sailors doing their jobs without paying him any mind.

Gilbert walked further along the street, away from the docks, ignoring the pain in his thigh. It was, at least, nothing to the injury on his chest that plagued every breath he took and left him feeling ready to faint. His fight with the mercenary Sir Hugh and his army, the fight that had killed his only true friend Henry, had left him rather battered and bruised; but he had a job to do, for Henry's sake if not his own, so his physical discomfort simply had to be ignored.

He'd been visiting every inn and tavern in Dover trying to discover if Robin Hood and his gang had made it here and if they had, where they had gone from there. As of yet, he had not had much luck. Everyone was eager to talk about Robin Hood and his remarkable exploits and how they had a cousin the great Robin Hood had actually rescued from one execution or another or a grandmother who lived in Nottingham and knew the famous outlaw personally. But no one had information on Robin's whereabouts now, in the present tense.

Gilbert approached the latest inn slowly, both hands hovering at his sides where his two swords rested against each hip. After his near-death experience fighting off an entire army single-handedly, he was far more wary than he used to be.

The only way he'd survived that day was to play dead.

And he'd lost his oldest, dearest, and possibly only real friend that day. Henry hadn't played dead, Henry had simply died.

All because of Gilbert.

They'd chosen to distract Sir Hugh so that Robin Hood could get away, but Gilbert was certain that Henry never would have done anything as foolish as attempt to stave off an entire army alone if Gilbert hadn't chosen to do so.

Gilbert and his arrogance had killed Henry.

Gilbert shook his head to clear it. It wouldn't do to think about Henry right now.

There were two men leaning against the side of the inn near the door as Gilbert approached, but they were talking amiably to each other and paid Gilbert no mind.

He entered the door, which creaked loudly as he pushed past it, and stood gazing around the common room. A handful of people were seated at various tables eating their morning repast.

No one appeared particularly threatening. No one resembled Robin Hood or his gang. No one had Sir Hugh's fiery red hair.

Gilbert sighed and made his way toward a young woman who was just setting a platter of food down before a massive man who looked like he might have simply grown in that chair and never moved from it.

"Excuse me, miss?"

She turned toward him, her braided blonde hair whipping over her shoulder in her haste. "Yes?"

"I'm trying to find a friend of mine. We were separated on the road by . . .unforeseen circumstances. I'm hoping he stopped here, as he hasn't been at the other inns I've been looking into."

"Does this friend have a name?"

Gilbert deliberated half a second whether to ask for Robin Hood or for Sir Hugh, and decided on the latter. "Sir Hugh. A Scotsman; fiery red hair. You'd certainly know him if he's staying here."

"I do remember Sir Hugh!" The woman said cheerfully. "But he isn't here anymore. There was a ruckus at the docks a week ago or so. I guess he tried to chase someone down but they got away across the channel. Not sure who he was chasing. At any rate, he went off the next day and didn't follow them. It was probably a simple misunderstanding between a Scot and an Englishman," she continued on gleefully. "We get that sort of thing all the time."

Gilbert doubted very much that a mercenary from Scotland chasing Robin Hood out of England was something the girl saw all the time. But there was hardly anyone else that Sir Hugh would be chasing down.

So Robin had gotten away after all.

"Do you know where he went? I would like to catch up to him eventually."

"Rather rude of him not to wait for you, isn't it?"

"Indeed."

"Sorry, I don't know more about your friend."

"That's alright."

Gilbert let her walk away, back toward the kitchen.

What to do next? Figure out where Sir Hugh had gone, of course. He had to pay for what he'd done to Henry.

Gilbert felt a hand on his elbow and swung around to face his attacker, half drawing one of his swords before he realized it was a small boy who was now staring at him with the widest eyes Gilbert had ever seen.

"Uh . . .sir?" the boy squeaked.

"What, lad?" Gilbert let go of his sword hilt, slightly raising his hands towards the boy, trying to look less terrifying.

"I remember Sir Hugh, too."

Gilbert studied the boy, wide-eyed and currently eyeing Gilbert's swords. Gilbert crossed his arms. The fat man at the table was watching with twinkling eyes, a chicken bone hanging out of the side of his mouth."What do you remember?"

"I ran messages for him while he was looking for someone." The boy frowned deeply and youthful anger laced his voice as he continued, "He's chasing down Robin Hood. Are you an enemy of Robin Hood?"

"Not at all. I'm his friend. I'm chasing down Sir Hugh."

The boy grinned. "Good. He got a message the day Robin crossed the channel and he went off to find the other outlaws."

"Other outlaws?"

"Sir Gisbourne and them."

"Do you know where?"

"At Gisbourne estate," the boy said simply.

Gilbert raised his eyebrows. Seriously? Sir Guy and his friends had gone home? And they didn't think that would be the first place they'd be looked for? Gilbert refrained from calling his new friends idiots, at least out loud.

"Thank you, lad." Gilbert dropped a coin in the boy's hand, causing his already wide eyes to widen further, and then he strode out of the inn.

That had been simple enough. Gilbert had expected much more of a hassle finding either Robin Hood or Sir Hugh.

At least now he had a destination, and a definite trail to follow. Sir Hugh was going to Gisbourne Estate. Robin had crossed the channel.

JANE

Despite the bitter cold, Jane removed her cloak in order to move more freely. The wind chilled her to the bone, and the hand that gripped her sword was stiff, but she ignored her discomfort.

Allen appeared equally cold and miserable, but he stretched his arms a bit and grinned at her before drawing his sword, the claymore of his father's that he'd found during their little trip to Scotland before Sir Hugh had chased them to Dover.

They were currently in a small courtyard behind the inn they were lodging at, surrounded by a small wall over which they could see the street behind and buildings stretching in either direction as far as they might look. A few windows were bright with firelight, but for the most part the city was dark and slumbering. Firelight danced from the windows of the inn to partially light the courtyard, and the moon was bright overhead.

They had stopped for the night in the city of Amiens. A river, the name of which Jane could not recall as Robin had said it so quickly in passing, and was not a word she instinctively recognized, surrounded part of the city while smaller forks broke off and divided various districts. It was a beautiful place, what little of it that Jane had seen in the dark of night. Robin had gotten them rooms at an inn once more and had ordered them all to bed. Jane, however, had dragged Allen outside—leaving his twins and her son Richard in the care of Lucy.

Jane wanted to train. She had very little knowledge or skill with weapons, but considering the current state of their lives, she knew she needed to know how to wield a sword, and to wield it well. Ida and Mark had begun training her when they first returned to Sherwood after John became King, and Jane had already lived through her first fight when Sir Hugh and his army chased them out of Sherwood shortly after that. Even so, she was woefully inadequate.

Which is why she was now shivering in the bitter cold of a wintry night in France, demanding Allen continue her training. She hadn't gone to Mark, though he had initiated her training in Sherwood, because he had been in a sour mood for several days.

Jane wasn't sure he would agree to help, and even if he did, he wouldn't be much fun to be around.

"Let's walk through a few simple stances," Allen suggested. "Get you warmed up before I teach you some simple ways to strike."

Jane followed Allen's movements closely, trying to imitate them. He had a slightly different style than Ida or Mark, which she commented on.

After a few more minutes, Allen suggested they duel for a bit. Having been thoroughly warmed up from the exertion, Jane moved more freely and confidently, though breathing was difficult given how thin and cold the air was.

"Good," Allen grunted as he blocked another strike.

Jane didn't believe him. How could it be "good" when he so easily stopped every attack? He hardly had to work at all to keep her blows in check; his wrist lazily flicking his sword to and fro to meet her oncoming blade.

"Jane, you're doing fine," Allen grinned, seeming to read her mind.

"I'm not so sure I am."

"Well, I am sure. You're far better than you were in Sherwood." Allen might have said more, but she'd managed to smack the flat of her sword against his side and he stepped away from her, grimacing.

"Alright, maybe I'm not too shabby," Jane grinned.

They continued to trade blows back and forth, and Jane thought maybe, if she kept persuading Allen to help her as they traveled along, she just might be acceptable.

Jane wondered briefly what Andrew would think of her new skills. He had, of course, been present for the start of her training back in Sherwood, but she would likely—hopefully—be much more proficient the next time she saw her husband.

If she saw her husband again.

She had no idea where Andrew was; lost somewhere in England with Guy and Ida. Or perhaps not with them at all, but alone somewhere, injured, or even dead. Surely he would have tried to get to Scotland to meet up with them when the gang gathered there immediately after Sir Hugh's attack on Sherwood. That had been the plan, after all. But he'd never showed up.

Jane felt the sharp sting of the flat of Allen's sword smack into her shoulder and winced.

"You're getting distracted," Allen commented.

"Sorry. I wasn't thinking about what I was doing anymore."

"Andrew?" Allen asked, lowering his sword. His face was shadowed in the relative darkness, but Jane could hear the heaviness in his voice. "I get it. I can hardly go a few minutes without thinking about Ida, wondering what became of her."

"Do you think we'll find them again?"

"I want to believe that."

"Me, too."

The door creaked behind them and Jane turned to see Robin exit the inn and stride towards them.

"You're going to wake the city," Robin said, "All the racket you're making with those swords. I think you've had enough training for one night; to bed with both of you."

"But we're just getting started!" Jane protested, though she was less concerned with continuing her training than simply commiserating with Allen over their lost spouses.

"You've been hacking at each other for over an hour," Robin chuckled. "Besides, the last thing we need is to draw attention to ourselves. So please, don't wake the city and go to bed."

Allen sheathed his sword and Jane reluctantly did as well, following him and Robin back inside. Now that Andrew had come to mind once more, Jane doubted she would sleep at all. As they parted to go to their separate rooms Allen gave her shoulder an encouraging squeeze.

It didn't help.

As soon as she crawled onto her straw mattress, she pulled the covers over her head and cried into her pillow.

MARK

Mark drew his whetstone slowly down his blade, watching Lucy out of the corner of his eye. She was on the other side of the room, speaking softly to Robin.

Two more days of rising early, riding all day, and finding a village or a farmhouse to house them while they slept and they had finally made it to Paris. Robin felt sure they could hide in the city without fear of being found by Sir Hugh or King John, even though King John was presently on the continent fighting with his nephew Arthur.

Paris was not a particularly beautiful city when they first entered it; the market by the gate was noisy and dirty, and the streets they traveled through in their search for a suitable inn to lodge for a few days were filled with filth. None of this sat well with Mark.

He could be home by now, living in the village of Wetherby outside of Nottingham. Though his childhood home had burned down years prior—all thanks to Sir Guy of Gisbourne—his home had been rebuilt in the same place, so his mother's garden still grew cheerfully out front, and the stream leading to the Sherwood Forest gleefully danced along the path to the woods not too far from his home. The air was clean and fresh, and certainly less smelly.

And it was Lucy's fault that he'd traded his ideal home for Paris, a city he was growing to hate though he'd only just arrived.

Little Marian came and plopped on the floor in front of him, her eyes bright. "Sword!"

Mark drew his sword closer to himself and out of reach of her outstretched hand. "Don't touch, Marian. It's sharp and it could hurt you."

Marian giggled, her eyes lighting up with mischief.

"Oohhh . . .scary!" Marian placed both hands on either side of her face, feigning a terrified expression. "Sword!" She reached for it again, so Mark set it aside, pulling Marian into his lap and tickling her while she shrieked with laughter.

Marian, he adored. Her mother, not so much.

If she'd killed Sir Hugh back in Dover, little Marian could be sleeping in her own bed tonight rather than a strange one in a strange city, surrounded by people she couldn't even understand because they spoke a strange language. It wasn't fair to Marian, or the rest of them, that Lucy had sent them on this unnecessary journey to escape the mercenary who ought to be dead by now.

They had made amends in the city of Hesdin not too long after the flight from Calais, but somehow it hadn't helped as much as Mark thought it would. That night after the argument and subsequent conversation with Lucy he'd felt better. The anger had eased and he could look her in the face and not feel an overwhelming desire to scream. But in the days that followed, his anger returned. They were still in a terrible predicament that they could have avoided if she'd simply killed the mercenary following them. However many times Mark tried to forgive her, he always came back around to that fact—she hadn't killed Sir Hugh and now they were fugitives in Paris.

GILBERT

Gilbert whistled cheerfully as he walked along, desperately trying to convince his body that he was no longer in any pain. It wasn't true, of course. The cut in his thigh still twinged when he put any weight on his leg—which made walking uncomfortable—and his wrist still bothered him. He could hardly hold anything without searing pain shooting up his arm and his wrist feeling a deep-seated burn. There was also the stab wound on his back that was taking an annoyingly long time to heal.

The dry grass crunched loudly beneath his feet as Gilbert kept up his steady pace; he wasn't about to take things slowly simply because he was wounded. The air was cold and crisp, and despite the pain he was in, he felt a level of joyful anticipation. Sir Hugh was almost in his grasp again and that man was going to die in the most pain-inflicting way that Gilbert could think of. He had several entertaining ideas in mind.

The choice Gilbert had faced in Dover had been an easy decision. Protecting Robin Hood was only in his interest because it had been Henry's interest; but avenging Henry's death by killing Sir Hugh was far more enticing. So Gilbert had set off from Dover by following Sir Hugh's army and heading toward Gisbourne estate.

ALLEN

Allen kept a tight grip on both William and Edward's hands as he followed Robin down the busy, narrow street. After nearly a week on the road, spending the night in whatever inn or farmhouse Robin could find, they were now, mercifully, in Paris at last.

The city was large, and constantly growing. Philip, unlike most of the kings before him, kept court within Paris. That, along with the ever-growing schools within different monasteries and churches—including Notre Dame—and the trading routes to various places that ran through the city, encouraged the growth of Paris.

Robin had found them rooms in one of the many inns that were scattered about Paris. They were running low on funds and were at times relying on Robin's reputation—both as an Earl and as the hero of England—to acquire what they needed. Robin, of course, had every intention of paying back everything they owed. It was simply hard to pay upfront when they were fugitives on the run.

Sometimes the mention of Robin Hood opened doors to them that were previously closed, though sometimes it slammed doors in their faces instead. However, Robin had managed to find them rooms at last and they had quickly settled into their Paris life. For the most part, that meant staying in their rooms and discussing among themselves the ever-present threat of Sir Hugh following them.

They'd been holed up in their lodgings for several days and the twins had gotten antsy. Thus, Allen had taken them for a walk which Robin had decided to join him for, apparently eager for any excuse to escape the inn. The walk, in hindsight, was perhaps not the wisest thing Allen could have done. Keeping track of his sons was hard in Nottingham where he knew every street and shop and citizen, here in Paris it was nearly impossible.

Allen had resorted to holding tightly to each son's wrist as they pulled him first one way and then the other, eager to see everything. They wanted to see all the merchants and nobles and servants that were scurrying along the narrow streets. They wanted to chase every carriage that lumbered along—and there were many—sending people diving out of its way, as it carried nobles and foreign ambassadors to various places around the city.

"Papa, look!"

"Papa, pretty lady!"

"Papa, her dress is purple!"

"I hate purple."

"Papa! There's a carriage!"

"Look at the big wheels!"

"Can I ride it?"

"Papa! She's got a gold necklace!"

"Can I have a gold necklace?"

"Papa!"

"Papa!"

Allen rarely had to respond to their outbursts, as they would immediately follow it up with another, sparing him having to make any observations and leaving him to focus on keeping hold of their hands as they strained against his grip. Edward would dart to the left and William to the right, jerking Allen in all directions in their excitement.

It was at moments like these that Allen missed his wife the most. Not because it would have been simpler if she were here, as they could each keep track of one son. No, he missed her because of how well they worked together as a team. He relied on her in all things, and this was one of those times when he would have done so.

Allen missed his wife more than words could express. It had been far too long since he had last seen her, last held her in his arms, heard her laugh or listened to her scold the boys. He ached to see her again or to at least know that she was even alive, or safe.

They had no news of Ida or the rest of the gang that had been separated from them since the escape from Sherwood and Sir Hugh. No news. And no way of obtaining news either.

Robin had been walking with Allen for a while, but when they'd turned to head back to their lodgings he had picked up his pace and was now several yards ahead. He turned and grinned at Allen every now and then, teasing him for the chaos the boys created.

"Papa! Another carriage!" Edward called out. Allen calmly pulled his son out of the way so as not to be run over and barely glanced at the carriage.

And then as it passed he felt a jolt of terror run through him.

He knew the man riding in that carriage!

Before Allen had time to think, the carriage was gone down the narrow road and William was crying out about a shiny stone he'd seen on the ground and was straining to pick up. Allen scooped his boys off the ground, tucking each under an arm, and sprinted to catch up with Robin—doing some impressive ducking and dodging around other people on the streets to avoid a collision.

"Robin!"

"What is it?" Robin slowed and turned toward him.

"Nothing good, hurry!" Allen said, running past him.

Robin gave him a questioning look but hurried after him as Allen continued his reckless charge down the street.

Allen had only met a handful of the royal family of England. He knew the late King Richard well, as he'd been one of his personal guards during the Crusades. He knew the late princess Joan, Richard's sister, and Berengaria, Richard's wife, from that same period of time. King John, on the other hand, he'd never met. He had, however, seen plenty of paintings of the man.

And now he'd seen him in person, sitting in a carriage riding through Paris and looking entirely displeased with the world.

What was he doing in Paris?

As soon as they reached the inn, Allen dropped his sons and steered them upstairs toward the rooms where the gang was living.

"What is going on?" Robin asked, following him.

"I saw King John in one of those carriages in the street," Allen said, pausing to lean against the wall and catch his breath. Running with two children in his arms was a terrible idea that he didn't intend to repeat any time soon.

"King John! Are you certain?"

"As certain as I can be of anything, Robin. He's here in Paris."

Robin moved down the hall towards their rooms, the boys having already invaded his own judging by their shrieks of laughter accompanied by Marian's young voice.

"We need to gather the gang," Robin said. "We have to discuss this."

KING JOHN

John tried to ignore the bouncing of the carriage as he made his way slowly through the narrow streets of Paris toward the French palace. He'd been sending and receiving messages with Philip for weeks and now he was headed to meet the King of France in person.

John was tired of the wars, and Philip was equally ready to bring them to an end. Thus, they were meeting to discuss possible peace. John was sure that by the time they were finished here, Philip would have renounced Arthur and removed his support of Arthur's claim to the English throne and to the English lands on the continent—leaving John's nephew alone for John to deal with —and given up his own right to the lands he'd been trying to take from John as well. That is, at least, what John was hoping would come of this meeting. It remained to be seen whether Philip would cooperate.

Given their less than satisfactory dealings up to this point, it was perhaps naive to think Philip would renounce Arthur and give up his claims to John's lands so easily, but John was tired. He wanted to end the conflict—without giving up his own rights —so that he could go home and rest. He wasn't suited to war.

When he'd tried to take over England during his brother Richard's absence, things had been more to his liking. Politics in London were easily maneuvered, and he had men like the Sheriff of Nottingham or Sir Guy of Gisbourne to do his dirtier work. Though Robin Hood, of course, had been a sincere nuisance.

But now? Now he was traveling around with an army, fighting his nephew and Philip at every turn and it was exhausting. He wished nothing more than to be done with it all.

Which is why, as he uncomfortably bounced along the streets of Paris, he hoped that Philip would simply concede to him rather than make his life more difficult.

ROBIN

Robin had gathered the gang from the several rooms they were occupying in the inn and brought them all to his own lodging space. They were now scattered about the room, some sitting on the bed, some in the few chairs that surrounded a small table in one corner, some leaning against walls. They all showed Robin's own worry in the expressions on their faces. He'd told them what Allen had seen and none of them were pleased.

"Why is King John in Paris?" Mary asked, hugging her daughter—who was seated in her lap and eyeing the world with the sort of oblivious fascination that only an eight-month-old could muster.

"He's come for us!" Mark said from his place in one of the chairs by the table. "How he knows we came here, I don't know. But we're all—"

"We aren't going to die," Lucy said sharply before Mark could finish his sentence.

Robin glanced at his wife, standing by his side facing the group. Since the argument in Hesdin she had little patience with Mark's melodramatic reactions to everything.

"What if he has come for us though?" Jane asked from her perch on the bed where she was trying to contain most of the children. "What do we do?"

"It's possible he isn't here for us at all," Dusty said, leaning against the wall across from Jane, with Will standing beside her. "He could have other business here that doesn't concern us."

"Why else would he arrive in Paris directly after we did?" Much asked. "It seems too coincidental."

"I can see two possible reasons for King John being in Paris," Robin said quietly, and the buzz around the room died down—other than the children who continued to talk to each other—Marian, in particular, declaring her views on William's silly-looking hair.

"One reason, the one which most of us seemed to consider first, is that he has somehow learned of our escape from Sir Hugh and the subsequent race to find refuge in Paris. Thus, he came looking for us and will soon be knocking on our door."

"So we have to run again," Elinor said.

"Or," Robin continued, "He is here to see Philip of France. That, I hope, is his real cause for being in Paris. There has been fighting with France, and now here is John in Paris. Perhaps they are negotiating peace."

"Or he's here for us and we're doomed," Mark said.

"When did we all become such pessimists?" Dusty asked, giving Mark a knowing look. "Even if he is here for us, we are not doomed. I, however, believe Robin's second guess to be the truth. It makes all the sense in the world. Philip and John are struggling over who has rights to lands on the continent, Philip and John disagree on Arthur's inheritance and right to the throne of England. Now here amid the fighting, John visits Paris. I'd say negotiations are exactly what is in order and we have nothing to worry about."

"So what are we doing?" Little John asked. "Staying here and simply watching for trouble?"

"Exactly that," Robin said. "We have to be careful. Now that John *is* in Paris going out and about will be a dangerous business on the off chance that he might recognize one of us, or one of his vassals might recognize us. However, if he isn't aware of our presence here and is only here to sue for peace, then we have no cause to go running off into the wild again. We can stay here in relative comfort and simply watch and wait."

WILL

The discussion of King John's presence in Paris had lasted a while longer, and even now that they had all dispersed to their own rooms, Will knew most of the gang were still reviewing the topic.

Will had stayed behind as everyone had returned to their rooms, letting Dusty take John and Daniyah away. Robin was sitting in a chair now, his head in his hands. Lucy was watching him with concern while also trying to keep Marian from leaping off the bed for sport.

Will approached Robin's chair and simply stood before him, arms crossed. It took a few minutes, but Robin eventually looked up.

"If we have no cause for worry; that is, if indeed King John is merely here to sue for peace with Philip, why do you look so downcast, my friend?"

Robin sighed. "I said we'd watch and wait."

"I know. I agree with your decision whole-heartedly. If we don't have to be running around in the wild without purpose, why would we subject our children to that fate?"

"I decided to stay in Nottingham to watch and wait; to stay in Sherwood."

"Robin—"

"I chose to wait, and we all came close to dying because of it. And now I've chosen to wait again."

"There is no immediate danger in this case—"

"That's what we said last time!"

"Robin," Lucy spoke from the bed, Marian contained in her lap now, "you needn't borrow trouble. Will is right; King John may not be aware of our presence here. In which case, running to who knows where with all of our children—and Rachel already nearly ill—is unwise. And if King John is aware of our presence here, we may yet escape him. Even if he knows we're in the city, it will take him time to find us among all the residents here. And even then, if we don't escape his notice, the Lord will watch over us in any event."

"I know."

"You shouldn't let this weigh so heavily on you," Will said. "King John's hatred for us, Sir Hugh attacking us, being fugitives, losing a portion of our gang . . .none of this is your fault or a reflection of your leadership, Robin."

"I find that hard to believe."

"I can see that, but you'll have to believe me. You aren't always going to make the right decisions, Robin. That much is true. The important thing is that you continue to make the decisions. Where would any of us be without you to lead us? Do you remember, back in the Sherwood days, after Marian's death when you broke down and stopped leading our gang?"

"You led them," Robin said, "and you didn't need me."

"I did lead them," Will replied, "but we were not what we once were, we were not what we had been under your guidance. You are good at this, Robin, even when you make mistakes."

Robin stared at him, grinning slightly although his eyes still seemed guarded.

"You will make mistakes, we all will. And you, and we, will learn from them and be better for it. But you can't give up on yourself or doubt every decision you make, Robin, or you will be a hindrance rather than the brilliant leader that you are."

Robin sighed, but he got out of his chair and his eyes had brightened at least a little. "I'll take that into consideration, Will. And in the meantime, if I falter, you'll carry them for me?"

Will smiled. "I will carry them *with* you, old friend. Always."

Chapter 4

GUY

Guy paced slowly around the men sparring. There were roughly a hundred of them, ranging from twelve to sixty-two years old. The last month of training had seen great improvement with some of them, and minor improvements with others. As it turned out, some people simply had an aptitude for weapons that others did not possess.

Andrew had gathered all of the serfs together this morning to spar, rather than setting them into smaller groups to learn different weapons as they did most days. They had a sword, a dagger, whatever weapons they preferred—except a bow—and were given a partner and told to disarm him, or in some way "win" the fight. Preferably without actually wounding each other or killing their opponent.

As they fought, Guy walked around the large circle of sparring pairs, watching closely. He studied their technique, searching for weaknesses and problems to address once the sparring had finished. He'd already seen a myriad of things to add to his mental list and he was only halfway around the group.

This wasn't the first time Guy had been in charge of training an impromptu and unlikely army of soldiers. The late sheriff of Nottingham had given him that particular job as soon as

73

they arrived in Nottingham all those years ago. That was why Guy was not surprised by the progress—or lack thereof—that he encountered now. However, he hadn't been training farmers and cottagers and simple country-folk in Nottingham. He'd been training soldiers; young and inexperienced ones to be sure, but not as thoroughly unfamiliar with weaponry as his serfs here on Gisbourne estate. There was, of course, the odd villager who was proficient with a sword, and more than a few of them made good use of bows on their own time. Yet, on the whole, they had come to him as entirely unprepared as a person could be for warfare, and the progress—what little there was of it—was encouraging.

The sounds of metal striking metal and men grunting and groaning filled the air. The day was cool, but not freezing as the weather had previously been. Even so, as it was January and still cold, the men were dressed in more clothing than was particularly conducive to effective fighting.

As Guy continued his walk, Ida came towards him from the opposite direction, having made the same sweep around the men taking mental notes on those who would need more guidance.

"What do you think?"

"They're better than I expected they would be," Ida replied to Guy's inquiry. "We might be able to defend ourselves if King John or Sir Hugh ever come calling, at least for a time. A hundred men wouldn't hold off the army of the King, or Sir Hugh for that matter, for very long."

74

"Still insisting we're doomed?" Guy asked with a smile. Ida and Andrew had become more than a little pessimistic over the last few weeks.

"Being realistic," Ida replied, though the darkness in her eyes belied her cheerful tone of voice.

"We don't even know if the King or Sir Hugh knows we're here yet," Guy said. "So all this doom and gloom has got to stop. It's groundless."

"We might need little Lucy to learn how to fight," Ida replied, referring to Guy's two-year-old daughter. "Fill out the numbers a bit more."

"Lucy isn't a fighter," Guy laughed. "She takes after her mother."

Ida wrinkled her nose. "Of course she does."

For a time they walked together in silence, watching the villagers and farmers who were fast becoming soldiers. Guy alternated between watching his vassals and watching Ida. Her negativity was not a new trait; she had never been a sunny disposition in all the time Guy had known her. However, the bitterness and despair that were beginning to be evident in her every word and deed were not usual for her.

"How are you doing, Ida?"

"What do you mean?"

"With Allen and your boys being gone? Not knowing what happened to them? I know you're worried."

Ida frowned and didn't respond.

"Faith told me—"

"Faith told you what?" Ida snapped. "That she caught me crying in the library? That I've been riding Midnight every evening so I can be alone to cry without being caught by your wife again? That I've given up hope of ever hearing good news of my husband and sons?"

Guy slowed his walk, watching with surprise as Ida's eyes filled with tears.

"I didn't mean to bring this all up," Guy said, placing a hand on her arm. Ida jerked away from his touch. "I am worried about you, that is all."

"Worried about me?" Ida scoffed. "Why would you care?"

"Because you are under my care," Guy replied. "Robin would worry if he were here, but now that we've been separated, you're under my care. It's my job to look after your welfare. That's why I care. And also because you *are* a friend, Ida."

"I never would have described our relationship as a friendship," Ida replied. "I despise you."

"You certainly took longer to forgive me for working with King John and the late Sheriff than most of our extended family did," Guy conceded. "But I would say in the last six months we have developed a relationship resembling friendship."

Ida didn't respond.

"However that may be," Guy continued, "I do care. And I worry. I don't want you to be hurting."

"I won't stop hurting until I have Allen, Edward, and William in my life again. You don't get it. You have your wife and your daughter and even your best friend here. I have no one."

"You have me—"

Ida scoffed at that, and Guy ignored her.

"You have Faith, and you have Andrew. You even have my daughter Lucy. You aren't alone. Just don't shut us out, Ida. Heaven forbid we only hear bad news about the rest of the gang," Guy's heart constricted at the thought. He loved this misfit family. "We may be all we have left of our gang. We need each other."

Ida sighed. "That did not cheer me up. That just made me feel worse."

"Ida—"

"Leave it, Guy. I don't really care right now." Ida strode away from him and Guy stopped his walk to watch her go.

That had not gone well.

Guy was all too aware that he was the means of keeping Ida from her family. When they'd scattered in Sherwood he'd made the impromptu decision to not follow the escape plan and travel to Scotland, instead choosing to come to his own home. Ida had been with him after the initial ambush in Sherwood Forest and he'd therefore insisted she stay with him rather than traveling alone to Scotland. They were safer in numbers. But it was possible that the rest of the gang had made it to Scotland safely, and if that were the case then Ida could have been with her husband and sons all these months rather than trapped at

Gisbourne estate. Guy felt bad about that, but he stood by his decision. If she'd traveled alone to Scotland, she could have easily been caught or killed by Sir Hugh along the way. Here, she had been safe for months. Her life was of more value to him at the time he'd made his decision than her emotional well-being. Now, however, her emotions were far more pressing than they had been.

Guy turned his attention back to his serfs and their training. Ida was unfortunately right in one regard: this measly lot would hardly hold off an army of King John's or Sir Hugh's, no matter how skilled they learned to be with their weapons. It was perhaps time to write to nearby lords and see if he could garner some allies for the coming fight, whenever that fight happened to arrive.

GILBERT

Gilbert strode along the well-worn path alongside the road, whistling to himself. He hadn't been this energized since just before facing off with Sir Hugh's army the last time they'd crossed paths. Fighting did that; it simply invigorated him. Something about a good fight brought a measure of joy to his heart that nothing else had ever done.

That was something Henry had never understood about him.

Henry.

Gilbert's whistling faltered for a second before he straightened his shoulders and put Henry from his mind. He was going to grieve, but not before he'd killed Sir Hugh and ensured that Robin Hood and his gang were absolutely safe from further harm.

Once he had begun his journey from Dover to Gisbourne estate it had not been hard to pick up Sir Hugh's trail. It was difficult to miss the mile-wide swath of trampled grass and the mass of boot and hoof prints that accompanied it.

Gilbert hadn't the least idea how far it was to Gisbourne estate, but he knew it wouldn't be hard to find it if he simply followed the not-so-subtle markings of an army. Particularly, in this case, Sir Hugh's army.

Gilbert could only hope he arrived before those he intended to rescue were already dead.

He was on foot, which made his journey slower than it might have been otherwise, but the army was slow-moving due to its size, so Gilbert anticipated catching up to them before they arrived at Gisbourne estate. Then it would be a small matter of infiltrating the army to get close enough to Sir Hugh to kill him.

Gilbert wished his wounds would heal faster so he could be entirely himself for such a momentous occasion. Killing Sir Hugh was meant to be enjoyed. But with his wrist making him one-handed and his ever-so-slowly healing back, the fight was going to be painful. Gilbert figured it would even things out, at least, which ought to prolong the joy of the fight but the idea of fighting with his broken wrist was not nearly as enticing as he tried to make it sound.

SIR HUGH

From the moment that Gisbourne estate came into view on the horizon, Sir Hugh's mood had lightened. This was a good day. A day that would see more outlaws killed. A day that would wound Robin Hood—the man Sir Hugh hated the most. A good day indeed.

Sir Hugh sat astride his horse at the head of his army, gazing over them with pride. They would kill the outlaws cowering in Gisbourne estate this day. And then they would march to France and find Robin Hood and kill him, too.

The weather was clear and bright, and almost warm. Spring was fast approaching. Isla, his daughter, would love a day like today. She'd called it beautiful and she'd make him take her outside so she could enjoy it. And he would do just that because he would do anything for Isla.

Today he was going to kill outlaws for her sake, as well as for his late sister.

"Alright, men!" Sir Hugh shouted to be heard by his army. It was doubtful every man could hear him, but he knew his captains would be shouting his message down the line.

"David! Robert! John! You are taking your men to surround Gisbourne estate. I will lead the rest of you in an assault on the front gate. Whatever pitiful army the outlaws have managed to put together, we will kill. David, Robert, John, and all of you who follow them will ensure no escape for the outlaws. Are we clear?"

His army roared back at him and Sir Hugh smiled grimly. "Then let's go kill some outlaws!"

Sir Hugh waited a minute for his three captains to move forward with their men and surround the estate. The manor was protected by a wall on three sides and a forest on the fourth. The forest was the most likely means of escape, but Sir Hugh had little fear of that becoming a problem. Judging by the reports he'd received while in Dover, there were only a handful of outlaws in Gisbourne estate, and Sir Hugh had an army. This was going to be over before it began.

Sir Hugh wanted to savor it, so he relaxed in his saddle and watched his men march around the wall to surround the estate. The death of outlaws was always something to enjoy.

IDA

Ida took a long drink of ale as she watched little Lucy across the table. She wasn't really interested in little Lucy or the way she picked at her food, but the sight of a child was putting her twins in mind so she watched little Lucy and dreamed of William and Edward.

Guy was discussing the training session they could do that day with Andrew, but Ida paid little attention to them. Her heart was aching, but something about watching little Lucy was soothing.

The calm of the breakfast table was soon interrupted, however, when a servant came running in, breathless and looking terrified.

"What is the matter, Isaac?" Guy asked.

"They . . .they are . . .coming," Isaac gasped.

"Who is coming?"

"The army . . .we saw them, in the distance. They are coming!"

Guy was on his feet immediately. "Andrew, get the villagers together, now! Ida, with me—let's see how far off they are. If we have time to send for the lords who agreed to lend men to our cause, we will need to send riders immediately."

Ida followed Guy out of the manor, striding through the courtyard toward the gate. "An army; do you think it is Sir Hugh or King John?"

"As King John is likely still abroad, I would assume Sir Hugh. But we will see."

And see they certainly did. After exiting the gate at the front of the manor, they could clearly see the army marching toward them, still a few miles distant. The individual men were not particularly visible, but the bright red hair belonging to Sir Hugh could be distinctly seen.

"Your allies will not be able to send men in time," Ida said quietly.

"There may yet be time."

Guy turned on his heel and Ida followed him. The next hour was spent in gathering the men they'd been training to prepare for the fight to come, and sending servants on swift horses to get word to the lords who had agreed to help them. Ida didn't believe those lords or their men would arrive before the fight began, but if they came late to give them reprieve that would work just as well.

It wasn't long before they could hear the roar of the army, cheering and chanting as they split apart and surrounded the estate on all sides.

All thoughts of her sons had vanished entirely as Ida prepared to fight for her life yet again.

Chapter 5

MARK

An equal measure of laughter and grunts of exertion filled the air as Mark leaned against a low stone wall that marked the edge of the field where he and his companions had traversed for the day. They were only a short distance outside of Paris, far enough to reach open fields where they could move more freely yet without having to travel too far. The scare that came with sighting King John in Paris has passed. It had been weeks since his appearance and nothing had come of it. It appeared Robin and Dusty were correct; he was negotiating peace, not coming for them.

Allen was currently sparring with Jane, as the latter was insistent upon becoming as proficient with weapons as the hardened warriors among the gang. She'd been begging Allen to train her nearly every day, and as soon as Robin had given them permission to roam Paris and move about freely yet again, Allen had taken her up on the proposition, training with her nearly every day. Often other members of the gang would go with them to keep up their own training. With nothing better to do with his time, Mark tagged along.

Today, Robin and Will were sparring nearby, both laughing and talking as they swung their swords at each other.

The long years of their friendship and the many battles they'd fought through side by side were evident in every movement they made.

Little John and Lucy were off to one side, deep in conversation. They had been sparring like the others for a time, but now Little John was leaning heavily on his sword and Lucy's hands were waving about as she spoke animatedly to her companion.

Mark still had some reservations in regard to Lucy. His anger from the beginning of the flight through foreign lands had dissipated after the argument in Hesdin; he could understand how none of the terrible things happening to their family were Lucy's fault entirely. Even so, he still felt they would be better off if she had killed Sir Hugh in Dover.

His anger may not have been as white-hot, but the bitterness that Mark had thought long gone was coming back to the surface; bitterness he'd begun to feel when his sister Marian was murdered and which had intensified when Robin fell in love with Lucy back in the days of living in Sherwood Forest.

Mark had learned to love Lucy as well as the rest of the gang; she was family. He thought he had moved past his initial feelings toward her; they certainly hadn't been at the forefront of his mind for many years now. But here in Paris, they'd begun to fester once more. Awakened by her refusal to kill Sir Hugh in order to save them—the sort of thing Marian would have had no qualms about doing.

Robin belonged with Marian; he always had.

They had grown up together; Robin, Much, Mark, and Marian. The inseparable foursome. Even as children, Marian and Robin had been destined for each other. Mark had always known it.

When Robin had left on the Crusades, Mark had been sure Marian would wait for his return and not pledge her heart to anyone else, and he had been right. And after the Crusades, during the first years in Sherwood when Marian and Robin had been at the height of their love, Mark had been as happy as he ever had before or since. Yes, they had been outlaws confined to dwelling in a forest, and their lives were filled with hardship, but Marian and Robin—as one—had been the beacon of hope for all of England.

And then Marian had been murdered by Guy of Gisbourne in a fit of jealousy.

They had been in Austria at the time, freeing Richard the Lion-Heart from Durnstein castle where he'd been held prisoner after the Crusades. The previous sheriff of Nottingham, along with Guy, had been there as well, intent on killing the King in order to be rewarded by John Lackland, who was Prince of England at that time.

The King had been saved, but Marian had been lost. She was buried in Austria, far from her home, and far from those who had loved her in life.

Mark sighed, surveying his friends sparring in a lonely field in France. They were all far from home now. Would they ever return to England, or would they all—like Marian—be buried far from home?

Mark glanced back toward Little John and Lucy, the latter of whom was laughing at something Little John had said. She was kind and wise, and often exactly what Robin needed, but she wasn't Marian.

Mark shifted uncomfortably.

He wished he wasn't constantly thinking about his sister these days. There had been so many years of peace, and of being perfectly happy with Robin and Lucy's relationship. He'd told Lucy, before her marriage to Robin, that he was not going to be put out by it. And he hadn't been.

But now?

Whether because of their current circumstances or because it had been festering unnoticed for all these years, Mark could feel the resentment building inside of him.

DUSTY

Dusty leaned over the table, studying the parchment laying before her. Her hand running lightly along the words, almost a caress. Nottingham castle had a library, but it was nothing to the treasure trove of knowledge Dusty had discovered in Paris in the month they had lived here. Every monastery she visited was overflowing with wisdom to be gleaned from the pages of books or the words of monks and other students such as herself. For Dusty was not alone in haunting the halls of the monasteries to learn.

The school of Notre-Dame was filled with people thirsting for knowledge, and here at Saint Genevieve abbey, where Dusty was currently poring over an old parchment, there were as many students as the cathedral's school.

Since first visiting both the school of Notre-Dame and that of Saint Genevieve, Dusty had discovered there were scholars from all around the world who had come to Paris to study. She found herself delightfully surrounded by brilliant minds who challenged her minimal knowledge of the world and stretched her imagination.

Dusty was currently holed up in the office of one Ernest Dartois, a teacher of medicine—Dusty's specialty.

Dusty set aside the parchment she had been studying and reached for a worn, leather-bound book beside a stack of scrolls. The table where she sat was filled with books, scrolls, and parchment, and several illuminated manuscripts. It was one of the latter that Dusty now opened to read.

Dusty's joy in the pursuit of learning kept her busy most days, but she had another task that occupied her days as well. Mark was melancholy since leaving England, and Dusty had taken it upon herself to lift his spirits. Will had told her of his conversation with Mark when they had first departed from Calais, and his resentment toward Lucy was only growing. After discovering the scholars from around the world and befriending Ernest Dartois in particular, Dusty had begun to drag Mark along on her trips to the abbey. He was less enthused by the dusty old volumes than she was, but he humored her. He was currently sitting on the floor near her chair, leaning against the leg of the table, a scroll in his hand.

While Dusty, and subsequently Mark, spent many of their days studying at the abbey or the Notre-Dame school, Robin had insisted the rest of them find work. They were low on funds before they arrived in Paris, having fled England all those months ago with almost nothing, and leaving Scotland with even less. Much had been the first to find employment, joining the ranks of cooks at the inn where they had their lodgings. The others were still searching for employment.

Lucy had found work, though unpaid, by offering her services at the hospitals in the city. When Dusty wasn't studying with Ernest and Mark, she also assisted in that regard; healing being, after all, her greatest skill.

Ernest Dartois soon came striding into the room. He was only a few years older than Dusty herself, with dark hair and eyes and a distinct twinkle in the way he looked and spoke.

"How are we getting along in here?" Ernest asked in English.

"Wonderfully," Dusty replied. "I think I may have simply died and gone to heaven."

Ernest laughed. "So much knowledge at one's fingertips; it does indeed feel like heaven." Ernest pulled up a chair to sit across from Dusty and picked up one of the scrolls off the table.

"Both of you disgust me," Mark snorted, though there was no malice in his voice.

"Knowledge is a beautiful thing," Ernest laughed in response. He couldn't see much more than Mark's head from where he was sitting on the other side of the table, but he could see the hand that Mark raised to wave him off like a pesky fly.

"Dusty, I have been thinking," Ernest began, grinning but ignoring Mark. "perhaps I can teach you a better understanding of my language as well as share knowledge of medicinal practices? There is only so much I can teach one such as yourself, who is already so proficient with medicine. But you are sorely lacking in understanding my language, and it might be useful to you as you are now living in Paris for . . ." Ernest studied her face, "an undetermined amount of time."

Dusty, when she first arrived at Saint Genevieve school asking to be allowed to study had been welcomed by Ernest. All she had told him of her life was that she and her family had recently come to Paris and might be staying for a while. She'd introduced Mark as a family member who needed something to occupy his time during their stay in Paris.

"I will agree to your tutoring me in French if you will allow me to teach you Arabic, the language of my birth."

Ernest laughed. "Arabic! I would be delighted! Arabic is one of the few languages I have yet to learn."

"How many languages do you know?"

"Well, I can read and write English, French, Latin, Greek, and a bit of Hebrew."

"Oh, you should teach me Hebrew!"

"I don't know enough of that to be a good teacher," Ernest laughed, "But the Bishop of Notre-Dame might be able to assist you in that endeavor."

"I suppose I will content myself with French, for now."

"It's not too hard," Mark commented.

"Do you know my language so well?" Ernest asked.

Mark turned his head as though to look at Ernest, but considering Ernest was behind him there was no possible way he could actually see him. "As the son of a nobleman, I learned French and Latin at a young age."

"But do you know Arabic?" Ernest asked with a laugh. "That is the true test."

"He doesn't," Dusty replied, shaking her head at Mark. "I have tried to teach my family my language and a few of them have taken to it. But Mark is not one who studied enough to be proficient."

"I don't need to know Arabic," Mark chuckled. "It's not a language I encounter in my day-to-day life."

"In spite of your confidence in your knowledge of my language," Ernest said. "I would suggest that living in Paris will challenge your understanding of the language and perhaps teach you more. It is, as you say, a language you will most certainly encounter in your day-to-day life."

The smile on Mark's face faltered.

Dusty wasn't sure what was going through his head at the moment, but considering his many snide comments to Lucy over the past month, it was likely frustration over the fact that they were living in Paris at all.

Dusty fully intended to get to the bottom of his frustration and bring him back to a place of calm and peace during their stay in Paris.

LUCY

Lucy pulled a blanket gently over her patient who was, mercifully, finally sleeping. Her knees groaned as she was able to stand at last, stretching her back and rubbing her neck. She'd been kneeling over this particular patient for nearly an hour trying to ease the girl's discomfort.

Lucy glanced around the large, dimly lit room, taking in the myriad of beds filled with the sick, the poor, and the travelers with nowhere else to go. Monks, nuns, and even various members of nobility were scattered around the room, offering food, tending to the ill, praying with those who asked for it—and even some who didn't.

Lucy had been working at the Hotel-Dieu, located near the cathedral Notre-Dame, for several hours. It was rewarding to once again put her skills to use. She was quite overshadowed—not that she minded—within the gang because Dusty was a far superior healer. But here, at least, she could be useful.

Lucy moved away from the bed of the young woman she'd been tending, and walked toward another bed, mere feet away. An old man was lying there, covered with a sheen of sweat and coughing incessantly. She placed a hand on his forehead, and removed it almost as fast; he was as hot as a burning fire.

Lucy went in search of water and a cloth. She passed many ill along the way, and was nearly knocked down by several children with ragged clothes and runny noses who were chasing each other around the room—they were likely orphans taken in off the street. Lucy wished she could take them all home with her, as there were many orphans in the Hotel-Dieu; but, though she didn't have the accommodations to give them all a home, at the very least it was a relief they had a place to go that wasn't the street. By the time she got back to her patient with supplies in hand, he'd woken up.

The old man smiled feebly up at her as she soaked her cloth in ice water and then laid it across his forehead.

"Are you an angel sent to guide me to heaven?" he asked hoarsely in French.

"Not at all," Lucy smiled, placing another cool cloth behind his neck and speaking to him in his own tongue. "I am merely here to ensure you live."

"Didn't deny you were an angel," the man chuckled. His laughter sent him into a coughing fit, a cough that wracked his whole frame and left him gasping for air.

"Easy. Try not to talk too much until we get you feeling better."

"Bruno de la Forge," he whispered, as Lucy continued to try and bring his fever down.

"Lucy…" Lucy hesitated for a moment, and then added with a grin, "Hood."

Though she was the daughter of a nobleman, having been orphaned at a young age Lucy had rarely ever used her own father's surname. And after living in Nottingham for so long, where everyone knew who she and her husband were and everyone called them by their first names, she was unaccustomed to using a surname at all. If people didn't call her Lady Lucy or Aunt Lucy, then it was the Lady of Locksley as often as not. But she rather enjoyed telling her new friend Bruno to call her Lucy Hood. Hood was not, in fact, Robin's surname from birth, but it was the one he was most likely to use ever since his days in Sherwood, and Lucy thought it only fair she adopt it as well.

"I'm glad to have met you, Lucy Hood," Bruno said between coughing fits. "The angel who's going to save me."

"I will do my best."

94

Working in the hospital, while rewarding for Lucy, was not lucrative for the gang as she wasn't paid. However, with Much working as a baker at the inn where they lived for some time now, and Allen recently being hired by a blacksmith they were beginning to have enough income to survive on more than charity. Will and Robin were still looking for work of their own, but they were managing alright.

Despite many of the gang coming from noble families, they were none of them afraid of work or believing any job beneath their dignity—living as outlaws in a forest had taken any of that level of pride out of them. Having a proper job was almost a relief to many of them. And in any case, whatever funds they might have had as nobility in England were still there, in England, and were of little use to fugitives who didn't want their presence in Paris known.

Chapter 6

ANDREW

Andrew gripped his sword tightly in his hand, watching from atop the wall as Sir Hugh's army split into three distinct groups and began surrounding Gisbourne estate. The task of encircling the manor was easy enough to do to the west, north, and south, but as the forest to the back of the house shielded the manor and spread across more than just Gisbourne lands, Andrew thought they just might have a chance of escape should it come to that.

And it was likely to come to that.

A motley group of villagers defending the manor from an entire, well-trained, army of knights and mercenaries?

Andrew glanced down the wall to the men under his charge, all of them with arrows at the ready. In addition to training the men over the past months, Guy had also overseen the fortifying of the simple wall that encompassed the manor. He had done this by having it made taller and giving it ramparts and battlements like a castle. It looked a bit odd, perhaps, but it would hopefully be useful in the battle to come.

Currently, Andrew had about a third of the trained serfs on the western rampart, watching Sir Hugh's army approach. Guy had a third of the men to the north, and Ida the final third of the men to the south. They were counting on the forest to protect the rear of the house, though both Guy and Ida had stationed their men so as to easily move to the east if necessary.

Sir Hugh, with his fiery red hair, was at the head of the charge fast approaching Andrew's position.

"Steady now," Andrew called down the line of men on the rampart. "Don't let your arrows loose until they are within shooting distance!"

The army was drawing ever closer, and Andrew could feel his heart pounding in his chest. Sir Hugh's army far outnumbered them, and were far more skilled. Andrew knew they were likely doomed. But he had to survive this. He simply had to.

He had to find Jane and his son Richard. He couldn't die here without ever seeing them again.

Andrew kept his eyes on Sir Hugh, which was easy enough to do considering his distinctive hair.

And then the army was, at last, within range.

"Loose!" Andrew bellowed. All along the rampart arrows went flying. A handful bounced harmlessly off of breastplates, a few caused soldiers to stumble a little as the arrows bit into the leather covering their legs, and one went straight through a soldier's eye. Andrew glanced to his left, wondering who had managed that shot.

His men were all hurriedly reaching for a second arrow, and preparing to fire again. Some took their time choosing a target, but the majority of them simply let the arrows go without deliberation; most of these harmlessly bounced off of armor.

This was not going particularly well.

IDA

"Nock! Draw! Loose!"

Ida was sure she was going to be hoarse before this day was over. She'd never shouted so much in her life. Neither had she ever been a part of a battle, and the prospect was terrifying. The soldiers were coming in ceaseless waves toward the rampart where she and her men were kneeling, barely covered by the battlements Guy had built.

Ida had done her fair share of fighting over the years; being an outlaw in Sherwood Forest had seen to that. But the fighting during Prince John's rebellion had been mainly ambushing small caravans in the forest or else fighting a handful of soldiers to rescue someone from an execution. Never a full-scale battle.

As far as Ida was aware, none of those facing the battle today had ever faced such a thing before. Guy and Andrew hadn't gone on the Crusades as Robin, Much, and Allen had. Fighting a war was not something they were accustomed to, and the likelihood of winning with their inexperience, lack of training, and lack of men was practically none.

She was going to die.

98

But first, she was going to lose her voice.

"Nock!"

All along the rampart on either side of her, men drew arrows from their quivers and Ida did the same.

"Draw!"

Bowstrings were pulled taught. Ida held her arms steady, carefully selecting a soldier among the oncoming wave. She kept her eye trained on one who wasn't wearing full-plated armor, but a less expensive leather jerkin. Sir Hugh's soldiers varied in the amount of the armor they wore, but all of it was more than could be said of the servants and villagers defending the manor.

"Loose!"

Ida watched in some disappointment as her arrow grazed the soldier's cheek, drawing blood, but not causing any further damage as it came to a sudden halt when encountering the armor of the soldier behind her intended target.

They were all going to die.

GUY

The line of soldiers below the wall were inching forward, shields over their heads to avoid arrows from above, carrying what were unmistakably ladders.

"Swords at the ready!"

Those brave men weren't getting into Gisbourne estate if Guy could help it.

All along the line beside him men were unsheathing their swords, though a few of them kept firing arrows; Guy didn't mind. If they could stop the ladders from being propped against the wall that would be better than fighting men on them.

The first ladder was raised, and before it reached the wall a young farmer's lad, barely sixteen years old, dropped his sword and leaped onto the battlements; as the ladder came leaning toward the wall he grabbed it with both hands and threw it back the other direction. It wobbled for a moment, and then the force of the soldiers below sent it falling back toward the wall. The young lad sat down on the battlement and caught the ladder with his feet instead, kicking as hard as he could; the ladder toppled backward onto the soldiers below, but not before one of them had fired an arrow straight through the boy's leg.

Guy ran forward and dragged him off the wall. "What were you thinking?"

"I got it knocked down, didn't I?" the boy responded through gritted teeth.

"Don't drop your weapons again! You need those."

"Yes, my lord!" The boy struggled to stand up.

"Stay down! If they get over the wall you can help, if you can, otherwise stay out of the way."

More ladders were being lifted. One of Guy's men jumped off the rampart down to the ground, within Gisbourne estate, and began searching the ground. Guy wondered what on earth he

100

might have dropped and why he was searching for it now, of all times.

Before he could shout for the man to get back up on the rampart, a ladder was being lifted right in front of him. Guy grabbed hold of it and with one shove to the right sent it toppling over.

"That's much smarter than what I did," the boy with the arrow through his leg said, scooting himself along the rampart to be closer to Guy.

"What are you doing?" Guy asked, glancing at him, and then immediately turning his attention back to the soldiers attempting to climb the wall.

"I figured I'd be safest with the most experienced fighter here."

Two ladders were safely up and soldiers were now climbing them. Two of Guy's serfs moved forward, each grabbing a pole of the ladder, and together they sent it toppling.

A moment later the man who had jumped down was running back up, a make-shift torch in his hand; no more than a simple branch on fire.

"Found some flint! Let's burn those ladders!"

A cheer went up from Guy's men as the villager went running down the line, setting ladders on fire as he went. Guy watched with a measure of amusement as the stick eventually burned to the bottom and the man drew back his hand wincing from the sting of the flame. His men weren't particularly well-trained yet and it wasn't pretty to watch, but they were getting the job done.

ANDREW

They managed to stop the ladders from being placed against the wall, though Sir Hugh's soldiers continued to attempt to erect them. Sir Hugh himself, with a group of soldiers, was relentlessly pounding the gate.

Andrew glanced around; he needed to get men down to the gate should Sir Hugh get it open, but if he left the rampart open those ladders would shoot up and Sir Hugh's men would be over and into Gisbourne estate.

"Matthew! Robert! Simon!" Andrew began yelling down the line at specific men; he would divide his crew in half and hope for the best.

"You're with me! We're going down to hold the gate! The rest of you, don't let those ladders up!"

"You can count on us!"

"We won't let them through!"

Andrew leaped down off the rampart and ran for the gate, only yards away. He glanced over his shoulder to make sure his men were following; a dozen or more men were jogging along behind him. If Sir Hugh got through that gate, they had to hold them. There was no other option.

Andrew was not going to die today. He absolutely refused.

IDA

Though they had managed to knock down a handful of the ladders that Sir Hugh's men were trying to erect, two of them had stayed up long enough for several soldiers to leap onto the rampart before Ida's men managed to send the ladders tipping over.

Ida dropped to her knees to avoid a particularly wild swing of her opponent's sword and swiftly reached up to slam her dagger into his thigh. He jerked backward, and she took advantage of that, leaping up and stabbing her other dagger into his chest and then with a boot to his stomach she sent him flying down into the mass of soldiers below.

Sir Hugh's men weren't making it into Gisbourne estate on her watch.

She glanced down the line; several of her men were shooting arrows down at Sir Hugh's army—though with their shields now over their heads this wasn't very effective—some were still fighting off ladders that Sir Hugh's men were stubbornly trying to put up, and two of them were still locked in combat with the soldiers who had made it up top already.

Ida shoved her daggers into her boots and grabbed her bow. She deftly pulled an arrow from the quiver at her back and took aim. As long as that farmer didn't twitch the wrong way . . .

Ida's arrow pierced the neck of Sir Hugh's soldier and he stumbled backward and over the battlement, landing atop several shields of his comrades below. The farmer gave her a curt nod of thanks, and then moved to help another of Guy's serfs fighting to knock over a ladder.

If this was how battles were waged, it was a tedious business, Ida thought.

Knock a ladder over, another took its place. Again. And again.

It had almost been a relief when those few soldiers had actually made it onto the rampart, because then there was a break in the monotony.

Ida glanced down at the soldiers below, wondering how long it would take to kill them all if they could only kill them two at time.

She glanced to the side to make sure there was no sign of any soldiers coming from behind Gisbourne estate. So far the forest seemed to be keeping them away, though she doubted very much that such good fortune would last. They would be coming from all sides eventually, and Ida knew they didn't have the numbers to hold off Sir Hugh's army for long. She had expected to see soldiers coming from the forest because it seemed the easiest way to sneak into Gisbourne estate, but she hadn't seen anyone yet.

ANDREW

Andrew stood at the ready, his men all around him, swords in their hands. The gate was creaking unnaturally, and already it had splintered in several places. Sir Hugh was going to get through any minute now.

A quick glance told him several ladders had managed to stay erect long enough to deposit soldiers on the rampart. Andrew's men who had stayed up there were now locked in hand-to-hand combat. Andrew could only hope their meager training could withstand an army.

The gate suddenly crashed open. The first thing Andrew saw was Sir Hugh's fiery red hair and his vicious grin; the next thing he knew they were overrun by Sir Hugh's soldiers.

Andrew jumped out of the way of one blade and received a nasty cut in his side by a sword to his left. He parried, ducked, and struck when he could; his mind went blank. Any worry for Guy and Ida, any thought of his wife Jane or his son Richard, had completely vanished. All he knew now was the swords in front, behind, and to the sides of him.

Duck.

Block.

Strike.

Again.

Again.

Again.

105

It was all a blur. A sword here, another there; a cut on his cheek, then one on his arm.

His arms ached, his leg had developed a cramp, and his head was pounding after a particularly hard knock against a shield.

Would it ever end?

Andrew glanced around and realized with a jolt that his men were nearly all on the ground; wounded or dead he didn't know.

He shot a glance at the rampart only to find it overflowing with Sir Hugh's men who were still surging over it like a wave.

"Retreat!" he yelled hoarsely to any of his men who might still be able to hear him. "Back to the manor!"

Andrew spun on his heel, ducked under the swing of a sword, and sprinted for the home of his youth.

When he made it to the door, he crashed into it, sending a wave of pain all down his side. He wrenched open the door and spun around. Two villagers were running after him, and Sir Hugh was hot in pursuit with his men.

Andrew held the door open, bouncing on his heels as he waited what felt like an eternity for his two men to make it through. As soon as they did, he slammed it shut and dropped the bar across it.

"Quick! Bring that table over here to barricade it!"

Andrew, legs mere noodles from exhaustion and wounds, wobbled over to the table and tugged on it. The two farmers came to his aid, and inch by very slow inch they got it over to the door. They could hear shouts and pounding on the other side.

"They'll try to get through windows," one of the farmers said.

"We can't do much about that, Robert," the other responded. "Lord Gisbourne already had them barred with wood several days ago. If that won't stop them, we can't help it."

"I agree with Matthew," Andrew panted, leaning against the table they'd just moved. "We can't hold them out of the manor for long. We have to escape. We'll get Lady Gisbourne and little Lucy and the servants and get out."

"What of the other lords and their men?" Robert asked. "Have we heard from them?"

"We hadn't heard from them before the battle began, and you think Lord Andrew got word from them while on the rampart or defending the gate?" Matthew scoffed.

The pounding against the door was becoming more aggressive.

"We need to move now," Andrew said. "We have to get the women and children and get out."

GILBERT

Gilbert stepped gingerly over a fallen branch, wary of making too much noise. He knew there were soldiers in the forest nearby, sneaking toward the manor exactly as he was. He needed to get inside the manor without being found out, find Robin Hood's friends, and get them out again. They would probably head for Dover after that, but that didn't matter. All that mattered right now was getting inside without detection.

"No guards posted," the low rumble of a soldier's voice came drifting out of the trees to his right. Gilbert angled his steps to the left and continued on.

A tall wall was coming into view through the trees. Not at the edge of the forest, but rather marking the edge of Gisbourne property.

Gilbert grinned. How Guy of Gisbourne thought that wall, tall as it might be, was going to keep anyone out of his forest and the rest of the manor, was unclear. Gilbert shimmied up the tree closest to the wall that he could see, using his unharmed wrist to pull his weight, and suffering no more than minor scratches on his hand due to the rough bark. He swung lightly down onto the wall, wincing as his broken wrist protested, and then leaped down inside Gisbourne estate, dropping into a roll as he hit the ground so he wouldn't break his own legs.

He paused, but heard nothing from the other soldiers in the forest. Gilbert wasn't sure they had crossed the wall yet.

Gilbert continued on his way, sneaking through the forest ever closer to the manor, keeping his ear open to any sounds of the soldiers of Sir Hugh's that were doing the same. Gilbert's plan was to infiltrate the manor with the soldiers, hoping no one would realize he didn't belong until after he'd rescued those he'd come to save.

As the edge of the trees came into his line of sight, Gilbert could see several soldiers exiting the forest and making their way stealthily along the field that led toward the manor. Gilbert clambered into a tree to get a better view.

Half a dozen or so soldiers had now exited the forest at various places and were moving slowly across the field. Most of them were not wearing full plate armor, but rather thick leather.

To Gilbert's right he could see what looked to be a fierce battle for control of the northernmost part of the wall surrounding the manor. Farmers and soldiers were locked in combat both on the wall and below it inside the estate. To the left, Sir Hugh's army was surging over the wall and the few serfs who had been putting up a resistance were now fleeing toward the manor house in the far distance.

By the time Gilbert finished his quick perusal of the surroundings, thirty more soldiers had exited the forest and were running to join the fray.

Gilbert hesitated for only half a second, and then dropped from his perch in the tree and took off running after the soldiers. The wound on his thigh, though fully healed by now, thoroughly protested at such exertion. Gilbert gritted his teeth and kept moving.

More soldiers were still issuing forth from the forest, but they paid no mind to Gilbert. He was just one more soldier attacking the estate.

As he neared the house, Gilbert veered off from the soldiers who were headed to the scuffle at the wall. He ran up to the first door he came to and pushed it open. It was slow work. Someone had tried to barricade it with a wooden desk.

Gilbert soon had the desk dislodged and the door open. He leaped over the desk and glanced around. He had no idea how this building was laid out, how many of Sir Hugh's soldiers might already be inside, or where to find the outlaws he was looking for. Gilbert took a moment to shut the door and place the desk in front of it again. Then he looked about in search of anything that might add to that inefficient barricade that he'd so easily gotten through. He could see nothing large enough to be of use within the small room.

The floor was littered with parchment, a water basin, some flowers—as well as the shattered remains of a vase—, likely all contents of the now-empty desk poorly barricading the door. Gilbert shrugged to himself. He didn't have time to properly do the job; he needed to find his quarry and get out as quickly as possible, preferably without detection.

Hands at his side, ready to draw either of his swords should such a need arise, Gilbert set off at a jog, glancing in every room he came to, and pausing every time he heard a sound to ascertain whether it were friend or foe. More often than not, the sounds were too far away to make that distinction.

He found no sign of any of Sir Hugh's soldiers.

Gilbert continued his trek through the unfamiliar house, picking his way carefully through each well-furnished room and empty hallway.

He soon heard voices again and slowed down, leaning against the wall, hands on the hilts of his swords, waiting.

"I don't have the key!" a woman nearly shrieked, clearly frustrated.

"I think Guy has the key," a man replied, sounding equally urgent.

"How do we get Faith out without a key?" the woman asked.

"Where is Guy?" the man replied.

"He and his men are still fighting, as far as I know. I sent my men, what remained of them, to guard the servants where they were hiding at the back of the house."

"There's only the two of us left," a third voice spoke. "So we stayed with Andrew."

"I have to find Guy," the woman said. "We need to get Faith and Lucy out of here, and get out of the Gisbourne lands. Immediately."

"I might be able to help with that," Gilbert said, coming around the corner slowly, and quickly assessing the group.

111

A woman was leaning against a large oak door, her light brown hair coming out of the braid it had been in, her clothes torn and covered in bloodstains, a quiver and a bow slung over her back, a sword at her waist, and the subtle outline of daggers in her boots that most might not notice but Gilbert definitely did. There were three men; one was standing nearer to Gilbert than the rest of the group, and staring at him suspiciously, the other two were behind the woman, and judging by what remained of their clothes, were serfs rather than nobility.

"I am Gilbert of Ilkeston," Gilbert said slowly, raising his hands away from his swords. "I was in the employ of Sir Henry—" Gilbert stopped, a heavy weight pressing into his chest.

"I don't recognize either of those names," the woman snapped, whipping out her bow and deftly nocking an arrow to the string.

"Robin Hood," Gilbert said. "That's a name you'll recognize. If I am not wrong in my assumption, you are part of his gang. When they escaped Sherwood Forest, they came, injured and exhausted, to Ilkeston."

Gilbert took a deep breath to steady his beating heart as his friend came to mind once more. "Henry and I nursed them to health and then accompanied them back to Nottingham in order to rescue young Marian from one Sir Hugh of Scotland. We then traveled with them to Edinburgh in search of the rest of the gang, of which we found nearly all of them save yourselves. Sir Hugh caught up with us, and we were separated in the aftermath of a battle . . ." Gilbert paused again, struggling not to picture Henry's head being chopped off.

"How do we know any of that is true?" the woman demanded, taking a step closer and leaving her arrow pointed at his heart.

"Ida, be reasonable," the man who didn't appear to be a farmer said. "He knows—"

"He named names that anyone could know, places that Sir Hugh may have gone. None of that proves he isn't on Sir Hugh's side!"

"I appreciate your wary nature," Gilbert grinned. "Most people are too trusting. I like you."

Ida glared at him.

"What would you like me to do to offer assurance of my trustworthiness? Swear by drawing my own blood? Tell you a more detailed account of our travels to Edinburgh?"

No one answered.

There was a long pause, during which Ida and Gilbert stared each other down, and the three men looked on with confused expressions, clearly unsure of what to do or say.

"Little John and Elinor had their baby," Gilbert said at last.

Both Ida and the young man who appeared to be a nobleman startled visibly at his pronouncement.

"They had their baby?" the young man said. "When?"

"In Edinburgh, before the flight to the coast. Her name is Rachel." Gilbert tried to recall the birth, and what details might induce Ida to believe him. "Will paced throughout the entire ordeal, Robin and Allen enjoyed sitting on tables and making fun of Much."

Ida lowered her bow.

"There was much teasing over whether Rachel would grow up to be a Marian or a Lucy, whatever that means," Gilbert added.

The young man chuckled.

Ida put her arrow back in her quiver and slung her bow over her back once more.

"I can't believe we missed a birth," the young man said.

"So does that mean he's trustworthy?" One of the farmers asked.

"Yes, Matthew," the young man replied. "Gilbert can be trusted."

"Based on his description of the birth of a child, or rather, how various adults acted during that birth?" the other farmer asked.

"I know it sounds absurd," Ida said, "but honestly, no one could relate such detail about our family without living with them, and no one could live with our family and not be trustworthy."

The young nobleman raised his eyebrows at her, questions and laughter in his eyes. Gilbert wasn't sure what that was about, but he didn't have time to ask.

"Well, if I am trustworthy, we need to leave. Immediately."

"We can't!" Ida said. "We have to get Faith out of this locked room that Guy created, but he's the only one with a key. Do we have an axe handy nearby?"

"Why is Lady Gisbourne locked inside a room?"

"It was for her protection," the nobleman said. "I'm Andrew, by the way."

Gilbert crossed his arms. "I'm still not understanding why Lady Gisbourne is locked in a room."

"Guy fortified this room specifically for her," Ida said. "And provided her with provision. So if the initial siege failed, she could potentially survive her own siege in here until help arrived."

"Or she could end up locked in a room and slowly starve to death on her own," Gilbert shook his head. "I admired Sir Guy of Gisbourne in my youth for he was one of the most feared men in England, but his reputation, at least in the area of intelligence, is slowly dropping. Perhaps his prowess with the sword will make up for such disappointment."

Chapter 7

SIR HUGH

The miserable farmers had fled without much resistance. It was true, of course, that getting through the gate and over the walls had taken a small amount of time, but now everyone who hadn't been cut down had fled inside the manor house.

Sir Hugh wondered whether the pleasure of swooping inside the house and killing the outlaws might be less than simply laying siege to the house for months on end and watching them suffer for a greater period of time.

He was still debating that point when his general Torin came walking up to him.

"It will be easy enough to get inside. The three doors we've checked so far have no more than tables or chairs shoved against them. It will stall us no more than a minute or two."

"Surround the house, so they can't escape."

"Already doing so, Sir Hugh."

"Of course, of course."

"Give the order and we'll kill them all. This job will be over within the hour and then we will collect our payment from King John."

"First of all, soldier," Sir Hugh replied icily, "I alone will be killing the outlaws. You can have your way with the peasants, but not the outlaws. Second, you will not harm any more of the servants or farmers than *necessary*, or this land will no longer be worth anything because there will be no working farms. Third, and this is very important for you to remember so pay attention: this job is not over until Robin Hood himself is dead."

Torin watched Sir Hugh lazily as this tirade came out, along with some spittle, clearly unimpressed by his friend's anger. "So can I give the order to enter the house yet?"

"Fine. So long as the outlaws are mine to kill and—"

"We don't kill all the tenants so you can retain the revenue when you ask King John to give you this property as your payment. Got it."

Sir Hugh watched Torin march away with a small measure of exasperation. Torin was the best there was, which is why Sir Hugh always sought him out when he was in need of an army to command, but he certainly didn't fear Sir Hugh which was equally admirable and annoying.

Still, in spite of Torin, Sir Hugh was going to enjoy today. And tomorrow the hunt for Robin Hood would begin in earnest.

GUY

Guy had just made it inside the house, with a dozen of his serfs. They were hastily throwing chairs and the like against the door they had entered in the hopes of keeping Sir Hugh's men out. Guy knew it was relatively pointless; the soldiers would get through regardless.

"What now, my lord?" the injured young man from the rampart asked, hobbling towards him.

"Now you and your fellow farmers go to where my servants are hiding and you protect them with your lives. It is likely that Sir Hugh will let you live, rather than fight you again, so that my land will continue to be profitable. He'll want that profit himself no doubt, or King John will take it himself. Either way, your lives will be spared."

"But what about you?"

"I am going to get my wife, and find a way out of this estate before the day is done."

"Why don't you leave her with us," a farmer suggested. "With the servants. Do Sir Hugh or the other men know her? Because if not, she can pretend to be one of your servants and therefore won't be harmed, and you can escape unburdened and come back for her, and us, with an army."

Guy considered this. It might be the better course of action, not only for Faith but for little Lucy as well.

"Guy!"

Guy spun around. Ida was running into the room, looking as haggard as he felt himself, covered in sweat and blood.

"You have to come quickly! We can't get Faith's room opened, but Andrew said you have a key, and Gilbert is already

118

trying to rush Andrew out the door, so come on! He's not a patient man!"

"Who's Gilbert? Why are we rushing out the door?"

"Robin sent him...I think...I don't know. He's a friend, he's trying to rescue us, but we can't do that without Faith out of her room. So come unlock the door already so that we can leave, NOW." Ida grabbed his arm and dragged him down the hallway.

"Ida, wait—"

"We'll find the hiding servants," his tenants called after him. "Don't worry about us!"

Ida dragged him down hallways and up staircases, all through his home until they reached the corridor where he'd built the safe room for Faith and Lucy. Andrew was there, as well as two of Guy's serfs and a man he didn't know who was sporting a sword on either hip.

The man with two swords had black hair and equally dark eyes; his physical resemblance coupled with his stern face left Guy feeling like he was looking at himself in a mirror—a mirror that reflected how one might have looked if they hadn't turned their lives around before it went too far.

"I'm Gilbert," the man said. "Now if you have a key, please, for all our sakes', get your wife and daughter, and let's go."

Guy pulled out the key he'd hung with twine around his neck and tucked into his tunic for the battle, and moved forward to unlock the door while Ida explained everything Gilbert had said about the whereabouts of the rest of the gang. In another moment, the door swung inward, and there was Faith, little Lucy in her arms. She sprang from the bed she was sitting on and ran into her arms, still carrying little Lucy. Guy wrapped his arms around them both and held on tightly.

"That's enough of that!" Gilbert snapped from behind Guy.

Guy let go of Faith enough to turn around, keeping one arm around her shoulders. "Can't a man hug his beloved wife?"

"Not when all of our lives depend on it."

"This is Gilbert," Guy explained to Faith. "He's offered to get us out of Gisbourne estate as well as he can, and then help us track down the rest of the gang who have, apparently, fled to France."

"France?" Faith asked, surprised.

"It's a long story that we don't have time for," Ida said sharply. "Gilbert said he'd explain everything after we're free of Sir Hugh."

Faith nodded silently.

Gilbert spun on his heel, hands held loosely near his sword hilts, and trotted off down the hallway. Andrew, Ida, and Guy followed; Guy still holding tightly to Faith. There were also two farmers who were part of the unlikely group currently traversing the halls of Gisbourne manor.

Gilbert led them a short way down the hall and then ushered them into a random bedchamber.

"You two," he addressed the farmers, "would you mind changing clothes with Andrew and Sir Guy? If I can pass them off as serfs I am rounding up—in the event we meet any of Sir Hugh's soldiers—that would be better than the alternative."

"I'm not sure Lord Gisbourne can fit in our clothes," one said hesitantly.

The other shrugged. "It's better than nothing, right?"

Guy and Andrew and the two farmers moved to change, and Ida and Faith, the latter still holding onto little Lucy, stepped out into the hall with Gilbert.

FAITH

Faith was unsure how Gilbert was planning on getting them out of the manor and off of Gisbourne lands without detection. Sir Hugh was surrounding the house, or so she'd been told, so there was no way out. Gisbourne estate didn't have the secret passages that Nottingham castle boasted. But the one thing that was truly occupying her mind at the moment was not how they would escape.

"Has Elinor had her baby?"

Gilbert glanced at her, eyebrows raised, an amused look on his face.

"Well? Tell us about it!"

"About . . .the baby? She's a baby; healthy, relatively happy, loved."

"But how was the birth?"

"Messy?"

"No, I mean, Elinor."

"Everyone is healthy, or they were, months ago, when last I saw them before they set sail for the continent. You'll have to wait to ask Elinor all your questions; I can't answer them."

Gilbert, though speaking seriously, had a distinct twinkle in his eye and Faith decided he looked slightly more friendly than she'd originally given him credit for.

The door to the bedchamber opened again and the four men came out. Guy looked a bit ridiculous in trousers far too short for his legs. Ida smirked and even little Lucy giggled.

"Papa! Too small!" The little girl pointed down at his legs. Guy grinned.

"This is to our advantage," Gilbert said. "He's not a wealthy lord, he doesn't have the money for decent clothes. Now, you two," nodding to the farmers who were looking quite odd in Guy and Andrew's finer clothes. "Go find the other serfs and stay with them."

As the two men set off down the hallway, Gilbert turned to Guy, Faith, Ida, and Andrew.

"Sir Hugh will likely have the entirety of the house surrounded by now and is already entering it wherever he can. My only goal is to get you out. You can make your own way to France to find Robin Hood if I don't make it."

Andrew and Faith started to object but Gilbert held up his hands to stop them.

"We need to get down to a door, and then I will dispatch whatever soldiers are in our way, and you will run through the hole I create in their line. Run for the forest, scatter, and meet up in a designated spot tomorrow."

"Tomorrow?" Ida asked.

"If you're being followed, you'll know by then. We want to be well sure that we are free of Sir Hugh and his soldiers before setting off for Dover," Gilbert said.

"That makes sense," Guy said. "We can meet at that little village on the edge of my estate, by the woods . . ."

"I know the one," Andrew said.

Ida nodded in agreement.

"Well that's that," Gilbert said, spinning on his heel once more and marching off. Faith and the others hurried to keep up.

Gilbert led them carefully through the manor, down staircases, through hallways, across wide-open spaces. Every time they had to turn a corner or cross an open room Gilbert would pause, check for soldiers, and then let them go on again. He was leading them toward the back of the house, where they could run for the woods.

"Andrew," Guy said softly as they walked along behind Gilbert. Faith turned toward her husband, wondering what he was going to ask Andrew to do.

Andrew turned toward him but said nothing.

"Do you think we'll be able to get to the stables long enough to get horses?"

"Likely not. I know Gilbert is planning on making us a hole to run through, but he can't hold off the whole army as we take the time to saddle horses."

"Are we going all the way to France on foot, then?" Faith asked. Her arms were already aching from carrying little Lucy; if she had to do this all the way to France, her arms might just fall off.

"Right now all we can focus on is getting *out*," Ida said firmly.

Gilbert suddenly stopped, throwing out his arm to catch Ida, and causing Andrew, Faith, and Guy to nearly walk into them. Gilbert placed his finger to his lips.

Voices and the sound of boots tramping along on the stone floor came gliding toward them.

"So far no sign of those outlaws," a deep voice said.

"Perhaps. But we don't really know what they look like, do we? They could be hiding with those serfs we found for all we know."

"Sir Hugh will know when he sees them; I imagine that's why he's having us round everyone up in the front room."

Faith held her breath. Not ten feet in front of them was the room from where the voices were coming.

A moment later, two soldiers came into view at the end of the hallway, but they weren't turning into it, rather they walked right past and continued on their way.

Gilbert crept forward, and the others followed. Faith's heart was pounding in her ears, and she was acutely aware of every little giggle and gurgle escaping from her two-year-old's lips.

As they reached the entrance to the room where the soldiers had been, Gilbert stopped again.

Three more soldiers had just entered the room from another doorway.

They hailed Gilbert.

"Find more serfs?" the youngest of them, blonde-haired and blue-eyed, asked.

"Indeed," Gilbert replied. "Any sign of the outlaws yet?"

"Not that I know of," the oldest of the three soldiers said, eyeing the group. "Why haven't you relieved them of their weapons?"

"They surrendered but I could hardly carry all their weapons myself."

"We can help," the young blond soldier offered.

Gilbert turned toward them and Guy and Andrew immediately took their sword belts off. Ida, however, did not immediately move to hand over her bow and quiver.

The oldest soldier seized her arm and pinned her to the wall, with Ida struggling futilely against him, and the third soldier, dark-haired and sporting a nasty cut across his eye from the recent battle, ripped the bow and quiver from her back.

"Don't hurt her!" Faith cried out. "We're surrendering!"

The oldest of the soldiers didn't let go of Ida, but he moved her from the wall. She glared furiously at Gilbert.

The soldiers set off toward the front of the manor, the young lad carrying the weapons and the oldest one pulling Ida along.

Gilbert roughly pushed Guy forward, and Andrew and Faith followed behind.

Gilbert turned his head to catch Andrew's eye, jerking his head toward the doorway that the three soldiers had originally entered.

Faith wasn't sure what that was supposed to mean, because he turned back around immediately and shoved Guy forward again.

Andrew, however, stopped following the group of soldiers accompanying Gilbert, Ida, and Guy. Before Faith could ask what he was doing, he grabbed her shoulder and steered her toward the other door.

"Andrew—"

"Shut up!" Andrew hissed quietly, glancing back at the other group disappearing out of sight.

Andrew pulled her along the corridor and out of sight and then stepped into the empty library.

"Andrew! What are you doing?"

"Getting you out. Gilbert will find a way to get Guy and Ida, and in any case, they can all three of them take care of themselves."

"We can't just leave them!"

"We most certainly can." Andrew opened the library door and peeked out.

"Well, *how* are we getting out?"

"I don't know yet."

GILBERT

They entered the front hall, which was packed with people. Villagers and farmers, all sporting various bloody wounds, were packed in the middle of the room with servants who were fortunately without injury, having been hiding within the manor throughout the battle; some standing, some sitting in tight little groups. Soldiers were surrounding them on all sides; more every minute as they continued to arrive after finishing their sweep of the manor house.

Sir Hugh was at the front of the group, by the entrance to the house, surveying the villagers and servants, searching.

"Keep low," Gilbert hissed at Guy.

Guy obediently went to take a seat by several other servants kneeling nearby.

The soldier who had been carrying all the weapons deposited them in a neat little pile by the wall and then went to take his place with the other soldiers surrounding the serfs along the walls, as did the other two soldiers. The one dragging Ida finally let go. She rubbed her arm, glaring at the soldier as he surveyed the other gathered servants. Gilbert was impressed with the amount of fire she seemed to possess.

Gilbert moved slowly forward among the soldiers and serfs to where Ida was currently trying to burn Sir Hugh into ash with the sparks flying from her eyes.

"Sit with Guy," he said quietly, before backing away to the wall, to watch the proceedings and figure out how to get out of this mess.

Ida very slowly and carefully wandered over to the group where Guy was sitting. Many of them were speaking to Guy in hushed voices and he seemed to be trying to silence them. They must find it odd, Gilbert thought, to find their liege lord in commoner's clothes and sitting as though one of them.

Gilbert surveyed the room, trying to decide how hard it would be to sneak Guy and Ida back out.

A soldier approached him, frowning. "Name?"

"Gilbert."

"I don't recognize you."

"It's a large army."

"Where did you fight?"

"I was part of the group sneaking in through the forest to stop any escape that way."

The soldier studied him, still frowning. He was young, with short brown hair and expressive grey eyes. He was also in full armor, his helmet tucked under his arm as he sized Gilbert up the way Gilbert was eyeing him. "No armor?"

"I'm not the only soldier here without armor," Gilbert laughed. "Some of us prefer the free use of our limbs, even at the cost of a little protection."

The soldier shook his head. "Idiots. That armor could save your life."

"I'll bear that in mind next time Sir Hugh sends us to attack someone."

"I hear we're going to France next."

"That's what I heard as well; that is after all, where Robin Hood is rumored to have run."

The soldier's eyes flashed.

"Is that who we're chasing? Captain Robert said 'outlaws' and I thought . . .well, Sir Guy of Gisbourne isn't a well-liked man, is he? He could have outlaw friends for all I know."

Gilbert studied him. The soldier shifted under his gaze.

"Torin, the general that Sir Hugh hired to create this army, the one we really owe allegiance to, asked me to join as a favor. I'm not usually part of this army. I joined the ranks just before the chase to Scotland, and Torin wasn't forthcoming on details. I didn't realize…"

"You owe your life to Robin Hood, don't you?"

"Don't we all?" The soldier studied him. "Did you know that's who we were tracking down to kill?"

"He is an outlaw."

"*Was*, and for good reason. Thankfully, for all of England."

Gilbert tried not to smile. He studied the soldier a moment longer; the dark look on his face, as though he'd been betrayed by this knowledge of who their real target was. Gilbert decided to take a chance.

"I am also a friend of Robin Hood," he said quietly. "And I am currently trying to rescue his friends, Guy and Ida, before Sir Hugh realizes they are among the serfs gathered here."

The soldier swung toward him, but Gilbert kept his face impassive, looking forward.

"You're a friend of Robin Hood?" he asked softly, trying not to draw attention to their conversation. There were numerous soldiers within earshot of them, as well as the serfs not too far in front of them.

"I am."

The soldier stared at him, then back at the serfs, and then turned to stare at Sir Hugh whose shouting at serfs and soldiers in an effort to glean where the outlaws were hiding was causing enough ruckus to distract any nearby listeners. Gilbert waited, wondering what the soldier would do with this information.

"King John hired him," he said at last, watching Sir Hugh interrogate the serfs. Gilbert turned to watch the soldier, watching the understanding dawning on his face. "King John . . .Robin Hood . . ."

Gilbert waited patiently. It was taking this man a ludicrously long time to put the pieces of this puzzle together. If he was a friend to Robin Hood, then the next logical course of action would be to help Gilbert.

The soldier looked at Gilbert again, and then back to Sir Hugh.

"Do you have a name, soldier?" Gilbert asked.

"Roger."

"Well, Roger, will you help me save Guy and Ida and get them safely back to Robin Hood, for the sake of all that he did for this country?"

Roger thought about this, still staring at Sir Hugh, who was now walking among the serfs, grabbing first one then another by the hair and turning their heads this way and that, trying to decide if he recognized them.

"How will we manage it?"

"Very carefully."

Chapter 8

MARK

Mark's eyes skipped across the old parchment in his hand, hardly taking in the strange characters it presented to him. He had told Ernest Dartois and Dusty that he had no desire to learn Arabic, but as he visited the abbey almost every time Dusty did, he was present when she had her lessons with Ernest and therefore had taken to passively participating. Ernest would give Dusty an hour or so of French lessons, and then they would take a break and read for leisure, after which Dusty would instruct both Ernest and Mark in Arabic.

At the moment, Ernest and Dusty were seated on the floor in front of his desk, leaning over a stack of old parchments that contained various information regarding Arabic. Some of it was old parchments, like the one in Mark's hand, that Ernest had found in one of the libraries in the abbey, and some of it was fresh parchment that Dusty was writing her own notes on in order to help Ernest; a mixture of both Arabic, English, and French.

Dusty was always content and rarely unhappy, but Mark had never seen her so excited since he'd met her so many years before. She loved the abbey, she loved the school there, and she seemed to draw more delight from learning and teaching than she did from almost anything else in her life. She was certainly settling into their new life with a vigor, and Mark was pleased for her sake. He wished he could do the same.

But he couldn't.

The fact that Dusty loved her life in Paris more than her life in England was great for her, but irksome nonetheless. The fact that Lucy was delighted with their new living arrangements and working at the hospitals, the fact that Robin had found a job working for a fletcher and seemed content to live in Paris for the rest of his life. The fact that all of them were happy and building lives; Mark hated it. Every time someone got a job, he felt more annoyance than the day before. Every time he heard the language of love slip easily off the tongue of the gang's children, he felt a flash of anger. They shouldn't be living in Paris; they should be home. They shouldn't be happy in Paris; they should be home. The youngest of the children shouldn't be learning French as their first spoken language. It was all wrong. And it was all Lucy's fault.

Dusty tapped Mark's knee, and he lowered the parchment to see her face, realizing he had been gripping it too tightly and it had begun to crumple in his hand.

"You are not focused."

"I was thinking."

"About?"

Mark sighed. "You don't want to know."

"Not Lucy again?" Dusty's eyes were kind and understanding, and that almost made Mark angrier. "We've talked about this. It isn't her fault we are in this predicament. King John put us here, and Sir Hugh, but not Lucy."

"I know."

Ernest glanced between them but said nothing. Dusty had been slowly filling Ernest in on the details of who they were and why they were in Paris, and he'd already been witness to more than one outburst by Mark on this particular subject so this conversation would hardly come as a surprise to him.

Mark sighed again, attempting to straighten the parchment he'd crushed. He'd been wavering for weeks, filled with so much anger toward Lucy because of Sir Hugh and because of his own sister Marian and yet desperately trying to forgive her. He appeared entirely indecisive on that point. Forgive Lucy or not? It really depended on the day. And today he was leaning towards definitely not.

"I hate that everyone is settling into life here in Paris," Mark finally said. "No offense to you or your city, Ernest."

"None taken," Ernest laughed. "I have no desire to pack up everything and move to live in your Nottingham either."

"Maybe if you tried to find some enjoyment or purpose here, Mark," Dusty suggested, "you might find yourself calling it home like the rest of us."

"But it *isn't* home!" Mark hissed.

"I grew up in Palestine," Dusty said softly. "And I loved my life. I had my family, and my best friend and I had my mentor Daniyah . . .everything about my life was perfect. And then

Saladin came and destroyed everything that I once knew and loved. I lost my family and my home. But I found a new family and a new home with Robin and the rest of you, in Nottingham. It isn't as hard or as terrible as you make it out to be, Mark. You still have your family, that hasn't changed. All you have to get used to is a place, a location. That isn't nearly as hard. Trust me, I know."

Mark hadn't considered that fact before; Dusty had lost everything and started over. She was always so content with every twist and turn of fate that Mark sometimes didn't even consider the emotional toll her life must have taken on her over the years.

"Did you ever forgive Saladin?"

"He was a vile man," Dusty said, "But for my part, yes. I did. Because living in bitterness was making my life miserable and I would rather live free of pain. And when I let go of that anger, God showed me to Robin and Allen and Much, and my new life and new family began. Everything since then has been a delight."

"Everything?" Ernest asked, his eyes twinkling. "The rebellion in England, delightful?"

Dusty chuckled. "Perhaps not every detail; but the whole of it has been well worth living. I wouldn't trade my new family for anything. Palestine, England, France, I do not care where I live. A place is a place. It is the people who make my life a delight."

"It is difficult to say the people are where I can derive my enjoyment or find contentment when it's the people who are making me angry," Mark said. "I think about Robin and it reminds me of Lucy and I'm angry all over again. I see Allen and it reminds me of his betrayal during the rebellion and I'm angry all over again. I see Jane and I think of her husband Andrew working for Sir Guy on the wrong side of the rebellion and I'm angry."

"You have quite the eclectic family," Ernest said. "So many quarrels and differences, some of truly momentous proportions, and yet you live in harmony."

"That's Jesus for you," Dusty grinned. "We were enemies, and now we are a family through the grace of God."

Mark snorted in disgust. It wasn't that he didn't agree with Dusty, but at the moment he'd prefer not to be family with certain members of the gang. Anyone who reminded him of Lucy failing to kill evil men or of Sir Guy killing his beloved sister during the rebellion.

IDA

The room was getting stifling. Too many bodies crammed into too small of a space. Hot, sweating bodies, covered with the filth of war and permeating the stench of fear.

Ida was going to throw up if she had to stay here much longer.

Guy was kneeling on one side of her, and all around were villagers and farmers that she'd been training over the last few months. Sir Hugh's soldiers, everywhere. Sir Hugh himself, nearly cracking necks as he grabbed chins or hair to turn faces this way and that to determine if they were the outlaws he was searching for.

Gilbert's rescue had not gone as planned.

Ida's stomach roiled again as the farmer next to her shifted. He stank. She stank. And she was seriously going to throw up.

"This way, miss."

Ida turned quickly at the sound of a voice behind her. A soldier was standing there, holding out his hand, and glancing furtively at the soldiers around the room.

Ida didn't know him, but as he was a soldier he was the enemy. She didn't take his outstretched arm.

Guy was also studying the soldier with suspicion.

"I won't harm you," the soldier said softly, kneeling down. He glanced around at the other soldiers moving around the room again. "But if you don't move now, and gently, we'll attract attention and I won't be able to get you over to Gilbert without Sir Hugh stopping us."

At the mention of Gilbert, Guy took her hand and placed it in the soldier's, giving her a look that said she didn't have a choice in this matter. As the soldier pulled her to her feet, Guy turned resolutely back to Sir Hugh, who was getting ever nearer to their little group.

The soldier slowly inched her backward, away from the serfs. Most of the soldiers next to the serfs were eyeing Sir Hugh's progress, and as for the rest they were packed so tightly together around the edge of the room they could hardly see over one another's shoulders.

The soldier led her slowly to the doorway Ida had been dragged through not too long ago. Gilbert was there, his eyes twinkling, though his mouth was set resolutely in a way that reminded Ida of Robin.

"Sir Hugh!"

Ida spun around at the sound of Guy's voice, but Gilbert grabbed her and began sprinting up the corridor away from the front room.

The soldier followed.

Ida heard Sir Hugh's voice echoing down the hallway after them.

"Well, well, well. What do we have here? Sir Guy of Gisbourne, a simple farmer?"

Ida wrenched herself free of Gilbert, realizing that Guy had made himself the distraction necessary for her escape. "We can't leave him!"

"We have to!" The soldier behind her grabbed her shoulders and pushed her toward Gilbert.

A moment later, though Ida struggled with all her might, the soldier and Gilbert each had one of her arms pinned to their sides and were dragging her to the back of the manor.

138

"We can't leave him!"

"We don't have a choice," Gilbert hissed, "and if you don't shut up you're going to attract unwanted attention!"

FAITH

Andrew had led her to one of the back doors of the house and was crouching by the window, cautiously peering over to see who might be out there stopping their progress. Before the fight began all the windows had been boarded up, but now the wood was smashed to pieces, some of it still hanging haphazardly from the window and some lying on the ground.

The house was eerily quiet. No sounds of servants scurrying here and there, no distant echo of Guy giving orders, no din of voices ringing from the kitchens or the crowded tables where all the serfs had been gathering to eat over the last few months of training.

Silence reigned.

Faith's heart was pounding, her breathing ragged. Little Lucy was growing increasingly heavier in her arms. Her little giggles and gurgles had devolved to quiet crying, her arms wrapped tightly around Faith's neck, her face buried in her shoulder.

Faith had never been this terrified, and she could understand why her daughter was now feeling that as well.

And what could have become of the others? A small part of Faith wondered if watching Gilbert shove Guy forward would be the last she ever saw of her husband.

Andrew slowly stood and moved toward the door, motioning for her to follow.

Little Lucy grabbed a fistful of her mother's hair as Faith walked toward Andrew, her crying pausing now that her mother was on the move again.

"Are there soldiers?" Faith whispered.

"A handful, but they are moving around to the other side of the house. A captain or someone just came and talked to them. I couldn't hear what was said, but I imagine they must believe they've rounded up everyone by now."

Andrew cautiously opened the door and stuck his head out. There was no shout from soldiers outside, and Faith drew a deep breath.

Andrew moved all the way outside, glanced both ways, and then turned back to Faith. "Come on!"

He took little Lucy from her arms, causing her to cry out in fear, shifted her to one hip as he grabbed Faith's hand, and sprinted for the distant stables with Faith struggling to keep up with his long strides. She expected to hear shouts from behind, or feel arrows pierce her back, but nothing happened.

When they reached the stables, Andrew threw the door open, dragged her inside, and slammed it shut again.

They stood there in the doorway, breathing heavily, not saying a word, for quite some time.

"That felt too easy," Andrew said at last, straightening and moving down the stalls with little Lucy.

Faith's fear was easing and her quiet confidence returning. "Why would it not have been easy? We have the Creator of everything on our side."

Andrew paused in opening one of the horses' stalls to grin at her. "Yeah, there's that, I suppose."

"What are we doing now, Andrew? Where do we go?"

"We go to the little village, as planned, and wait till tomorrow to see if the others show. If they don't, we go to France."

Andrew had placed little Lucy on a pile of hay, and she was not fond of her predicament, pushing at the hay beneath her as though to get it away from her. Her crying had stopped, but she was staring at her mother with wide, terrified eyes.

"This feels too familiar," Faith sighed, remembering their plans in Sherwood before Sir Hugh had first attacked them all those months ago; meet in Middlesborough and if no one shows, go to Scotland. Well, Guy had changed that plan and gone on to Gisbourne estate instead. Faith wondered if the others believed them dead, as they'd never turned up either in Middlesborough or in Scotland.

Andrew soon approached Faith, leading two horses toward her. One was a bay mare named Promise, who was Faith's own

141

mount and she moved forward eagerly to take her reins and pat her nose. The other horse was Quest, another bay, one of Guy's horses that Andrew had borrowed when they'd run from Nottingham and Sherwood six months ago.

"Are you ready?" Andrew asked.

"I don't know, but we don't have a choice. We need to get out of here before someone sees us, don't we?"

Andrew nodded. He helped her mount Promise, fetched little Lucy, hastily dusting hay off of her, and passed her to Faith before moving to open the barn door.

"Well, here goes nothing," Andrew said as he swung into Quest's saddle.

Faith followed Andrew out of the barn, turning Promise toward the forest on the edge of Gisbourne property.

They broke into a gallop and before long were hidden among the trees.

GILBERT

Gilbert took a careful look out of the window to be sure no soldiers were lurking behind the house. What he saw was not soldiers at all, but rather Andrew and Faith galloping toward the forest.

Gilbert grinned.

This just might work after all.

There had been more than a few minutes of uncertainty. Gilbert didn't often find himself in situations where he wasn't entirely in control of the outcome. Yet ever since joining up with Robin Hood some months before, he was continuously being thrown into, or running headlong into, situations where he had to use more of his brain than simply wielding his two swords and easily cutting down opponents.

It was exhausting.

He might have to insist Robin Hood payed him handsomely if he expected Gilbert to continue helping the gang out of ridiculous situations.

But they were nearly free of this particular situation.

"No soldiers," Gilbert said, turning to Roger and Ida, the latter of whom was glaring daggers at him.

"Roger, escort Ida to the stables where you will find her a horse and get her to the forest safely, please."

Roger nodded. "Yes, sir."

"Where are you going?" Ida demanded. "If the answer is going back to save Guy, then I'm coming, too!"

"No. You are going with Roger, and you will meet Andrew and Ida, who I just saw running for the forest mere moments ago. If I do not arrive or Guy does not arrive tomorrow at the meeting place, then you will escort Andrew and Faith and the child safely to Robin Hood. I'm entrusting them to you, Ida."

Ida was still glaring at him, but at least she seemed to be considering this plan. Gilbert was sure a charge to care for the others would be enough to convince her to go. The little he had gleaned of her nature in the last few hours suggested she was undoubtedly the sort to thrive given the opportunity to protect others.

Ida slowly nodded. "Alright, I'll go. But take Roger with you to save Guy."

"No. He needs to see you safely off—"

"I can take care of myself, thank you very much. Take Roger, get Guy, and make it to the designated meeting place or I will find you and kill you myself."

"I will do my best to be there."

Ida hesitated a moment, and then said, "My husband, and sons . . .they were with everyone in Scotland?"

"I told you, though it has been months since I lost contact with them, everyone was healthy and relatively safe when last I saw them. Of course, we were running from an army at the time—the army currently camped in front of this manor, in fact."

Ida nodded and drew a deep breath. "Okay. Good luck, Gilbert."

When she slipped out the door and toward the barn, Gilbert turned to Roger. "Thank you for your help. If you want to slip back among your ranks, I will not judge you. I am, however, going to steal Lord Gisbourne from under Sir Hugh's nose, one way or the other, and will likely die in the process."

"You're a grim fellow, aren't you?"

"The last time I tried to take on this army single-handedly, my friend lost his head."

Roger blinked, and then stared open-mouthed at Gilbert. "Oh."

Gilbert turned from him, trying not to remember that fateful night in vivid detail, and failing utterly.

"You were . . .oh. Oh."

"If you keep saying 'oh,' I'm going to kill you."

"You were the duel-wielding knight. I should have recognized you, there's only so many people in this world who wield two swords, but you died!"

Gilbert was marching down the corridor back toward the front of the house, and Roger was jogging to keep up with his determined strides.

"You were definitely dead."

"I was definitely determined to survive."

"But—"

"Were you there?" Gilbert spun on him. "You were! You—"

"I didn't kill your friend!" Roger leaped backwards away from Gilbert's reach, throwing his hands up in surrender. "And I didn't know we were chasing Robin Hood or I never would have agreed to follow Torin. It's just that I needed money, and I've worked with Torin before, and all he said was that Sir Hugh was chasing down outlaws. I assumed you and the other fellow were just that."

"Sir Henry was not an outlaw, and neither am I, though I'm not exactly what one might call a savory sort."

"I'm sorry."

"Did you kill him?" Gilbert clenched his fists to keep himself from drawing both his swords then and there and slicing off Roger's head.

"No. I didn't wound either of you, I was farther back in the circle of soldiers."

Gilbert studied him a moment longer, then nodded curtly and resumed his march back to where Sir Guy of Gisbourne was likely being killed, or already dead.

ROGER

Roger Sparr hurried to keep up with his new friend. He wasn't sure if he was terrified of Gilbert or impressed by him, though it was likely both. He'd infiltrated Sir Hugh's army today, which had impressed Roger to begin with, but when he'd made the connection to the night in Scotland when Sir Hugh had his army massacre those two men—who Roger now knew had been protecting Robin Hood himself—he was nearly in awe of the duel-wielding man striding down the corridor in front of him.

That man had been dead.

Fully. Completely. Dead.

Facedown in the dirt, littered with wounds, blood seeping out from underneath him and spreading in a large pool. Sir Hugh

146

had even had another soldier stab him one last time for good measure before they'd moved on in pursuit of the other outlaws. Roger shuddered to think he'd been on the opposing side of Robin Hood. He had never intended this. He had nearly finished his stint protecting a caravan and was in search of work. Torin had approached him with a job opportunity; hunt some outlaws. Roger knew that in the future he would demand more detail from his potential employers. Chasing down Robin Hood, indeed. Gilbert was slowing down as they neared the front hall, and Roger followed his lead.

They entered the front hall to Sir Hugh giving a lecture and hesitated just inside the door.

". . .expect you to continue to work your farms for me, and run the manor. You'll all be going about your lives exactly as you were under Lord Gisbourne, and Lord Ancel, and the previous Lord Gisbourne as well. For those of you who lost family members today, that is no one's fault but your own. You should not have joined in the war. I merely wanted the outlaws. Now go home."

There was a pause and a moment's uncertainty, and then the serfs slowly began to disperse; villagers and farmers heading out the front door, and the servants, with nervous glances at the soldiers, heading deeper into the house to resume their duties. Roger doubted if this estate would run smoothly immediately, after all that had transpired here.

He scanned the serfs leaving the front hall, trying to find Sir Guy of Gisbourne. He wasn't anywhere to be found. Yet neither was there a pool of blood staining the floor, so there was still hope he was alive.

Gilbert started to move through the crowd, easing around servants headed in the opposite direction, who stared at him suspiciously as they passed, and soldiers milling about waiting for new orders. Roger followed uncertainly, unaware of what Gilbert might be planning to do now.

Gilbert went straight across the hall and out the front door. He stopped there, and Roger paused as well, taking in the scene in front of them.

There were groups of soldiers all around, some of them sporting wounds. A few healers were moving about among them, dealing with the worst of the injuries. The dead still littered the courtyard and Roger could see more bodies in the distance near the wall. Farther down the road that led away from the manor house, through the broken gate in the wall, tents were being erected. Roger supposed Sir Hugh would let them spend all of one night licking their wounds, and then would have the army marching for Dover to sail across the channel and find Robin Hood.

Sir Hugh himself, with his red hair flying about in the cool wind, was talking to Torin in the courtyard just outside the manor, gesturing wildly.

Behind him was his horse, waiting to be mounted. Behind the horse was Sir Guy of Gisbourne, laying face down in the dirt. His hands and feet were bound together, and a rope led from his bound limbs to the horse's saddle.

Sir Hugh, apparently, intended to have Sir Guy dragged along behind him. It was not the way Roger would have expected Sir Hugh to kill him, but it would certainly be excruciating.

GUY

He was going to die. He knew it with certainty.

Guy could feel blood slowly trickling around his wrists and ankles where the ropes binding them together were cutting into his skin. The horse he was tied to was stamping its feet impatiently, as though it were eager to send Guy to his death. Though it was entirely possible it simply wanted to get out of the cold.

Guy was laying on his stomach, his arms and legs pulled up over his back where they were tied together and then tied to the horse. He was craning his neck to see around him. Vaguely, he thought this must have been how little Lucy felt as an infant before she could crawl.

There were soldiers milling about the courtyard, many of them looking unsure as to what to do now that the battle was over. A number of horses were attempting to graze among the stubble of grass that the front of the manor boasted. What little there had been left from the winter they were still experiencing, the training of Guy's serfs had effectively trampled.

If Guy turned to his right he could see the gate down the road, and beyond it tents being pitched. It looked like Sir Hugh's men would be staying. If that were true, then likely he wasn't planning on chasing down the others yet. That, at least, was a relief.

Guy lowered his head to ease the ache in his neck, letting his forehead rest on the frozen ground.

He was going to die.

He prayed Andrew had gotten Faith and little Lucy out. Prayed Gilbert could safely get Ida away. Prayed his death would come swiftly and not prolong his agony.

When Guy had shouted at Sir Hugh in the front hall to distract his attention from Gilbert and Ida leaving, he had known he would die. He had thought, however, that it would be quick and relatively painless. A public beheading, at least. Instead of killing him, however, Sir Hugh had first demanded to know where the other outlaws were hiding, gesturing among the serfs. Guy had told him plainly they were gone.

Sir Hugh had enjoyed beating him after that, to which Guy had calmly submitted in order to buy the others more time to get off of Gisbourne lands. Being beaten in that front hall was not a first for him; it was where his father had often chosen to deal out his punishment.

150

Then Sir Hugh had dragged him outside, bound him, and tied him to his horse's saddle.

"Let's begin, shall we?" Sir Hugh snarled, kicking Guy's shoulder.

Guy could hear him mounting his horse, and he gritted his teeth. This was not going to be pleasant.

Sir Hugh's horse shifted; every time a hoof hit the ground, Guy winced. His anticipated excruciatingly painful death was imminent. But Sir Hugh wasn't moving yet.

"I wonder, do you think this is how I should kill your friend Robin Hood? Or something more extreme, perhaps?"

Guy ignored him, and focused on Faith and little Lucy. He pictured them safe, and happy. Faith with flowers braided into her hair, as she so loved to do. Little Lucy's bubbly laughter filling the air, surrounding Guy with warmth.

"I believe I'll wait and see how effective this is, in terms of maximum pain, before I make my decision about Robin Hood."

Guy clenched his fists, causing the ropes cutting into his wrists to sink further beneath his skin. He wanted to shout that Sir Hugh simply get it over with, but refrained. He wasn't going to give Sir Hugh the satisfaction.

"Should we gallop? Or take this more slowly? I do wonder how slowly you'd die if I simply walked from here to Dover."

151

Apparently Sir Hugh had no intention of ever actually killing him. Guy nearly banged his head against the frozen ground in frustration.

"Perhaps simply walking wouldn't do the trick after all, and I have no intention of letting you live. So gallop it is."

Sir Hugh laughed.

Guy wondered if that would be the last sound he'd ever hear.

Lord, into your hands, I commit my spirit.

Sir Hugh's cluck to get his horse moving rang in Guy's ears, louder than any cluck had a right to be, and then suddenly he was rushing along the ground. The frozen earth grated against his chest and thighs, the only parts of his body on the ground as he did his utmost to hold his head up. Every rock he encountered sliced open a new cut on the portion of his body hurtling across the rough ground.

They flew past the gate and outside the manor.

Guy's head dropped for an instant and he felt a searing pain cut across his cheek, as though he'd just fallen into a fire. He jerked his head back up a moment later, feeling the blood now oozing down the side of his face. He wasn't entirely sure he still had his left ear, but it was impossible to tell. His chest was on fire, his thighs equally burning with pain.

Small twigs were stabbing him as he rushed over them, and lodging themselves into his legs and his chest. What dirt there was that wasn't solidly frozen to the ground was wrapping around him like a blanket as he was dragged along. Every ragged breath was harder to take than the previous one had been.

Every muscle in his body was throbbing. He hit another rock, a larger one, and his world blinked out of focus as the gash it created in his side sent him tumbling even deeper into the pool of agony he now lived in. He could feel his clothes slowly shredding beneath him, and his legs had gone numb from being held up by the rope.

And then suddenly Guy was rolling over and over. His brain told him he was rolling in the opposite direction that Sir Hugh had been galloping before it was shut out by the roaring anguish that now inflamed his entire body.

He'd come to a stop.

Guy let out an involuntary whimper.

He lay there, blood oozing from nearly the entire surface of his body, unaware of anything but the agony burning through him. Once again, his vision blurred to black.

Guy could feel arms pulling him up. He wondered if his mother had come once again to comfort him in the night as she so often did after his father beat him to a pulp. He listened intently for the sound of her gentle voice soothing him.

For a moment he could see again, and his eyes told him a man was dragging him onto a horse, and that said man also had an arrow sprout in his arm as Guy watched him. . .

And then all was darkness again.

There was a fire. It was raging violently and someone needed to put it out! It was going to destroy the manor and everything else in its path.

No. It wasn't a fire. It was pain.

Pain searing up and down his body. Guy writhed and convulsed, trying to get away from the pain, to no avail.

Slowly, Guy became aware of the thudding of hooves.

Pounding, pounding, pounding in his head.

He'd just killed the woman he loved.

The Sheriff was taking him back to Nottingham.

All the long ride from Austria, the Sheriff's horse's hooves pounded into the ground, driving into Guy's mind.

You killed Marian.

You *killed* Marian.

Murderer.

Thud. Thud. Thud.

You killed her. You killed her. You killed her.

The horse's hooves were chanting at him. With every hoofbeat, Guy felt the jarring pain in his body heighten.

He was in hell.

Chapter 9

SIR HUGH

He had, for one glorious moment, been killing an outlaw;
the one thing that truly gave him joy, apart from his daughter. And
then his joy was snatched away and replaced by annoyance and
frustration.

Sir Hugh had felt the weight that he was dragging behind
Night, his horse, suddenly cease to exist. He'd spun around in the
saddle, dragging Night's head around to go back the way they'd
come. Night hadn't appreciated the abrupt turn and had reared
unexpectedly and sent Sir Hugh tumbling, and then sprawling on
the ground like an idiot.

Sir Hugh was not an idiot.

He'd leaped to his feet, and grabbed for Night's reins, but
his horse had had enough for one day and sidestepped out of his
reach. Sir Hugh had looked back, to see why Guy of Gisbourne
had come loose from his bonds and saw, to his fury, the duel-
wielding knight he'd met twice before dragging Guy onto a horse.
Beside him, also mounted, was a soldier Sir Hugh was sure was
one of Torin's men.

The question of why Torin's soldier was betraying him
was overshadowed by the question of how that duel-wielding
knight was even alive.

That man had, rather stupidly, tried to hold off Sir Hugh's entire army by himself—with the help of one other man. Both had died that night.

And yet here Gilbert was, stealing the outlaw Sir Hugh had been so looking forward to killing.

Gilbert was now second on Sir Hugh's list of men to kill, directly after Robin Hood—the man who'd kidnapped his daughter. Not least because he'd just spoiled the execution of an outlaw, but also because the one time that Sir Hugh had fought him in a duel, the knight had bested him.

Sir Hugh managed to regain control of Night with a little more difficulty; he really wasn't interested in behaving at the moment. Then he took off after Torin's rebellious soldier and the knight who had stolen Sir Guy.

He hadn't waited to give orders to Torin, or anyone else, but he wasn't alone in his pursuit. Some of Torin's men, it turned out, had the presence of mind to realize someone interfering with the outlaw's execution must not, in fact, be on their side and had therefore taken up the chase as well.

Sir Hugh could see Sir Guy slumped over the saddle in front of the duel-wielding knight, looking quite dead. That, at least, was something positive.

Yet the pleasure of it was rather ruined by the fact that the dead man in question was on a horse galloping away from him rather than laying in the dirt where he could gloat over him.

Robin Hood and his friends were proving far more of a nuisance than Sir Hugh thought any outlaws had a right to be. Killing people was his business, and he was good at it. So why were they causing him so much trouble?

Twilight was fast approaching. Between the brief battle to gain control of Gisbourne manor and then interrogating the serfs until Sir Guy had stepped forward, the day had passed swiftly. The dual-wielding Gilbert and the traitor of a soldier were riding hard to the east which meant they, and Sir Hugh as well, were casting long shadows that stretched beneath them and reached for the horizon in front of them.

If Sir Hugh could only catch those traitors as fast as his shadow could, he'd already have the outlaw—dead or alive, whatever state he was currently in—back in his custody.

IDA

Dawn came and went with Ida pacing the small room where she, Andrew, Faith, and little Lucy had holed up in the small village on the edge of the forest still on Gisbourne lands. The wife of one of the serfs who had bravely defended the manor gladly let them hide in her little house as they waited for Gilbert and Guy to make an appearance. It was one small room, with a straw mattress in one corner. There was a door that entered a small kitchen that made up what could be considered a second room, but it was small and only used for cooking. So they were

157

all gathered in the small living space waiting for Gilbert and Guy to arrive.

Ida was getting uncomfortable.

This was exactly what had happened before when they'd fled Sherwood. She, Guy, Andrew, and Faith had simply sat around Middlesborough waiting for the rest of the gang and no one had showed. Guy had then made the decision to head for Gisbourne estate, as that would be—in his mind—the safest place for them. And it had been safe, and their lives quiet, for some months.

Now, however, Sir Hugh had arrived and everything had gone to hell. Ida was now facing the same decision that Guy had been back in Middlesborough. Wait for the others, or take those already with her to a safer place?

"Would you like to eat?"

Ida glanced toward the open door where their host, Emma, was standing. She had an old apron on over her simple brown dress and was covered in flour from her hem to her hair.

"I've just begun baking," Emma said, shaking some flour off her hands. "And I'll have some bread for you later. But before that, I'm sure I could scrounge something up."

Ida glanced at her companions. Little Lucy was curled up on the simple straw mattress that made up the only bed in the house. Faith was sitting beside her daughter, stroking her hair absentmindedly as she prayed; she'd been praying since their arrival and Ida found it simultaneously annoying and reassuring.

Andrew was, as Ida had been, pacing. They'd been matching each other's strides on either side of the room.

Andrew now turned toward Emma with a blank expression on his face.

"I suppose you must be hungry," Emma said hesitantly, looking first at Ida, then at Andrew. "I'm sure you haven't eaten since before the battle."

Ida sighed. "Right. Food. I'll come help you, Emma, and we can scrounge something up for me and my friends."

Ida followed Emma to the only other room in the house, the small kitchen.

Emma had done more than simply shelter them. Though she wasn't as well-versed in medicine as Dusty or Lucy, she had done her best to patch up both Ida and Andrew's various wounds they'd received during the brief battle of Gisbourne manor. Ida was grateful for everything, no matter how small. Any help they received was welcome.

But now she had to decide what to do. Stay and wait, hoping for the best? Or simply take Faith and Andrew to safety elsewhere?

FAITH

Ida was going to tell them they had to leave. Faith was sure of it. They'd eaten what Ida and Emma had prepared, and then Ida and Andrew had resumed their pacing. Little Lucy had

159

woken up eventually and had been having a lovely time helping Emma baking bread. Faith sat on the straw mattress and studied her companions.

Andrew seemed lost, as lost as she'd ever seen him. She could understand; Guy was, after all, his oldest and dearest friend. She ached to be sure her husband was still alive, but even so, she couldn't wallow in that despair the way that Andrew seemed to be doing because she knew full well Who was in charge of their present situation. And anyway, though it would hurt tremendously, she knew if her husband *had* died, then he would be safe with the Lord already.

Faith shuddered, thinking of Guy being dead. She certainly didn't want him to be dead. But she couldn't deny a certain calm assurance that even if he was, she would be okay.

Faith glanced over at Ida, still pacing by the window. Ida would scoff at Faith's assurance, of that Faith had no doubt. And Ida was going to insist they go to France to find Robin and the others without waiting for Guy and Gilbert. Faith watched her friend's face and knew with certainty that was what Ida was going to say, if she could only bring herself to say it.

Faith heard little Lucy giggling in the kitchen with Emma, and her heart ached. Would her husband ever hear that laugh again? Would little Lucy ever know her father? She was young enough that if he was, indeed, dead then she would likely forget him before she was all grown up.

Emma returned with little Lucy, bearing a wooden tray with steaming bowls, spoons, and chunks of bread.

"Soup!" Little Lucy said gleefully, her small tray wobbling dangerously as she toddled toward her mother.

"We brought sustenance," Emma said. "You all must be hungry again." Emma glanced at Ida and Andrew, still pacing, and shook her head. "I should put you all to work to get your minds off of things."

"Thank you, Emma," Faith said, taking little Lucy's tray before it could tumble to the floor and setting it beside her on the bed. "We are all grateful for what you are doing for us right now."

"I just hope Lord Gisbourne comes along soon . . .and Matthew, too." Emma smiled, but it barely reached her eyes.

Ida stopped pacing and took a bowl, spoon, and a piece of bread from Emma's platter and settled onto the dirt floor under the window.

As they all began to eat, Faith wondered when Ida would make her decision.

They couldn't stay here. Sir Hugh would likely inspect all the villages and farms on the Gisbourne estate. Andrew said he was likely to claim it for himself and would see to it that it ran smoothly so that he could collect revenue and add to his wealth.

When they'd finished eating, Emma took all the bowls, spoons, and trays back to her little kitchen.

Ida sighed. Faith looked to her expectantly as little Lucy clambered into her lap, her chin wet with soup that had not made it into her mouth, and was now dripping down onto her dress.

"Mama!"

"Yes, little one?"

"When is Papa coming?"

Faith could feel tears forming in her eyes, though she tried to stop them. "I don't know, little one. I don't know."

"We can't wait," Ida said, finally voicing what Faith had known she eventually would. "We have to leave."

Andrew groaned from where he was now laying on his back on the floor by the wall where he had previously been pacing, a bowl of uneaten soup steaming beside him..

"We can't stay here," Ida said defensively, glaring at Andrew, whose eyes were closed. "We'll leave first thing in the morning, head south to Dover, and then go to France and see if, by some miracle, we can locate the others. Gilbert is sure they've gone to France, but he doesn't know where. . ."

Ida lapsed into silence.

Little Lucy looked from one adult to the next, unsure why they all seemed so upset. Faith pulled her daughter to her chest, hugging her tightly. She didn't disagree with Ida's decision and had known it was the conclusion she would come to eventually, but somehow it still hurt to think they were giving up on Guy.

"We should all rest, not that we've been doing much else," Ida sighed. "Andrew and I both need to heal, and though I doubt that will happen overnight, the least we can do is get some rest before we leave tomorrow."

"I can make sure you have food to take with you," Emma said, coming back into the room. "We don't have much, of course, but I can't let Lady Gisbourne travel empty-handed."

"Thank you, Emma," Faith forced the words past the lump in her throat.

Little Lucy pulled away from her mother's embrace to stare at her, placing her tiny hands on Faith's cheeks. "Mama's sad? I'll make it better!"

Little Lucy wrapped her arms around Faith's neck and planted a slobbery kiss on her jaw.

Faith couldn't hold back the tears after that.

GILBERT

Gilbert wondered idly if he'd ever hear another sound apart from the pounding of hooves driving into the hardened dirt. His left arm was struggling to keep hold of the reins, the gash where an arrow had pierced his wrist during his rescue of Sir Guy making every movement intensely painful. That wrist still hadn't completely healed from its break, and now it had another wound. He could no longer feel his fingers. His right arm was keeping Sir Guy secure so he didn't fall off the horse.

Sir Guy flopped across Gilbert's lap in a rather ridiculous manner, his legs dangling over one side of the horse and his arms and head flopping around on the other side. The blood from his wounds had long ago seeped into Gilbert's trousers and stained them permanently. A few sticks that had managed to lodge themselves in the man's chest were now rather rudely poking Gilbert, but he didn't have time to remove them from his helpless charge. The horse Gilbert had rather unceremoniously stolen was not at all fond of Sir Guy's helpless flapping around or the unfamiliar presence of Gilbert and was skittish as a result.

Sir Hugh and his stubborn band of men—thankfully, at least, not the entire army—were keeping pace behind Gilbert and Roger. Gilbert didn't spare even a glance over his shoulder for fear of it slowing his race to freedom, but Roger was continuously looking behind with terror written across his face.

Gilbert wasn't afraid. Fear was not a commodity he dealt in. What he was feeling though was incredibly annoyed.

His rescue of Robin Hood's friends had not gone well. It was likely that four of them—counting the child—were at least free, but he had no way to confirm that. He wasn't going to rendezvous with the others as Sir Hugh would then know precisely where they were. He would instead lead Sir Hugh as far from the others as he could and then deal with the soldiers in the only way he knew how.

Gilbert and Roger had watched from just outside the manor as Sir Hugh had taunted Guy and then proceeded to gallop off down the road, gleefully enjoying the excruciating pain he was inflicting on his victim. Roger had been the one to dart for one of the nearby soldier's horses, and Gilbert had followed his example. They'd raced after Sir Hugh, unsure whether Guy would even be alive to save by the time they caught up.

Gilbert had followed the thick trail of blood that Guy created behind Sir Hugh's horse until he was within throwing distance; at which point, he removed a dagger from his boot and —rather impressively, in his opinion—he'd managed to send his dagger flying straight through the ropes that held Guy to Sir Hugh's horse.

Guy had come to a rolling stop and Gilbert had leaped to the ground beside him, untying him as quickly as possible and dragging him back toward the horse he'd stolen, which Roger was dutifully holding steady.

He'd mounted, struggling to keep the unconscious Guy from falling from his stolen steed, and then made for the opposite direction. Sir Hugh had, of course, given chase along with a number of soldiers who realized what was happening and thought it best to stop the rescue. They left to shouts from other soldiers, particularly the two who were now without horses because Gilbert and Roger had had need of their mounts.

Gilbert and Roger had galloped through the night, with Sir Hugh and his soldiers not far behind them. The horses they'd stolen were coated with a thick sheen of sweat, their breath was coming in great noisy gasps—each one reverberated along their bodies so violently that Gilbert was sure they would knock Guy right off. Their heads were drooping ever lower; it was a wonder the poor beasts weren't tripping over their own noses.

It was small comfort that Sir Hugh and his men's horses were not faring much better. It had been a long ride through the night and into the next day and all of them were exhausted; the men as well as the horses.

The horse beneath him faltered and for a moment Gilbert thought he was going to lose Guy right over the horse's neck. It struggled to right its footing, however, and on they ran—if the stumbling slow pace they were keeping could be called running.

"We can't keep this up!" Roger yelled, bringing his horse closer to Gilbert's, although the horse protested with a loud cry of pain, and tripped over a rock, stumbling several feet before finding its footing again. Roger eyed his horse with some trepidation. "Gilbert, we can't keep this up."

Gilbert knew he was right. They were going to kill the horses trying to keep up this pace; they'd become progressively slower through the day. The sun was reaching its zenith and Gilbert knew that by nightfall, or sooner, the horses would not be able to go a step further.

A scream punctuated Gilbert's thoughts, and for once he did turn in his saddle to see what had caused an animal's cry of pain and fear.

One of Sir Hugh's men had gone down. The horse was laying on the ground, and the soldier was several feet in front of it, sprawled on the grass. The horse didn't appear to be getting back up, but Gilbert thought he could still see its chest rising and falling as it ingested great gulps of air.

The question that burned in Gilbert's mind was how he was going to shake Sir Hugh and his remaining men off of his tail when his own horse was as likely to collapse as that poor devil back there.

He did not, in fact, have an answer to that question, but he wasn't entirely worried.

Guy groaned, and Gilbert tightened his arm around Guy's torso as he flailed. ". . .Mar . . .ian . . ."

Gilbert worried what this frantic ride was doing to Guy's already serious injuries. The man might not live to see another day under the best of circumstances, but as it was, Gilbert was jostling his wounds, and he wasn't likely to see a physician of any sort for quite some time.

Another yell behind them, this time from a man rather than a horse. Gilbert didn't look back to see what had caused the disturbance.

". . .I didn't mean to . . .please! . . .sorry . . ."

Guy was moaning pitifully, bouncing along across Gilbert's knees, his head smacking into the side of the horse every few steps, which was causing the horse to become increasingly more jittery on top of its exhaustion. Guy was delirious, that much Gilbert knew. What Guy was going on about, he had no idea, but the man's current state of mind didn't bode well with the injuries he'd sustained. If he was still alive when they dealt with

Sir Hugh and the soldiers, Gilbert would be surprised. Yet, even so, he had to try to save him.

A moment later, Roger's horse tripped and crashed to its knees. Roger managed to stay on its back and turned to watch Sir Hugh with open terror as Gilbert ran—as fast as a near-dead horse can run—past.

Gilbert hesitated for a split second, and then swung his horse—slowly—back around.

"Up! Quickly!"

Roger glanced up at him and his outstretched hand, doubt written across his features.

"Now!" Gilbert roared.

Roger clambered onto the back of the horse, grabbing Gilbert's shoulders, and Gilbert turned his mount forward again.

The steed slowed even further, stumbling with each step; the sound of its breathing was growing steadily louder.

They weren't going to make it much further.

The sound of something large smashing into the ground echoed behind them, and Gilbert was sure another horse had collapsed. Perhaps if they could just hold out long enough, they'd be the only ones on horseback.

But considering the extra weight his poor mount was having to carry, Gilbert thought it more likely he'd be the next one down. He might as well get this over with before the horse had to suffer for it.

Gilbert pulled his horse to an abrupt stop. Roger slipped off and landed with a thud on the ground, although Gilbert had miraculously kept hold of Guy.

Gilbert dropped to the ground, pulling Guy down as well and rather roughly dropping him on the ground. He then turned to face the oncoming soldiers. There were about a dozen of them, counting Sir Hugh.

Gilbert strode toward them, closing his eyes and breathing deeply. Twelve men. Gilbert let his confidence wash over him. His prowess with the sword—or in his case, swords—could not be matched. It was true that trying to take on the entire army single-handedly had ended very badly, but twelve men? This was too easy.

Gilbert opened his eyes. Roger was now by his side, looking positively petrified. Gilbert ignored him and focused on the twelve men whose horses were faltering ever closer. They were staggering toward him in a line, not all at once.

He drew his two swords, grinning.

This was what he lived for.

He ignored the pain reverberating throughout his body from his wounds of the past few days, and the bruises and cuts that hadn't entirely healed from his last encounter with Sir Hugh's army two months before. His wrist was particularly angry with him, but that couldn't be helped.

Wounds or not, he could do this. He'd beaten Sir Hugh back in Nottingham in a sword fight, so Gilbert knew he had nothing to worry about there. And taking down eleven soldiers was hardly a challenge, even in his wounded state.

His confidence, so frail after the failed rescue, was returning full force. No one was better than he was with a sword. This was going to be over before it began.

Seeing as the soldiers came within range in shifts, as their horses weren't all moving the same pace and several had been reduced to walking when their horses gave out on them, Gilbert never had more than three opponents at a time. His wrist screamed in agony with every swing of his left sword, but executing the eleven soldiers was done without too much trouble.

Sir Hugh had rushed passed him entirely while he fought off the other soldiers, his eyes only for Guy, sprawled on the ground and bleeding out. Roger, however, despite his obvious terror, stood over Guy's body valiantly.

When Gilbert had finished with the rest of the soldiers, sporting a handful of fresh cuts on his arms and legs, none of which were too serious, he moved forward to help Roger.

Roger was now on his knees, bleeding from his arms, but what concerned Gilbert more was the gash in his chest. Sir Hugh was bearing down on Roger for the fatal strike when Gilbert had struck him from behind; no fanfare, just a wallop on the back of the head with Gilbert's heavy pommel and down he'd gone.

Gilbert dragged Roger, bleeding and broken, away from Sir Hugh quickly, and then spun around when he heard Sir Hugh rising from the ground.

He jumped toward him, bringing both swords in broad swings in front of his chest. Sir Hugh stepped back, struggling to bring his own blade up to block.

Gilbert flicked his wrists and danced forward, both swords moving with as much speed as he could muster in his exhausted state. Sir Hugh had to continually step back out of his way to avoid being sliced in half.

The sight of Henry's head being chopped off filled Gilbert's mind, and he surged forward. Sir Hugh had to die.

In another moment, Sir Hugh tripped over a rock as he scooted backward and he stumbled to his knees. Gilbert took that opportunity to plunge one of his swords into Sir Hugh's chest.

Letting loose a satisfying roar, Gilbert pulled his sword free and stepped back, breathing heavily. Sir Hugh stared at him, seemingly shocked to find himself losing the duel. In his eagerness, Gilbert had swung wide of the heart, but it would do the job.

"That's for Henry," Gilbert hissed.

Gilbert would have loved to gloat further, watching as the life slowly left Sir Hugh's eyes, but Guy and Roger were now both fatally wounded and needed attention.

Chapter 10

ANDREW

Emma had provided them with bread, cheese, and water from her well. They'd woken little Lucy long before she was ready to open her eyes, mounted their horses, and set off. They were headed to Dover, and from there they would attempt to find the rest of their family.

For the first time in a long time, Andrew had hope that he would see his wife Jane again, hold his son Richard again. His heart skipped at the thought.

The sky was grey and the morning cold and clear as they trotted along.

They were headed toward Jane and Richard, and for that Andrew's heart was light. Yet they were leaving behind Guy, who was more than likely dead. That was enough to snuff out the light that had begun to shine when Andrew thought of Jane.

Guy.

Dead.

Andrew could not claim a closer friend in the world than Sir Guy of Gisbourne. At the very beginning, it had been only them. The two of them surviving Lord Gisbourne's abusive hand, thriving under Lady Gisbourne's gentle nature. The two of them, horror-struck by Lord Gisbourne's murder of Guy's mother. The two of them, alone in the world, turning to one another for comfort. Even as Guy had risen to prominence, become friends with Prince John and the Sheriff of Nottingham, he'd always kept Andrew by his side. They were brothers; their bond ran deeper than blood.

But now it was severed, perhaps forever.

It wasn't forever, though, as Andrew well knew. He shared Faith's assurance that they would one day be reunited in heaven.

Yet, even so, that comfort was only enough to assuage the pain, not remove it entirely.

Guy was dead.

His best friend was gone, and how was he supposed to survive without him? Who would he tease about being impressively brooding? Who would he commiserate with when the rest of the gang continued to distrust him due to his past associations with Prince John?

Andrew's heart constricted, his throat closing over, and his vision blurring. He wanted, more than anything else at this moment, to be with Jane. Jane would know how to comfort him, despite the loss of his dearest friend.

They plodded along for hours, stopping when the sun was directly overhead to eat some of Emma's provisions before setting off again. Little Lucy sat in front of her mother, watching the world with her wide, expressive eyes. Sometimes she'd point at a field of flowers that had caught her eye, or clap delightedly when a bird would soar overhead. Her laughter would bubble up and wash over the landscape; her joy complete.

Guy would never see her grow up.

Andrew turned away from little Lucy, staring resolutely ahead. The road they were taking was not lonely. There were occasionally other travelers headed in either direction; merchants with small caravans of produce carted along behind them, knights in full armor riding along the road alone, a farmer and his family riding their rickety old wagon to one place or another, all of whom would wave politely as they passed.

To keep Guy from his mind, Andrew focused on how wonderful it would be to see Jane and Richard again. His son was likely going to be unrecognizable. It had already been six months and would likely be more before they found where Robin and the others were hiding. So long a period of time in a child Richard's age was an eternity. His son had not even lived one full year in the world when they had been separated in Sherwood; he would be nearing two if they didn't find Robin and the others quickly. Andrew missed his son dearly, and his wife as well. Yet he was going to see them soon if all went well. Guy, on the other hand, he would likely never see again in this lifetime.

Andrew could once again no longer see the road through his tears.

IDA

They'd been traveling for over a week, stopping in taverns along the road, very quickly running through what little they had of money. Ida had hoped to procure more weapons, as she now only had her daggers stuffed in her boots; her bow and sword having been taken by Sir Hugh's soldiers. Andrew was entirely without weapons, having never taken up the practice of carrying daggers in his boots, and Faith had never carried any weapons at all in her life.

If they met any trouble, they would be hard-pressed to get out of it. But they didn't have the money to spend on weapons. They might not even have enough to reach France and find the others.

The others . . .

Ida's despair, ever-mounting since arriving on Gisbourne estate, had seen at least a pinprick of light in the last week. She would see her husband and sons unless some unforeseen obstacle arose to detain them.

Ida wanted to believe that nothing of the sort would occur; they would reach France, easily find Robin and the others, she'd be reunited with her family and all would be well. But she didn't truly believe that, not even close. Something was sure to happen to stop their progress. Ever since the attack on Sherwood six months ago, their lives were forever marked by obstacles.

Mountains to climb, Faith might call them. But Ida knew they were impassable.

She wanted to see her husband, to hold her sons, more than anything. It made her heart pound and her hands shake just to think of them. Yet she couldn't hope; hope only led to more heartache when it was inevitably snatched away. But hope was a hard thing to destroy or ignore.

When another small town came into view on the horizon, Ida made the decision to stop for the night. She procured them rooms in a tavern with what little remained of their money and then left Faith to look after little Lucy, and Andrew to brood—if he kept this up, he was going to look remarkably like their deceased friend soon—and she went to care for the horses.

The small stable behind the tavern was dark, with only one lantern swinging from a post near the middle of the stable. Along both sides were stalls, about a dozen in total. Half of them were occupied by horses, three of which were the gang's. The stable smelled strongly of manure, with an underlying scent of leather. It was far from the most pleasant smell, but, as Ida had grown up on a farm, she ignored it and went to groom Midnight. There was a small lad employed by the tavern who was also in the stable, already in the midst of grooming their other two horses.

Ida tied Midnight to the gate of his stall and grabbed a brush. She hadn't finished her thorough brushing of Midnight when she set the brush aside and leaned against her horse, wrapping her arms around his neck and burying her face against his velvety nose.

Guy was probably dead.

How could she possibly continue to face Faith every day of their journey knowing she hadn't been able to save her husband? She hadn't even tried. She'd simply left with that soldier Roger and then listened to Gilbert when he said to run.

What would she say to Lucy if they ever found the other members of the gang? Apart from his wife Faith, no one cared more for Guy than Lucy did and now he was dead.

And why did she care so much? Guy's likely death laid heavy on Ida's heart. She didn't respect him or like him and for many years she had hated him, but now that he was probably dead she felt some amount of remorse for her treatment of him. And more concern for Faith than she thought possible. She was as close to grieving Guy's death as she could get without actually crying for him, and it shocked and disturbed her.

Ida finished caring for Midnight, made sure the stable boy had done a decent job with Promise and Quest, and then returned to their rooms to sleep. Leading this small portion of their family while aching for her husband and sons, grieving for Guy, and wondering where on earth they would find the others, not to mention worried about Sir Hugh following them, it was nearly too much for Ida to stand. If they ever found the others, she was going to kiss Robin just for holding up under the ever-mounting pressures of leadership for so many years.

ROBIN

Robin reached into the basket of feathers by his side and snatched one up, glancing at it briefly to ascertain its length and then deftly cutting it down to seven inches with a flick of his knife. He was sitting on the wooden floor in the backroom of the fletcher's shop where he worked, surrounded by a basket of feathers, an unruly pile of arrow shafts, and a large pot of hide glue. He carefully attached the feather he'd just cut to an arrow shaft with thread, and then covered the spine of the feather in hide glue to ensure it didn't come off, before setting it to one side to grab another feather.

Once he'd attached three feathers to the shaft, he picked up his knife again, and carefully trimmed the fletching to be as effective as possible in flight. Robin tossed his fletched arrow into the ever-growing pile against the opposite wall and then grabbed the next shaft and feather to begin again.

Pepin Grasson, the fletcher who had so graciously agreed to hire Robin, was busy in the front of the shop with a customer; a knight demanding a large number of arrows as fast as humanly possible. Robin listened through the open door between the rooms, though he couldn't see the encounter due to where he was sitting against the wall.

"I need five thousand arrows, now!"

"We will get your arrows to you as soon as we can," Pepin responded quietly.

"Now!"

"Five thousand arrows cannot be cut, sharpened, and fletched all in a minute," Pepin said calmly. "But we will do our best to fill your order within the week, sir."

"Week! No, no, no. That won't do at all. I need them now!"

"Are you leaving for a battle immediately, sir?"

"No."

"Then your arrows can wait the time necessary to create them, yes?"

"I am in a hurry—"

"But you are not entering any conflict within the week?"

"We set out in a fortnight."

"Then you will certainly have your arrows before you leave. Good day to you."

Robin grinned as the knight expressed his displeasure in loud sighs before leaving.

Pepin peeked in a moment later, his long brown hair hiding most of his face as he leaned around the door. "Five thousand arrows, Robin."

"I heard."

"Finish the order you're working on first. Sir Henri can wait."

"Whatever you say, Pepin."

Pepin nodded curtly and then disappeared back into the other room. Very little could disturb Pepin Grasson, Robin had realized soon after starting his job. He was a man of eternal calm; not exactly pleasantly calm, but certainly not wishing anyone ill. He wouldn't be riled into anger, but he wasn't likely to dance with joy either.

When Robin had first approached him for work some weeks before, Pepin had initially turned him away with an explanation of not wanting an Englishman in his business. He insisted it would prove him untrustworthy to the locals. Robin had tried to convince him otherwise and had inadvertently succeeded when he let slip he was, in fact, Robin Hood.

Robin had realized soon after arriving in France that being Robin Hood did not carry the weight that it did in England. The Frenchmen, on the whole, did not care that he was champion of the downtrodden of England. Robin had not, therefore, expected the knowledge of who he was to play any role in getting employment when he began looking for a job.

Pepin Grasson had no great love for the late Richard the Lion-Heart or hatred for John Lackland, but his admiration for the reputation of the famed archer was enough to land Robin a job fletching arrows. Pepin was of the opinion that no one could fletch an arrow better than the great Robin Hood, though until Robin started working for him he really had no basis for that belief at all. Robin found Pepin's complete faith in him rather amusing.

He was certainly adept at fletching arrows, but his mind often wandered from his work. They had been living in Paris for almost three months now. King John and his politics with Philip and Arthur hardly played any role in their lives at all, and Sir Hugh was nowhere to be found.

They had settled into a peaceful, productive life among the French. Robin working with Pepin nearly every day, Lucy volunteering at the various hospitals, Marian being looked after by Elinor, Mary, or Jane throughout the day. Their evenings were spent in comfort in their rooms at the inn, Lucy often reading Scripture to them, while Robin played on the floor with Marian or vice versa. Sometimes the whole of the gang would gather for a night of fun and games, or simply conversing with one another while the children caused chaos, other times it would be mere factions of the gang that enjoyed each other's company for a meal.

They were practically happy, and certainly giving themselves purpose and building a home. Friendships were being born among those they worked with, such as Pepin, or the scholars that Dusty would bring by for a meal from the schools she spent nearly every day at.

They could live here for the rest of their lives, Robin was sure of it. They would be safe, and they would be happy.

The only thing missing from their lives were the five members of their family that were still at large. Guy, Faith, little Lucy, Andrew, and Ida. Otherwise, everything was as perfect as living as fugitives could be. Robin could raise Marian here without complaint.

Yet, even so, he missed Nottingham. He missed his home, he missed being surrounded by people he'd known all his life. He missed being the Sheriff of Nottingham and helping his people by ruling them well. He missed Sherwood Forest.

He didn't believe there was ever a chance of them returning home, however, so he resigned himself to the fact that their lives now, such as they were, would be the template for the rest of their lives. It wasn't a bad life, truth be told. They had a place to live, an income, jobs they genuinely enjoyed, friends to break the mundane of everyday life, and most of their extended family surrounding them. If Paris was his home till his death, Robin could live with that.

It had been amusing, over the last three months, to watch the members of the gang who had not been raised with access to the education that others among them had been blessed with. Those who already knew French had integrated nearly seamlessly into the culture of Paris, although life in Paris was far different from that in Nottingham. But those who had not spoken a word of French before coming here, or who knew only a little, had had more of a struggle. It was not their struggle that amused Robin, but rather their attempts to learn the language. There had been many a night when Little John, Elinor, and Jane had sat around the fire quizzing each other on new words they'd picked up in the last day and being corrected in pronunciation by Will or Allen or even Mary when she was in a particularly feisty mood.

The result was that three months into their stay in Paris, all of them could at least carry on a conversation with the locals, some more adeptly than others. Then there was Dusty, who spent every waking hour at the monasteries and schools, conversing with scholars from around the world, and learning to speak, read, and write fluently in French from her private tutor Ernest Dartois. Dusty astounded Robin with her aptitude for learning languages as well as every other subject known to man. Robin was sure she was soon going to rival any of the other scholars that the schools boasted about with her ever-increasing knowledge in all subjects.

Much was cheerfully toiling away in the kitchens of the inn where they lived, happy to be doing what he loved and unconcerned with anything else. His daughter, little Mary, was nearly a year old now. She wasn't yet walking, and though she knew very few words as of yet, what she did know was a smattering of both French and English words. Robin's own daughter Marian was also picking up on the language faster than the adults of the gang who were trying to learn, and most of the children were the same way, the only exception being three-month-old Rachel.

Robin carefully wrapped the thread around another feather, securing it to the shaft of an arrow. The pile of shafts at his feet was dwindling. He would have to fetch more of the completed shafts from Pepin if he was going to continue much farther in his work today. As Robin took his knife and trimmed the vanes of the feather, he continued to think about his family.

Mark, as of yet unemployed, spent much of his time wandering the countryside and growing moodier by the day. Robin wasn't entirely sure what was bothering him. He'd tried to draw it out of him a few times and received sullen responses. It was possible he was still seething over Lucy's insistence to never take a life, resulting in her not killing Sir Hugh when she had the chance.

This wasn't the first time Mark had taken to being quiet and moody. When his sister, Robin's first wife Marian, had died, Mark hadn't said a single word for months. Yet no one had died yet in this instance, so grief could hardly be the culprit responsible for Mark's increasingly brooding nature. Will and Dusty were the only people Mark seemed willing to speak to without a sullen expression on his face, and Robin trusted that whatever was disturbing him could be dealt with by the two of them. When Mark wasn't wandering aimlessly around the countryside, he spent his time with Dusty at the various monasteries and schools she had begun to call home.

Will was keeping busy working as a carpenter's apprentice. He often brought home various blocks of different shapes and sizes, the unwanted ends and leftovers from projects, and carved and whittled these blocks into animals or other toys for the children. Little John, though unemployed, was kept busy every day by Elinor and Mary, who would send him on errands to fetch things from the market or various shops, or by Jane who would take him to the countryside to spar and otherwise continue her training with weapons and hand-to-hand combat. Every couple of weeks, the whole gang would make a day of it in the countryside, taking a picnic along and letting the children run wild as the adults all sparred and trained.

Robin ran his fingers along a feather, idly counting the shafts still left beside him as he continued to run through his gang in his mind. He liked to consider them all every few days, gauging how they were faring emotionally and physically depending on their circumstances.

Allen was working with a blacksmith, and coming home every day far dirtier than anyone else, covered in grime and sweat that none of the rest of them could complain of. He was happy though, as happy as a man still longing for his missing wife could be. He was, at least, more content in his new life than Mark could boast.

Robin wished there was something he could do to find Allen's wife Ida, and Jane's husband Andrew, as well as Guy, Faith, and little Lucy. He didn't like that part of the family, the people under his care and charge, were beyond his reach. He felt helpless when he thought of them, and helpless was not a feeling Robin was either used to or enjoyed. Yet there was nothing that he could do about it except trust that the Lord was keeping watch over them.

LUCY

Warmer weather was just around the corner. Lucy could feel spring beginning to creep over the landscape whenever she went for a walk outside of the city. Inside Paris, it was still dark, dreary, and generally smelling of human and animal waste at all hours of the day. Nottingham had never carried this stench in every narrow street, for which Lucy was immensely grateful. Despite being surrounded by the height of fashion, education, and the arts here in Paris, Lucy truly missed Nottingham. Her days were hardly lacking in things to do; she was far too busy to dwell on her homesickness. And in any case, she was surrounded by her family, who were far more important than the clean smelling streets of Nottingham.

Her life in Nottingham had been full, and so it was here in Paris as well, though the routine that she followed was entirely different. Lucy woke every morning in time to feed Robin before he went off to his employment as a fletcher, crafting arrows for others' use. A lot of mornings before her trek to the hospital, Lucy would take one or another of the horses the gang had brought to France on a ride through the countryside. She loved riding, and their horses certainly needed the exercise, being cooped up in the city every day and night. And Marian loved getting out of the city nearly as much as the horses did. Generally, Marian would then be taken to Elinor, Jane, or Mary—or all three, if they'd decided to keep all the children in one place for the day—and Lucy would make the long walk to the hospital near Notre-Dame to spend the rest of the day easing the discomfort of the sick and homeless.

On this particular morning, however, Lucy had chosen not to visit the hospital but to spend the day with her daughter. They were far from home, and despite being loved by the other women of the gang, Lucy didn't want Marian to feel neglected. So she chose a day every week to spend entirely with Marian.

They had gone walking in the countryside one afternoon, though it had been so cold that Marian's little hands had remained nearly purple for several hours and Dusty hadn't been at all pleased. Despite her purple hands and red nose, Marian had enjoyed frolicking in the fields where she could be her energetic self without five adults reaching out to contain her.

Once they'd gone to the market at the city gate, but Lucy decided that wasn't a trip to repeat after Marian had upset an entire cart of produce by chasing a stray dog beneath the mule pulling the cart and causing an uproar that resulted in the cart's contents spilling over a nearby booth which had toppled and sent its own products spilling across the street and impressively causing other booths nearby to wobble or fall over as well. More than one passerby had tripped over the bread, cloth, fruit, and other various items that were strewn about the road. Three merchants and the man with the cart had demanded retribution from Lucy and Lucy had decided taking Marian to the market was not something she was likely to do again.

Today Lucy decided that her day with Marian would remain closer to home; namely, in the stables belonging to the inn where they lived.

Lucy made sure her daughter's hand was securely within her own, and then led her down to the stables. It was a large building, with nearly thirty stalls down both sides of the aisle, many of them occupied by horses of all kinds although a few were empty and some housed grain of various kinds. Stacks of hay, barrels filled with oats, and even shelves of tack filled the middle of the stable. The overwhelming smell was that of manure, hay, and horse sweat.

Lucy led little Marian over to Hero's stall. Lucy hadn't been discriminating when riding and grooming the gang's horses. Her own horse, Scamper, hadn't been seen since the initial attack on Sherwood seven months before, so she wasn't personally attached to any of the horses, she simply loved them all. They all needed exercise and care, and she didn't mind giving them all a little love. She wasn't the only one caring for the horses, of course. The stables employed a number of grooms to look after any horses in their care, and the other members of the gang would occasionally stop by to groom or ride whatever horse they'd been stuck with since leaving England—as only Allen still had his own horse.

Lucy swung open the gate of Hero's stall, and the mare looked up at her expectantly.

"No ride today, Hero," Lucy said, moving forward and stroking her soft nose.

"I want to ride!" Marian said.

Lucy smiled, and scooped her daughter up, holding her close to Hero. Marian immediately reached out to touch her face.

"Gently, Marian."

"She's so soft!"

"I know."

Marian had spent a lot of time with horses over the last seven months, as they had practically been living on them as they ran from Sir Hugh. And even in Nottingham in the days of peace, Lucy's love of riding had led to Marian spending many hours on the back of a horse, or playing with a bit or bridle on the floor of the barn while her mother groomed one horse or another. She had rolled around in the hay and, unfortunately, in manure more times than Lucy could count.

Today, however, Lucy thought she might attempt something new with her nearly three-year-old daughter. She was going to teach her how to groom Hero, rather than simply letting her watch—and consequently cover herself in manure—as she had done in the past.

Marian planted a wet kiss on Hero's nose, and Lucy grinned, lowering her daughter to the floor again.

"Alright, Marian, stand back for a minute."

Marian skipped out into the aisle and scrambled up a pile of hay to perch herself on top of a covered barrel. Lucy coiled a rope around her shoulder and then moved forward toward Hero's shoulder, the mare turning to watch her movements. Lucy reached slowly under Hero's neck and caught hold of her mane, placing her other hand lightly on the mare's nose. She gently led Hero out of her stall and into the aisle where she had more space to work.

Lucy slipped the rope from her shoulder and over Hero's head, then tied it to one of the support posts holding up the roof of the barn.

"Marian, you can come over now."

Marian jumped down from her perch and ran over to her mother.

"Slowly, little one. We don't want to spook Hero."

"What are we going to do?" Marian asked, gazing up at Hero who towered over her little body.

"We're going to get a brush, and brush her body, mane, and tail."

"Why?"

"It cleans her, like when I give you a bath, and it is also a good time for me to check and make sure she doesn't have any injuries."

"Hero doesn't have an owie!"

"I certainly hope not, but that's something we have to watch for. Plus, Hero just loves being brushed, which is why I chose her for today. Dandy throws a fit when I have to brush him," Lucy laughed, adding as an afterthought, almost to herself, "Which is honestly quite odd for a horse."

190

Lucy went to the shelves of tack and supplies and found a brush to use and then returned to her daughter, who was jumping up and down to reach Hero's nose in an attempt to pet her.

Hero bent down benevolently and Marian squealed with delight as she threw her hands around Hero's nose. "She loves me!"

Lucy grinned. "She just might. Now come here." Lucy scooped up her daughter and placed her on her shoulders. "We're going to brush her neck first. Watch what I do, and then I'll give you the brush."

Lucy showed Marian how to brush in the direction of the hair growth and then gave the brush to Marian. Marian leaned over her mother, being perched on Lucy's shoulders placing her a bit higher than necessary, and roughly brushed Hero's neck. Lucy placed a hand over Marian's and guided the brush in more gentle and productive movements, all the while talking softly to Hero.

"I think she likes it!"

"I think she does."

As Lucy continued to guide her daughter's movements, her mind wandered to Marian's namesake, and subsequently to Mark. He couldn't speak to her anymore without a hint of annoyance in his voice, and that was on a good day. On the worst days, he would shout at her if he spoke to her, or ignore her entirely. He was furious she hadn't killed Sir Hugh, but Lucy knew that his anger and pain went far deeper than that. He'd never really been the same since witnessing his sister Marian's murder.

Chapter 11

GILBERT

When he'd beaten Sir Hugh, Gilbert had hurriedly strapped together a make-shift stretcher, made entirely of ropes, to pull Guy's broken body along behind Gilbert's exhausted steed. He'd then swung Roger up into the saddle. Roger clung to the horse's neck as Gilbert walked along beside the animal, encouraging it to continue moving forward for a few more miles at least. Just until he could find a place to stay. Roger's horse had dragged its feet slowly along behind him of its own accord. The other horses chose not to tag along, probably due to their exhaustion.

It had only been a few hours before Gilbert had come across a small village. He'd pounded on the first door he came to, demanded entry as friends of Robin Hood, and promptly dragged Guy inside as Roger stumbled along beside him.

The inhabitants of the house he'd accosted were an elderly couple. They'd put Guy into the only bed in the house, and made Roger comfortable on a pile of blankets by the fire. The wife, Rachel, had set about heating water and finding cloth to use for bandages while the husband, Michael, had run to his neighbors for help.

It wasn't long before a passel of women from the village were filling up the entirety of the little house, sending Gilbert rushing outside for the comfort of solitude. The women were debating whose grandmother's old remedies were the best and who knew the most about medicinal practices as they cleaned and dressed both Guy and Roger's wounds. Gilbert wasn't convinced any of the village women would actually succeed in saving Guy. Roger, whose wounds were not nearly as drastic they might, in fact, heal in the end.

That had been Gilbert's perspective that first night in the village. Two weeks had passed since then. Roger was on his feet now. Within a week of arriving, Roger had been well enough, and determined enough, to take his stolen horse and ride for the nearest city where he hoped to procure a real physician for Guy, rather than the eager to help but utterly clueless in the ways of medicine village women who'd been tending to the lord of Gisbourne estate. Roger had not yet returned. The longer he delayed, the less hope Gilbert had of Guy's survival.

Not that there had been much hope to begin with, and the simple fact that the village wives had managed to stave off death thus far was nothing short of a miracle.

The simple rope burns on Guy's wrists and ankles were healing nicely, though due to how deeply they had cut into his skin would likely scar. The side of his face that had been torn was also healing, and would also likely scar. He was missing a portion of his left ear, but Gilbert was sure he could survive without it just

194

fine. It was the rest of his wounds that Gilbert was concerned about.

His chest, torn open and bleeding profusely when Gilbert had brought him to the village, had, over the course of the last two weeks, maintained a moist, yellow consistency. His entire chest was inflamed and red, which offset the yellow dampness rather disgustingly. His abdomen had begun to harden while his stomach was swelling and his shoulders turned an unnatural green. The small punctures in his skin due to the twigs and rocks that had buried themselves inside him during his attempted execution were equally infected. And to top it all off, he had an angry, pus-filled gash in his right side that had Gilbert apprehensive about his internal organs—having never studied such, Gilbert didn't have the least idea what might be located around that hole in Guy's side, but it obviously didn't bode well. The wound was incessantly bleeding, and leaking the same moist yellow liquid that the rest of his chest was covered in.

Nothing short of a miracle was keeping that man alive.

For the first two days after arriving in the small village, Guy had been delusional, moaning about murdering Marian and crying for his mother by turn. He'd fallen silent after that, and hadn't truly woken up since. The women were force-feeding him daily, which often led to much choking and throwing up, but somehow they were keeping him nourished enough not to die. Gilbert could only attribute it to the miracle that was also keeping his wounds from killing him.

The satisfaction of killing Sir Hugh was overwhelmed with concern for Guy. And more than that, his pain over Henry's death was still as sharp as ever. Beating Sir Hugh hadn't assuaged it all in the way that he thought it should.

ROGER

Roger's search for a physician had led him through a handful of tiny hamlets and then eventually to the town of Oxford. It was a large town, though perhaps not quite a city, with a monastery, a few dozen homes, a handful of shops, a large open market, and of course the river Thames flowing lazily by.

Roger made for the shops first, tethering the poor horse he'd stolen and consequently dragged all over the kingdom to a post, and then bounding up to the door of a butcher's shop.

Inside all was darkness that his eyes slowly adjusted to, and the place smelled rancid. There were flies buzzing about in all directions, red meat on tables and hanging from hooks in the ceiling, and a skinny man with large arms wielding a giant knife was standing by one table. He looked up curiously as Roger ran in.

"Can I get you anything, sir?"

"Information, quickly!"

"You do know this is a butcher's shop. I deal in meat."

"Well right now I need to know if you have any physicians available for immediate use, if not sooner."

The butcher lowered his knife, looking at Roger rather thoughtfully. His deliberate movements and lack of verbal response had Roger bouncing on his heels in impatience, debating whether or not to throttle the butcher until he gave up the information Roger needed.

"The monks have some training with medicine over at the monastery, and of course there's that Walter fellow who set up an apothecary some ten years back. I believe he was trained by the monks, actually."

"Great. Where can I find this Walter fellow with the apothecary?"

"Just down four doors that way," the butcher waved his large knife and tiny droplets of blood went showering across the already dirty room. Roger jumped backward out of the way to avoid getting splattered.

"Thanks!"

Roger ducked back out of the butcher's shop and ran down the street in the direction the butcher had pointed, counting shops. Sure enough, four doors down was a small shop with dried plants hanging from the small awning over the door and a tiny wooden sign tacked on the door that read "apothecary."

Roger shoved open the door and hurried inside. He was greeted by an overwhelming wave of smells that permeated the room. Roger assumed the smells stinging his nose and making his eyes water were coming from the herbs and flowers; dried and hanging from the ceiling, filling bowls and plates along every shelf and table, and scattered across the floor in some places. There were rows of wooden shelves filling the small room, and tables scattered among them. Every surface was filled with jars, bowls, bottles, and the like and each one was filled with some plant—whole, fresh, dried, crushed—or various liquids that Roger didn't recognize. There was also one shelf devoted entirely to wine. Each bottle, jar, or bowl was labeled with a small strip of paper written across with the tiniest script Roger had ever seen.

That Walter fellow, as the butcher had called him, was bending over one of the tables, dried plants scattered around him. He had a pestle and mortar before him and was concentrating on crushing whatever plant he was currently working with.

"Walter?"

The young man glanced up; he could hardly be older than Roger himself with blue eyes that bored into Roger, and brown hair that was littered with crushed plant the way a cook's hair might be littered with flour.

"You are Walter, yes? You are trained in medicine?"

"Do you need medicine for some ailment?"

"What I need is a physician, a good one if I can get it."

"Are you hurt?" Walter set aside his pestle and moved toward Roger, concern etched in every line of his face. "What can I do?"

"I'm not a hurt, a friend—well, a man anyway—there's an injured man."

"Where? Can you bring him to me?"

198

"Hardly. He might be dead already. He can't travel, not in his condition. If he's still alive, that is."

"Where is he?" Walter moved swiftly toward the wall where he pulled a bag off of a hook and began placing various jars and bottles inside it, his movements quick but controlled.

"Some nameless little village, miles from here. It took me days to reach Oxford."

Walter raised his eyebrows but didn't comment, continuing to fill his bag with supplies, moving to a chest of drawers now where he found fresh cloth for bandages.

"Is there something I can do to help?" Roger asked.

"I doubt it. I'll have all my instruments and ingredients in a moment, and then it will be down to the stables to borrow one of William's horses, after which I can follow you wherever you need me to go."

"Thank you."

Roger tried not to shuffle his feet too much as Walter methodically gathered his supplies. Sir Guy of Gisbourne was bleeding out in that tiny village with Gilbert keeping watch and this man, possibly Guy's only hope of survival—although hope was a strong word, considering the state of Guy's wounds—was taking all the time in the world to simply pack a bag.

Walter seemed to know Roger was impatient because he looked up and smiled as one might smile at a child. "Describe his wounds to me. I can more accurately assess what I need to take with me that way."

Roger began to describe the extensive nature of Guy's wounds, and Walter continued packing for what felt to Roger like an eternity.

Before long, however, Walter was moving toward Roger again. "If you'll follow me to the stables, we can be on our way."

"Actually, I need to go get my horse; I left him at the butcher's. I'll meet you on the road leading west outside of town."

"I will be there shortly."

Walter strode down the street and Roger ran to get his stolen steed. He mounted in a hurry and cantered out of town where he then had to pull his horse to a stop. Sitting still and waiting for the physician did not agree with the horse any more than it did with Roger, it stamped its feet and flicked its tail impatiently.

Less than five minutes later, Walter came trotting out of town. "After you," Walter half-bowed to Roger.

Roger dug his heels into his mount's flank and it sprang forward. If Walter was going to let Roger set the pace, then Roger intended to run the poor beast ragged in order to get back to Gilbert and Sir Guy before the latter died.

GUY

Guy leaned against the rough wooden table, poorly hewn, covered with cloth of the finest quality. Among the silks and

200

satins was the occasional wool or some other cloth as well, but it was the finer threads that had Marian's eye. She caressed the smooth surface of one such cloth of the deepest red and Guy wished she would use that gentle hand to caress his cheek in such a manner.

Marian glanced up at him, and immediately her eyebrows shot to her hairline. "I don't know what you're thinking, Guy, but whatever it is . . .the answer is no."

Guy smiled. "You don't know, so how could you know you'd say no."

"That sentence may have sounded good in your head, but I confess, I'm not entirely convinced your education was of the finest degree."

"My education was indeed poor for many years . . ." Guy's mind drifted to his abusive father for a moment, but he brought it back instantly. "I was merely wishing you would show me the affection you give to the cloth in your hand."

Marian arched her eyebrows, tossing her thick brown hair over her shoulder, her eyes flashing. Guy's heart skipped a beat.

"You are positively the most absurd man I have ever had the misfortune of attending the Nottingham Fair with."

"Have you been escorted by gentlemen before?" Guy frowned, gazing into the beautiful face so near his own.

"Wouldn't you like to know?" Marian set aside her purple cloth and moved toward the next booth, deftly weaving through the crowd of peasants and nobles who were filling the streets. The sounds of children laughing, merchants clamoring for attention, and the hum of a million different conversations filled the air.

Guy followed Marian, catching hold of her elbow as she leaned over a table to appreciatively take in the tantalizing smell of freshly baked foods. "Have you been here with other men in past years?" Guy asked quietly.

Marian ignored him, taking a warm roll the baker offered her with a smile. "Thank you, Peter."

"Anything for you, Marian. How is your father?"

"As well as he can be." Marian glanced at her escort and then caught the baker's eyes again only to roll her own. The baker smirked but quickly wiped his expression clear as he glanced at Guy.

Marian moved toward another booth, stepping around a woman with a large basket filled with purchases, and three soldiers deep in conversation. Guy, who still had hold of her elbow, followed.

"Marian, you're torturing me."

Marian smiled. "You won't like my answer."

"Who brought you to the Fair?"

"My father, generally, and we always came with the Earl of Locksley and his son."

"Robin Hood? That's who my rival is?" Guy frowned. "You do realize socializing with outlaws is entirely punishable by law."

"Is it a crime to help people, Sir Guy?" Marian turned to face him fully, her eyes shooting daggers.

"He's stealing."

"Not for himself."

"If you see him . . ."

Guy didn't have a chance to finish what he was about to say to Marian, because quite suddenly she was laying on the ground. The Fair had vanished. They were in lush green countryside, with the shadow of a castle looming nearby. There were shouts and the sounds of blades striking one another, but all Guy cared about was Marian.

She was prone on the grass in front of him, a sword protruding from her chest, tears wetting her cheeks.

"Marian!"

Guy tried to run to her but found himself further and further away from her with every step that he tried to take.

"Marian!"

Suddenly she was upright again, the sword gone, though she was still in that beautiful countryside.

"I would rather *die* than marry you! I *love* Robin."

Everything went black.

Guy was numb.

Slowly he became aware of pain. Excruciating pain.

His father was beating him again.

Guy opened his eyes, determined not to show weakness. That would only anger his father and cause the beating to last longer.

Lord Gisbourne's whip flashed through the air, striking Guy's chest and ripping out chunks of flesh. Guy could feel the blood gushing from his wounds, pooling on the floor beneath him.

He wanted to die.

But then there was his mother, tears in her eyes but an encouraging smile on her face.

Then she was throwing herself between Lord Gisbourne and Guy, and Guy wondered if he would ever be so brave as she was.

The pain was going to kill him. Guy curled into a ball on his bed, screaming to release the agony, but it refused to leave him. Andrew was beside him, patting his shoulder awkwardly. Every gentle pat felt like an axe slicing through him, cutting away at his flesh.

"Let go, let go! Stop, stop!"

Everything was fading to black again.

GILBERT

Gilbert leaned against the door frame, ill at ease, his arms crossed loosely, waiting for some sign of distress or call for help.

If there was a cruel man to kill or a selfish man to beat

into submission or any man at all that Gilbert could fight with, that would be ideal.

Instead, however, Gilbert was watching the young physician Roger had found. Walter. A man who could hardly be thirty years old. Roger was sitting on the floor near Guy's bed, sipping some herbal tea that Walter had concocted for him. Walter had also sent the owner of the home, Micheal, to care for Roger's horse, saying it was in about as bad shape as Guy was and it was hardly fair of Roger to have worked him to the point of death. He would, apparently, have gladly cared for the horse himself but for his desperation to save Guy first.

And desperate he was. That much Gilbert appreciated. But the waiting and watching and having nothing productive to do was driving Gilbert mad. He hardly knew Guy at all, had just met him when he was so brutally executed—or, nearly executed, as Gilbert ought to say. Though if he died despite Walter's best efforts it would have been an execution alright, albeit a very slow one.

Guy still hadn't woken up. Rachel had continued to force-feed him. The number of times the unconscious man had gagged and promptly thrown up all over her were impossible to count, but Rachel had been determined to keep Guy alive. The other women had been shooed out by Walter, who insisted on working alone unless it was necessary to have a second set of hands. So far, he hadn't asked for Gilbert's help. He had enlisted Rachel's help to mix up ointments and teas for him, giving her precise written instructions to follow.

Walter was leaning over Guy's chest now, concentrating, his brow furrowed slightly. Guy's raw, open wounds had hardly altered in the two days since Walter's arrival. Gilbert knew Guy was going to die, despite his apparent subconscious stubborn will to live.

Rachel and Michael's small house had begun to eternally smell of herbs; cloves, mint, myrrh, saffron, and every other plant Walter saw fit to use in his desperate attempt to revive Guy. The smells had been overpowering on the first day, leaving Gilbert's nose stinging and his eyes watering, but he was growing used to them. The atmosphere inside the house still felt suffocating upon first entering it, but it only took a moment or two for Gilbert to adjust.

Walter was carefully extracting a small rock he'd found near Guy's stomach that the annoyingly helpful village women had missed when they'd pulled out the rocks and twigs three weeks before. He moved slowly and gently, and Gilbert found himself leaning forward slightly to watch as the stone came up, cleared what remained of Guy's skin, and splashed blood back down on Guy's stomach. Walter sighed, eyeing Guy's raw bleeding body and frowning.

"I can't imagine how he has survived this long."

Gilbert couldn't imagine either, but somehow Guy was holding onto life; for now, at least.

SIR HUGH

Sir Hugh's fingers tightened and his quill snapped in half. He'd been writing to Nottingham to inform the Sheriff that his daughter Isla would need to remain in the Sheriff's custody for some time longer. It had been four months since Sir Hugh had seen the only light of his existence, and strangely enough, he missed her. But Isla was in no conceivable way more important than killing Robin Hood and his band of outlaws.

Sir Hugh had woken up in the middle of the field where he'd been so close to killing Torin's traitorous soldier and then dealing with the duel-wielding knight named Gilbert. The traitor, the knight, and the outlaw's possibly dead corpse had been nowhere to be seen. Sir Hugh had been surrounded by dead men and half-dead horses. Torin had found him there, bleeding to death, and dragged him back to Gisbourne estate. He'd spent two weeks healing from his wounds and every minute of those weeks he kept the faces of Robin Hood and Gilbert fresh in his mind. The two men he was most eager to kill. This was by no means about King John's money anymore; it was personal on both counts.

In those two weeks of healing, lords of neighboring estates had been dropping in to demand that Sir Hugh free Gisbourne estate and give it back to its rightful owner. Some of the idiots had even brought soldiers as a show of force. But even from his near-death bed, Sir Hugh had easily dealt with them. The signed and sealed letter of the King that he kept with him at all times put nearly everyone in their place. Sir Hugh had been hired to do this job by the King himself, and unless they wanted to incur that wrath of the King of England, they had best stay out of his way. And so they left him to heal in peace.

In the weeks since he'd been healed and back on his feet, Sir Hugh had been corresponding with every ally he had, trying to find the duel-wielding knight and his companions. The next time Sir Hugh saw Gilbert, he was going to kill him. Without any fanfare; simply kill him and have it over with. The man was becoming a terrible nuisance.

In fact, all of the outlaws were. First, they'd all escaped the attack on Sherwood, then Robin Hood had kidnapped Isla, after which they'd run to Scotland. When Sir Hugh had followed, they'd escaped again. He caught up in Dover, but once again they managed to elude him. Then the attack on Gisbourne estate, which had been successful up until the outlaws disappeared right under his nose, one of them even managing to escape mid-execution.

It was infuriating.

Sir Hugh threw aside the broken quill and snatched up another from his desk. He was in what he assumed was Sir Guy of Gisbourne's den, where he spent most of his days. Writing to allies for information and help, pacing, smashing every breakable object within reach that was easily thrown across a room.

The question now was whether to wait for information on the whereabouts of the possibly dead Sir Guy or go to France and find Robin Hood. Sir Hugh certainly planned on killing Gilbert eventually, but Robin Hood was a higher priority. And waiting for news of Sir Guy had wasted an entire month.

Chapter 12

IDA

Ida stroked Midnight's nose, enjoying the velvety feel of her horse's face and trying to remain calm. They were nearly to Dover. From there, they would sail to the continent and head for French lands. Where in that vast area Robin and the others were hiding, Ida didn't have the faintest idea. Yet, even so, her anticipation was growing, as was the certainty that she would see her husband and sons again.

It was barely dawn, and Ida had bullied Andrew and Faith out of bed minutes before, insisting they eat in their rooms and meet her in the stables as fast as possible. There had been no sign of Sir Hugh and his army in the past month; not even a whisper of someone trailing them. Even so, Ida had maintained a steady pace to get them as far out of his reach as possible. And now with Dover so near and France just beyond it, she rose earlier every day with more impatience than the day before.

She was terrified that they would reach the others only to have them snatched away again, but her desire to find them was overpowering her fear.

The stable was dark, with the light of one feeble lantern which Ida had brought with her casting its bright but ineffective light around, causing the deep shadows to grow yet darker.

210

Midnight nickered softly and Ida leaned into him. "We're almost there, Midnight, almost."

The stable door opened, emitting the grey light of morning into the stable, and Andrew sauntered in. He had grown increasingly taciturn and surly over the last month and Ida didn't know what to do about it. Although a realist and grounded, unlike Faith, Andrew had always been more of an optimist than not. Now, he didn't say a word, either positive or negative, and simply glared at the world.

"Is Faith nearly ready?"

"Coming," Andrew huffed, moving toward his horse's stall and preparing to saddle Quest.

It wasn't long before Faith joined them, by which time Ida had already saddled Promise for her friend. Faith's eyes were red-rimmed and puffy, but she smiled gratefully, passing little Lucy over to Ida long enough to mount before taking her little girl in her arms and holding her tight to her chest. Little Lucy squirmed but didn't protest.

Ida mounted Midnight, checked to make sure Andrew was still with them, and then led her small party out of the stable and back onto the road that would lead them to Dover and, eventually, to the rest of their family. Her desire for her husband and sons was overwhelming, and now she was nearly equally eager to get Andrew to his wife Jane and son Richard as that might be the only thing to save him from his depression, as well as

211

surrounding Faith with the love and support the rest of the family would provide; that was of the utmost importance.

WILL

The massive kitchen of the inn where they lived had been transformed. One small area was still being used to cook food for the guests of the inn, while the rest had been cleared and decorated. The tables and floor were spotless, rather than covered in utensils, meat, vegetables, flour, and the like as they always were when Will visited Much in the kitchen. Each table was surrounded by freshly hewn logs to form chairs, as the actual chairs the inn owned were left in the common room for the other guests of the inn. Vases filled with vibrant flowers, the first of the spring season, were on every table and strung in garlands along every wall. It was like being at a wedding, except this party was not for a wedding ceremony but rather to celebrate the birth of Robin and Lucy's daughter, Marian.

She was turning three, and Much had convinced his friends in the kitchen to go all out in honor of the little girl. They'd concocted special dishes just for the occasion; despite being a simple inn, they'd somehow managed to get their hands on a peacock for the main course. There were marinated leeks, sausage, spiced quince cakes, and as much freshly baked bread as Will had ever seen in one place. He could understand why Much, who had always been obsessed with food, loved working in the kitchen.

Much was with two of his fellow cooks even now, fretting over the peacock and discussing the uses of spices. Mary was sitting at one of the cleared tables, little Mary in her lap. Little Mary, who was nearly a year old now, had a handful of flowers she was waving about like a flag and her mother was attempting to save from being crushed without taking them away altogether. Will watched with amusement from his seat at a second table.

"The petals are falling!" Daniyah announced from the stump beside him. Sure enough, two purple petals went sailing gently to the table.

Dusty came and sat across from Will, John scrambling into the seat beside his mother.

"Did you see that bird?" John asked with obvious excitement.

"It's a peacock, John," Dusty laughed.

"Ever eaten peacock?" Will asked his wife, laughing.

"No. Have you?"

"I haven't had the pleasure."

Will glanced around the room, enjoying the spectacle. Robin and Allen were enacting some sort of Celtic dance. Robin looked utterly ridiculous, and Allen seemed entirely out of practice. William and Edward were watching their father and Robin with squeals of laughter, doubling over and occasionally even throwing themselves on the floor.

Little John and Mark were conversing at the end of the room opposite the Scottish dance, and Jane—with her son Richard in her arms—was nearby, swaying to the music provided by a handful of musicians that Lucy had hired. Elinor was seated at the same table as Mary, with three-month-old Rachel in her arms, nursing quietly.

Lucy was showing Marian the various extravagant courses that Much and his friends had put together for the meal. Both were talking animatedly and laughing often.

They were all happy, and all at peace.

Will grinned, glancing back at the Scottish dancers who were now attempting to teach Edward and William—who were not cooperating at all.

"So much joy in one room," Dusty commented. "The Lord is good."

"Indeed."

Will glanced back toward Little John and Mark. They were deep in conversation, and for once Mark wasn't glaring at the world in general. He didn't look exactly at peace, but he wasn't looking particularly angry which was progress.

Much finally decided the peacock was as good as it would get and called everyone to gather at the tables. Most sat down with smiles on their faces, and Robin, Allen, and the twins were still in fits of laughter.

The cooks not continuing their work of providing for the inn and its inhabitants but rather feeding the gang, with Much's help, were Bruno and Eloise. Will watched as they assembled a handful of servants and began to direct the first course. Everyone was given a quince cake, as well as a bowl full of sliced oranges, blackberries, apples, and pears.

Will watched with amusement as his daughter Daniyah and young Marian tasted each fruit and then began trading between each other for the ones they enjoyed the most.
The fruit was quickly followed by a thick pottage, and then again by the peacock, along with a plentiful supply of fresh bread.

"*C'est tellement merveilleux!*" Marian exclaimed, sampling a small bite of peacock.

Will looked down startled and then glanced up in time to see Lucy looking down at her daughter with a mixture of surprise, laughter, and sadness on her face.

They'd been living in Paris for only three months, but the children were taking to the language of the locals so easily. Will wondered how long they would live here. If it was the rest of their lives, then perhaps English would be the strange language to their children. Will rather hoped that someday they would be allowed to return to England, but if this was their life for the rest of their days, it wasn't a bad one. The only downside was that there were still five members of the gang missing. That, and Mark's constant underlying anger against Lucy.

DUSTY

"Myrrh would be the best option," Ernest Dartois said vehemently.

"I disagree," Dusty replied. "Cloves, especially with comfrey."

"*Quel malheur*! Please tell me you are not serious? Mixing cloves and comfrey?"

"The cloves are perfect for cleaning wounds and ensuring infection is held in check."

"That is what myrrh is for, my friend. Though I do admit cloves work just as well. But the comfrey as well?"

"It speeds up the healing processes—"

"I am well aware! It is the mixture I am astounded at. Cloves and comfrey."

Dusty laughed. She and Ernest were in his office debating the proper ways to use medicine, as they often did. If it wasn't medicine they were debating, it was philosophy, and if not that, then Ernest was bemoaning his task of teaching Dusty to read and write French. Dusty had actually picked up the language surprisingly well under Ernest's tutelage, and he often told her so, but he loved to tease her as well.

"We must come to a different topic," Ernest said now, leaning back in his chair at his desk, studying Dusty with twinkling eyes. "I am afraid my poor physician's heart cannot stand it."

"I'll have you know, I am a good physician."

Ernest laughed. "Oh I am aware; I have seen your work and thoroughly picked apart your brain. Your friend Lucy is not without her talents as well. How is your family, Dusty? It has been some days since you have invited me for dinner."

"Everyone is doing well." Dusty was seated in a large cushioned chair that Ernest had purchased for her use. She was in his office so often that he'd decided she needed her own corner, complete with a comfortable chair and a small desk. "You can come for a meal this evening if you're so desperate for our company. It will just be Will, John, Daniyah, and I, not the whole gang."

"And have you heard from your missing friends?"

"Nothing."

"And your friend Mark, still brooding?"

"Still brooding. The anger and hurt that is simmering in him concerns me greatly."

"Do you know the true cause?"

"Mark was frustrated with Lucy months ago for not killing the mercenary following us."

"That would be Sir Hugh, yes?"

"That's the one."

"And he is still angry over simply that, then?"

"Well he's angry about something, that's certain. Lucy says there was a huge argument on the trip to Paris, although I wasn't aware of it. Yet Lucy thought they'd patched it up, so when Mark first started being so moody, she didn't attribute it to that argument."

"But now she thinks that must be the reason?"

"Yes. I know he hates being here in Paris and wants to go home but there is something deeper; I feel it. I may have to approach Mark about it. He needs healing, though perhaps of a different sort than we were just discussing."

"Who would be the best candidate for such a job?" Ernest leaned forward, placing his elbows on his desk, in what little space wasn't occupied by parchment, books, and quills, tapping his fingers lightly together. "Robin would be his oldest friend, yes?"

"Yes," Dusty replied. "Robin would probably be the best option, or Much as he is also a childhood friend and even more, he's completely harmless. He won't get into a yelling match. Robin is less likely to remain calm in every situation."

"Then perhaps you should persuade Much to talk to Mark and weasel out whatever is making him brood. When once you have that information, you can set about the next course of action, whatever that needs to be."

"I may do exactly that. Now, on to more enjoyable subjects, how about we test your minimal knowledge of Arabic?" Dusty grinned.

Ernest groaned good-naturedly. "*Ca alors*! My Arabic will never reach the heights of your French. I do not have the aptitude for languages that you so apparently do."

"N'importe quoi! You speak, read, and write in half a
dozen languages. What is Arabic compared to that?"

"The hardest language I have ever set about trying to
learn," Ernest laughed.

IDA

Ida shook hands with Captain Anthony. She'd just paid for
berths on his ship, leaving the next morning, to take her, Andrew,
Faith, and little Lucy to Calais. From there, they would figure out
where in France they would look first for the others. Ida had
never been outside of England and didn't have the least idea
where to start. Andrew hadn't traveled abroad either, and anyway,
his recent brooding left him unapproachable. Faith, however, had
traveled often as a child, spending her youth in many different
countries. Her mother had died abroad, due to complications
giving birth to Faith's deceased little brother Richard. All of this
Ida knew from their days of living as outlaws in Sherwood Forest,
and now she finally had an opportunity to put Faith's knowledge
to good use.

Ida had enlisted Faith's help in procuring a ship, and she
intended to lean heavily on Faith's experiences abroad to decide
where they should travel first.

"Feel free to bring your belongings aboard the ship
tonight," Captain Anthony said. "But it would be better if we

don't stow the horses until morning. The less time they have to spend on the ship the better."

"I imagine they don't like it much, do they?" Faith asked.

"Not at all," the captain replied.

"Agreed," Ida said. "I will send a servant with our belongings; don't worry, they won't take up much space. I will see you in the morning, sir."

"I look forward to it," Captain Anthony replied.

"Thank you!" Faith called to the captain as Ida turned and marched back toward the tavern where they had put up for the night.

"Faith, I expect your help in looking over the captain's maps to decide where we will go to look for Robin and the others."

"I'll be glad to help in whatever way that I can."

Faith was quieter than usual these days, which was saying something because Faith was already the quietest member of the gang, except perhaps Little John. Ida often saw her hastily wiping tears away. Yet even so, she remained calm and comforted. Ida knew she herself would never be so collected if Allen died. Though it was entirely possible Allen was already dead and she simply didn't know of it. Gilbert had said the gang had gone to France and everyone had been healthy when last he saw them, but that was months ago.

They spent a restful night in Dover, and with dawn the four of them, plus their three horses, tramped down to the docks and to Captain Anthony's ship. The horses were loaded without too much difficulty, although Quest balked at being led up the gangplank and nearly knocked the sailor leading him into the water.

Faith settled below deck with little Lucy, and Andrew found a quiet corner of the deck to sulk. Ida stood by the railing, watching England disappear. Every day brought some new adventure, and she didn't like it. She wanted to go back to living on her little farm, with her husband Allen and her wild twins. Milking cows, collecting eggs, caring for horses, discussing crop growth and harvests with Allen. Simplicity. Safety. She wanted it back more than she could say.

She wasn't going to get it though, by the looks of things. She was leaving England for the first time in her life with no real knowledge of how long she'd be gone, or if she would ever return to those shores at all.

ROGER

Roger sipped the tea Rachel had made for him; it was simple chamomile, not some strange concoction of Walter's. Roger's wounds from the battle at Gisbourne estate were long since healed. Walter had seen to that when he wasn't busy dealing with Guy. Walter hadn't been with them many days before he realized Gilbert had been hiding wounds as well, not only from Gisbourne estate and the subsequent escape but also from a

221

previous battle with Sir Hugh's army weeks before even that. Walter had been indignant, calling Gilbert a fool, and then doing his utmost to right the wrongs done to Gilbert's body.

Roger was currently sitting outside the little house they'd lived in for what seemed like ages. Rachel and Michael remained the definition of hospitality. Gilbert was getting antsier by the day. And Walter continued to fight for Guy's life, as he had been doing for three weeks already.

Three weeks.

Would his city miss their apothecary? And was he ever planning on going home?

After the first week of Walter's attention, with no apparent change in Guy's situation, Roger thought it would be better to let the physician go back home and let Guy be put out of his misery. Walter, however, had refused to leave. He'd begun this work and he would see it to its conclusion. If Guy died, so be it, but Walter intended that he should live and until he either got better or stopped breathing, Walter wouldn't budge. Roger admired the fire in the young physician. He also admired Guy's resilience. How a person mortally wounded to the point that Guy had been could keep clinging to life for so long was a miracle; that was the only explanation that made sense. Roger wasn't an expert in medicine, but he was sure Guy should have been dead thrice over before Walter even saw him. Walter, intent on staying, had sent word to Oxford of his prolonged stay. He had friends who could look after his shop in his absence.

After the second week under Walter's skilled hands, Guy's wounds began to change appearance for the better, rather than the worse. And now after a third week, Roger thought Guy just might survive after all.

The wounds on his chest and thighs had begun to close over and were no longer leaking the disgusting yellow liquid they had been before. Both his chest and his thighs were still red and raw, but they were no longer open wounds. The gash in his side had closed over and appeared to be no more than a large cut rather than a life-threatening injury. His face had long since healed, though his left cheek was scarred and he was missing part of his ear. The cuts on his wrists and ankles were also healed, and also scarred.

The only problem was that Guy had yet to wake up. Rachel and Walter continued to force-feed him, Walter teaching Rachel to use fluids, such as thin broth, rather than the mashed vegetables she had been attempting before. This resulted in fewer choking episodes and Rachel no longer being thrown up on.

Guy continued to moan often in his sleep, sometimes babbling about Marian's death, a woman Roger only knew by association with Robin Hood, and sometimes crying like a terrified child. Walter was concerned at his continued lack of consciousness, but he didn't know how to change that situation so he simply continued to care for Guy's external wounds.

Roger surveyed the village around him, enjoying the peacefulness of the evening and watching the sky fill with brilliant colors as the sun set. Gilbert plopped onto the ground beside Roger, eyeing the tea in his hand.

"I'm sure Rachel would make you a cup of tea," Roger laughed.

"I don't want tea. I need a good strong ale, and a fight."

"You don't handle calm well, do you?"

"It isn't calm, it's torture. And what if Guy never wakes up? What am I supposed to do with him? Drag a hallucinating half-dead man to France for Robin Hood to look after?"

"Maybe."

"Or just leave him here? I can't do that."

"Well, whatever you decide to do, I've been thinking . . ."

"Have you?" Gilbert eyed him suspiciously.

"Wherever you go, will you let me tag along? I don't have a fixed abode, I'm a knight for hire," Roger chuckled. "Besides, I'd love to meet Robin Hood and thank him in person for all he's done for England. And anyway, I'm too invested in Guy's health now to abandon him."

Gilbert snorted but didn't disagree.

Roger knew that Gilbert, too, felt responsible for Guy and wouldn't leave him. Though the prospect of carting Guy in his current state of mind all over France seemed like a terrible idea. It would be better if the poor man would just wake up of his own accord.

"I won't say no to your company," Gilbert said at last. "You've proven yourself a decent fighter. And I'll need help with Guy if he ever wakes up."

"I shall gladly help in any way that I can."

Gilbert sighed heavily. "It appears I may need help killing Sir Hugh after all, as well."

"I was equally shocked when we heard he was still alive. I can hardly believe it; although considering how Guy is still alive from far more extensive wounds, I shouldn't truly be surprised."

"I am more disappointed than words can say. But he *will* die. I'll see to it before I meet my end."

Chapter 13

SIR HUGH

Dover. The last time Sir Hugh had been in this wretched little port, he'd been close to catching and killing Robin Hood. This time, he wasn't close at all. Yet he still had every intention of catching and killing Robin Hood.

Sir Hugh had brought Torin and the whole army to Dover, but they were hard-pressed to secure passage to Calais all at once. Sir Hugh hated the idea of transporting a hundred or more men at a time, then waiting impatiently in Calais until the rest of the army had crossed over in a matter of days or weeks as they found berths on various ships. Yet that appeared to be the only option unless he wanted to throw all his men and horses into the channel and tell them to swim.

"Another week won't delay your execution of Robin Hood anymore than your detour to Gisbourne estate," Torin said quietly as Sir Hugh glared at the retreating back of the captain who had just agreed to take a handful of men on his ship.

"This is going to take too long."

"Hardly. Be patient."

Sir Hugh glared at Torin, who looked mildly amused.

"I would like to bring to your attention once more the fact that the excursion to Gisbourne estate easily took more time than

226

crossing the channel will. Once we find Robin Hood, and you have your fun ending the lives of Robin and the other outlaws, you should go home to Scotland with Isla. You need a break. This job is taking a giant toll on you."

"Of course it is! Usually it only takes me weeks to track down and kill whoever I am hired to kill," Sir Hugh growled. "It has almost been a year since I first agreed to kill Robin Hood and his band of outlaws for King John. A *year*."

"I am well aware, having been a part of your schemes all the while," Torin replied. "As I said, you need a rest before you take on another job."

The idea of a rest, though it sounded pathetic and weak, was actually rather inviting. Robin Hood would have to be good and dead before Sir Hugh ever agreed to such a thing, however. And killing him or any of the other outlaws was proving to be a truly impossible task.

IDA

Ida sank into the chair beside Faith's, studying the map Captain Anthony had graciously given to them. They were still in Calais; Ida had decided they would stay there until they had news of the others or a solid plan as to where to look. Wandering the countryside aimlessly seemed pointless and stupid. So she had gotten them rooms at an inn near the docks. Andrew had already retired to his room, as he did every day, but Ida and Faith were still in the common room trying to make a plan worth following.

"I do have some old friends on the continent," Faith said, running her fingers over the map. "My parents loved to travel. I spent most of my childhood outside of England."

"I know. Are any of those contacts of yours in Aquitaine?"

"You think Robin is in the province of Aquitaine? Why?"

"He knows Queen Eleanor, King John's mother. They met on the crusades with Richard the Lion-Heart."

"I do remember hearing that," Faith moved her hand over Aquitaine, studying the cities labeled there.

"Allen knows her, too, and Dusty and Much. They all met her when they were part of the royal guard for King Richard. Robin might have gone to her for refuge. I imagine she's the only person King John won't defy."

"That is possible. We could see if we can discover where she's currently living and then seek her out. Even if our family isn't with the Queen Mother, she might be able to help us find them."

"Or help us stop her son. Robin was always a favorite of hers, or so Allen tells me. If she knows of his hunt for us, she likely doesn't approve of it."

"Most of my friends are in Paris," Faith said. "So we have two options, I think. Seek out Queen Eleanor, or go to my friends in Paris."

"Let's put both those ideas to Andrew tomorrow and see what he thinks."

There was a commotion at the door and then a handful of rowdy soldiers came pushing their way into the tavern.

"We need ale!"

"And a good meal!"

Ida shifted closer to Faith, one hand dropping to her lap where it would be closer to the daggers in her boots. The soldiers began settling into chairs around a table across the way, but Ida didn't relax. A moment later none other than Sir Hugh walked through the door. Faith tensed beside her.

The tavern keeper had approached a table of soldiers to discuss what they might want to eat and if they needed rooms. Sir Hugh tapped him on the shoulder.

"We need rooms, as many as you have. I have an entire army crossing the channel. It'll take a week or two for everyone to arrive."

"I won't be able to accommodate more than fifty or so men," the tavern keeper replied.

"That's fine. I can put the rest up at other taverns."

Ida wished she still had her cloak on so she could pull her hood over her head. If Sir Hugh glanced toward them there would be no mistaking who they were.

Ida reached out and gripped Faith's hand. "Go upstairs, now," she hissed.

Faith stared at her, eyes wide with terror.

"Just go. Walk, don't run. If they notice you, I'll deal with them."

"You can't take them all," Faith whispered.

"Then just pray to your God that they don't notice us."

Faith got up, trembling but surprisingly calm. She folded up their map with gentle, methodical movements. Every second that she dawdled was excruciating to Ida, who kept her eyes on Sir Hugh. Yet she was glad that Faith was acting naturally and not causing a scene.

In another moment Faith began her slow amble towards the stairs. She walked right past the table of soldiers, within arm's reach of Sir Hugh—thankfully, his back was to her.

The minute Faith was no longer visible, Ida stood. She walked carefully toward the stairs, trying not to look at the soldiers or Sir Hugh. If she inadvertently made eye contact all would be lost.

The walk across the common room felt never-ending. As she passed Sir Hugh's chair he turned his head to speak to the soldier next to him and Ida's heart stopped beating. But she kept walking forward with slow but determined strides.

Don't run. Don't run. Don't run.

As soon as she reached the stairs Ida bounded up them, forgetting not to draw attention to herself in her panic. She raced down the hallways to Andrew's room, shoved the door open, and then slammed it shut.

As Ida had suspected, Faith had come to Andrew's room. They were both standing near the window. They had been talking, but when Ida burst in the room, they'd stopped.

"Did he see you?" Andrew asked, stepping forward. "Do we need to run?"

"I don't think he noticed us," Ida said, placing a hand on her heart as she tried to slow her erratic breathing. "But we're leaving as soon as the soldiers settle down for the night. You'd better prepare; as soon as the common room is empty, we're getting out of this tavern."

KING JOHN

John leaned against the wall, a goose-feather pillow propped up behind his head for comfort. He was sitting on his bed at a tavern in the wilderness of Normandy, an array of letters and documents spread out before him. His meeting in Paris three months before had only led to more and more negotiations. Would he be allowed to keep his lands on the continent? Would Philip stop supporting Arthur as King of England? These were questions that apparently had no answer, as Philip remained vague and refused to settle on any treaty they drew up together. First he wanted more of John's lands than John was willing to let go of. Then he had the audacity to suggest he might still support Arthur. John was exhausted. He was tired of fighting the war, tired of wandering all over the continent, tired of the never-ending negotiations. He wanted peace and comfort, and an end to all this nonsense.

And on top of it all, he'd received word only that morning from the mercenary Sir Hugh that Robin Hood and the other outlaws he'd paid to have killed were still alive and apparently hiding in France, no less. If Philip was harboring the outlaws, it was almost enough for John to wish no treaty was signed after all. Yet his dislike of the war and desire to return to comfort outweighed his dislike of Robin Hood. Let him hide in France; Sir Hugh would find him regardless. And at any rate, an old enemy of years gone by was hardly important to John given his current situation.

It was true that one of the first things he did after becoming King was to hire the mercenary from Scotland to kill Robin Hood, but being King for a year and having nothing to show for it except a war with France and with Arthur as well had tempered John's hatred of Robin Hood and his gang. He was simply tired of it all.

He wanted Philip to come to a conclusion about their treaty, and then he wanted to go home. Nothing more. If Robin Hood and his outlaws lived in France for the rest of their lives, John didn't really care.

In some ways, John was jealous of his late brother's ability to attract the loyalty of men like Robin Hood. When Arthur tried to claim his throne, it might have been reassuring to have such a man fighting alongside him rather than against him.

FAITH

They were nearing Fontevraud Abbey and Faith's heart was lifting. There was tangible hope again that they were nearing their family and their long journey would come to a close. She only wished Guy could be alive to see it. But she knew he was in good hands.

A simple query to a few strangers here and there had produced the knowledge of where the Queen Mother had retired. Fontevraud Abbey, where she lived in peace with the monks and nuns there. Faith thought it sounded like the perfect home. Ida thought the opposite, but she was glad to have a destination and had pushed them hard every day. The near run-in with Sir Hugh in Calias had put her on edge. He hadn't discovered Faith and the others, but it had been far too close for comfort. Ida had them sneak out of the tavern that night and then ridden them hard and fast every day to reach the abbey. There had been no sign of the army following them, for which Faith was grateful.

The abbey was coming into view. Faith could see the very archway that would lead them into the first courtyard and garden in front of the church. The church spires were rising gracefully into the air, high enough to see over the wall and archway. Two towers surrounding the front door.

"Do you think they are in there?" Andrew asked softly.

"There's only one way to find out," Ida replied.

They passed under the archway and Faith could see gardens growing, filling the courtyard to their left in front of the church. There were also several other buildings besides the church itself to the left and right, spread out across the countryside.

Several monks were tending to the garden, and one hailed them. Ida dismounted, so Faith did as well, coming to stand beside her with little Lucy on one hip as the monk came to them.

"How may I assist you?" he inquired in his native French.

"We are here to see Eleanor of Aquitaine," Faith answered, as Ida only knew a smattering of french herself. "Is she here?"

"Of course she's here," the monk smiled. "I'm Alexis, by the way. If you'll follow me I'll take you to the Queen. Brother Pierre!"

Ida tensed when he shouted, her hand twitching to her waist where she was carrying one of her daggers. Faith took her hand and squeezed it. "He's going to take us to the Queen Mother," she whispered.

One of the other monks in the garden came wandering over after being called. "Yes?"

"This is Pierre," Alexis said.

"I'm Faith, and this is Ida and Andrew. Andrew can speak your language, but Ida only knows a little so don't be offended if she doesn't speak too much to you."

"Of course, of course. Pierre, will you see to it their horses are stabled? Thank you. Now follow me, my friends."

Faith followed after the monk, pulling Ida with her. Alexis led them to one of the outlying buildings, a stone's throw away from the church. Once inside he led them down a long hallway. There were several nuns moving about the place on business of their own, and they greeted the group following Alexis politely, but none of them stopped.

Alexis finally stopped before a door and knocked.

"Who is it?"

"Alexis, my lady. I bring guests who wish to speak to you."

"Guests?" The door opened, and there stood Queen Eleanor. She was tall, with grey hair and sparkling eyes. She eyed the three strangers at her door with some confusion and much amusement. "And who do I have the pleasure of meeting today?"

"I'm Faith," Faith spoke in English for Ida's sake, knowing the Queen would be able to do the same. "This is Ida. She's the wife of Allen. Perhaps you remember him from the Crusades. Robin Hood's friend? And this is our friend Andrew."

"Of course I remember Allen! Such fire in his young soul," the Queen chuckled. "Come in, come in." Eleanor ushered them inside her room, and Alexis said his farewell.

The room was furnished with a table and several chairs. There was also a bookcase in one corner. The Queen waved them into seats and Faith gratefully sank into one.

"So what brings you to me?"

"Your son," Ida growled. "He hired a mercenary to kill us all and we've been on the run ever since. We understand that Robin came to the continent some time ago, and we're trying to find him."

Queen Eleanor sighed, her eyes darkening. "I had heard rumors that John was going to try and have Robin killed. I didn't believe them."

"It's true, ma'am," Faith said. "I take it you haven't heard from Robin then?"

"No, I have not. He should have come straight to me," Eleanor sighed. "I can deal with my son."

Andrew leaned back in his chair, sighing. "They aren't here."

"We'll find them," Faith replied.

"I can help with that," the Queen said. "I have plenty of power and influence, not to mention my contacts here and in England. I will find Robin and have him and his family brought to me."

Chapter 14

GUY

Guy was watching Marian dance in an open field dotted with flowers. Her dark hair was streaming around her and her face was alight with joy. A golden light seemed to be emanating from the very air around her. It was spreading, covering the field with its glory.

Slowly it stretched out toward Guy, bright and warm. As the light swept over him, Guy was overwhelmed with a feeling of joy and goodness. He felt whole and safe and loved.

The light was growing brighter, and Guy found he could no longer bear it, despite the pleasant way it made him feel. He closed his eyes to stop the light from burning through him, and in an instant it was gone.

Darkness enveloped him.

Slowly, he became aware of sensations he was sure he hadn't felt in a very long time. A scratchy straw mattress beneath his back. The sound of someone slurping a drink. The gentle whisper of a skirt sliding across the ground. The sting of pain in his side. A pounding in his temples.

Guy's eyes felt as though they weighed more than a horse, but he struggled to open them anyway.

"Rachel, is the broth ready?" a male voice Guy didn't recognize spoke from near Guy's side.

"Just about!" called a woman's voice that Guy didn't recognize any more than the man's.

"I'm not sure how much longer we can keep force-feeding him," the man sighed quietly.

Guy fought to push his eyelids up, and then quite suddenly the dim light of a small room flooded into view. Guy blinked rapidly against the light, for however dim it might be it still caused his eyes to water with pain.

"You're awake!"

Guy opened his eyes again, glancing to his left. A young man he did not know was sitting there, looking concerned and relieved all at once.

"Wh . . ." Guy tried to talk, but found his throat was no longer in the practice of doing so and refused to cooperate.

"You're in a little village in the countryside of England," the young man smiled. "You were gravely injured. We've been fighting to save your life for two months."

Two months. Guy let that register slowly. Two months he'd been unconscious as the world moved on without him. He wondered if Faith and little Lucy had gotten away and were safe. If Ida and Andrew had survived.

The vague memories, suffused with agony, of his execution and rescue came trickling in. The man who had saved him, he realized now, was none other than Gilbert, the man who'd been trying to rescue them all in the first place.

"You need some rest, but first you need to eat. We were about to feed you anyway," the man said. "I'm Walter, by the way. Walter Tessel. An apothecary and healer from Oxford."

Guy nodded in response to this, and Walter leaned forward to help Guy sit up, putting a feather pillow behind him to prop him up. From this angle, Guy could see the entirety of the little room, which had a dirt floor, a low roof, a couple of hewn logs as chairs. In one of them was a soldier that Guy vaguely remembered. Had he been helping Gilbert? The soldier was sipping on a mug of some unknown drink and watching Guy with an expression of joy and confusion.

A woman entered the small room from what Guy assumed was the kitchen. She came bearing a bowl of steaming broth and she stopped abruptly when she saw Guy.

"You're awake!"

Guy nodded, and then wished he hadn't as the world began to fade in and out around him.

"How wonderful!" the woman brought the bowl to Walter, who took it in his hands and smiled at Guy.

"I'm going to feed you. I know you might find this demeaning, but your arms haven't been used in months and they'll need exercise before being used again. Okay?"

Guy nodded once more, though he didn't much like the thought of being fed like a child. He was alive, somehow, and for now that was enough.

GILBERT

Gilbert pushed open the door to the small house he'd been calling home for longer than he'd anticipated. Roger was sitting and sipping his tea as he always was; both Rachel and Walter insisted their concoctions were helping the man heal. Gilbert glanced to his left and then froze.

Guy had woken up.

He was propped up by pillows and Walter was sitting beside him, feeding him like a babe. One spoonful of broth at a time.

"He's going to live," Gilbert said quietly.

Walter glanced over his shoulder before turning back to his task. "There is still a long way to go in terms of recovery, but yes. He'll live."

Gilbert moved to stand by the bed. Guy made eye contact with him and seemed to want to say something.

"Easy," Walter said softly as Guy gagged on his unspoken words and began to cough. "It'll take time. You're alive, but barely. Whether you ever recover the use of your arms and legs is another matter. And I'm still concerned about damage done to your internal organs. The injuries you sustained," Walter

240

hesitated. "You're alive, Sir Guy, but I can't promise death wouldn't have been easier. What your life may look like moving forward likely won't be what you are used to."

He was going to live.

Gilbert stared in some awe at the man being fed like a helpless child, a bit of broth leaking from his mouth and dribbling down his chin.

In the days after Guy's miraculous awakening, Gilbert had sat beside Guy and recounted the escape, maintaining his belief that the others got away safely due to the diversion of Sir Hugh chasing Guy. Gilbert was sure Guy would want to travel to France to find them, and Gilbert agreed he would see him there safely. None of these conversations were particularly riveting. Guy couldn't speak, and merely nodded, shook his head, or grunted on occasion.

Still, things were looking up for Gilbert. After he reunited the whole of Robin Hood's gang he intended to take his leave, find Sir Hugh, and kill him. He'd make sure to wait this time; wait and watch the life drain from his eyes. He wasn't going to let him come back to life a second time. The news that he still lived stung nearly as much as watching Henry die.

That tragedy was beginning to feel an age ago, so much had happened since then. But Gilbert had not forgotten, and he was going to see his only friend avenged.

After that he might return to Robin Hood's service, feeling thoroughly responsible for the outlaws at this point. They'd certainly keep him entertained for the rest of his life. Robin Hood always seemed to be in one scrape or another, and the rest of the gang were equally as bad. But first things first, Guy had to be safely escorted to France and reunited with his wife, child, and the rest of the outlaws.

Then sweet revenge.

ANDREW

Andrew plucked a flower from the ground beside him and began to tear it into shreds. He and Faith had gone for a walk in the countryside and were now seated beneath a tree near the outer wall that encircled the abbey.

Faith watched him tearing up the flower from where she was leaning against the tree and then said softly, "You haven't talked about him yet."

"There's nothing to talk about. He's dead." Andrew winced as he said it and glanced up at Faith, hoping he hadn't offended her.

"Andrew . . ." Faith hesitated.

"I'm sorry—"

"No, no, it's alright. I understand. It's just that I spent years pulling my husband out of the darkness that you are now allowing yourself to fall into. Guy wouldn't want that. He'd want you to be happy, Andrew."

Andrew could feel his heart slowing inside his chest at the thought of Guy. He grabbed another flower and started tearing it apart, too.

"Andrew, he was your oldest friend. You knew him from the time you were children. You went through hell together under his father's hand. You were his only friend for a long time during the years when John was rebelling against King Richard," Faith took a deep breath as a single tear made it's way down her cheek. "I am always going to be grateful to you for your friendship to him. And because of that friendship, the way you always took care of him, I have to take care of you. I have to. And right now, you have to grieve. You can't bottle this up. I won't let you."

Andrew leaned back against the willow tree, letting the crushed flower petals fall from his hand.

"Andrew, please talk to me. Just tell me what you're feeling."

Andrew sighed, and closed his eyes. What was he feeling?

"I understand your pain, Andrew. I do. He was my husband. If you need to rail against God, I can patiently listen. I felt that, too, at the beginning. And if you need to cry, my tears are not yet spent."

"He's dead," Andrew said simply. He could already feel tears burning his eyelids in their desperate attempt to escape. "He sacrificed himself for all of us, so we could escape. He—" Andrew opened his eyes, a few tears leaking from his eyes.

Faith reached out and took his hand.

"I love everyone in the gang, don't get me wrong, and we have all developed deep and meaningful relationships over the years but," Andrew hesitated, but Faith simply watched him with her expressive eyes, so he continued, "no one really accepted us, deep down. Even before Sir Hugh showed up it was Guy and me, and then the rest of them."

"I know."

"It wasn't just Ida, though she was certainly the most vocal. And I know most of them will say it isn't true, Dusty and Lucy certainly thought they'd worked past it. But somehow it was always Guy and I all alone, set apart, different. Forgiven but not completely, trusted but never fully. We only had each other, you know that."

"I do know that. I have watched it happen all these years. I've heard Guy complain about it frequently. I've talked to Lucy about it."

"And now he's dead," Andrew said. "He died to save Ida, after all her mistrust and hatred." Anger was surging through his veins now. How could they all mistrust Guy for so long after all he'd done to prove his worthiness? He'd *died* for them.

From an objective point of view, Andrew knew exactly why they'd been the outcasts of the gang. They'd fought for Prince John for most of the rebellion rather than King Richard. And even after they'd switched sides and helped to spy on the Sheriff of Nottingham, the gang could hardly see past the fact that Guy had been responsible for Lady Marian's death. It was entirely

244

understandable. The fact that they had lived so long in harmony and peace was a miracle, the fact that Robin and Guy had not only been on speaking terms but even friends was a true testament of the power of the God they all served.

But Andrew didn't want to see things from an objective point of view. Guy was dead, and he wanted to blame Ida and the rest of them for ostracizing Guy for so many years.

"He was a hero," Faith said softly, more tears spilling down her cheeks.

"Yes, he was."

"And we don't know for sure that he's dead, do we? We didn't see him die."

"He gave himself to Sir Hugh so Ida could escape. What do you think Sir Hugh would have done with him? He hasn't been chasing us around this past year because he wanted to shake hands and part ways as friends."

"I know, I know. Even if there's no hope for him in this life at least you know he's safe in heaven."
Andrew sighed. It was true; he did believe that. But he didn't want Guy safe in heaven, he wanted him alive.

"I'm sorry you lost your friend, Andrew."

"Me, too. I'm sorry you lost your husband. You deserve better, you know."

"I don't deserve much, Andrew. I'm a human like everyone else, a sinner. And I have been given so much that I don't deserve." Faith wiped her tears away, smiling slightly. "I still have my family. I still have my own life. I have my daughter. I have you. Just don't shut out the rest of us, Andrew."

"I'll try not to."

"And you know, deep down, that the rest of the gang loves you, too. Don't shut them all out because of Guy's sacrifice. He didn't make sure we could escape just for you to lose all joy in life."

Andrew sighed. She was right, of course. It would just take him a while to get there.

IDA

Ida sat on the steps that led up to the chapel, her back to the church doors, watching Faith and a few nuns and monks working in the herbal gardens in front of the church. Faith was adjusting to life in the abbey remarkably well. She loved the simplicity and the routine, and the constantly being surrounded by people who shared her beliefs. Ida was impressed by how well she acclimated to their life after fleeing from Gisbourne estate.

She was calm, and relatively happy. How that could be was beyond Ida's understanding. Even with the hope dangling in front of her that she would soon see her husband and sons if the Queen Mother was able to find them, she still felt unsettled. There were times she couldn't breathe she was so afraid of something happening to stop her reunion with her family. And she found herself crying into her pillow more nights than she cared to admit.

But Faith, who had lost all hope of seeing her husband again was somehow cheerful and content.

It was unnerving and annoying.

Ida knew exactly what Faith would say about it, too; she trusted God. If Guy was dead, then he was safe in heaven. And if not, then God would bring him home to her. And she would tell Ida to trust Him to bring Allen and the boys to her, too.
Ida wasn't ready to do that though. She wanted the confidence that Faith had, but she wasn't sure she could trust God the way Faith did. It was too much to ask.

GUY

Guy grappled with his leg muscles, forcing them to do his bidding. There was a moment of nothing happening, and then slowly Guy shuffled forward the last two steps and collapsed down onto the mattress that had been his home for months. He'd just managed to shuffle to the wall and back and Walter appeared pleased.

"This is good, Guy! You are mending much faster than I imagined you would, considering the severity of your wounds. Let's work on stretching your legs again. We need to build up those muscles once more."

'Good' was not the word Guy would use to describe limping from one end of the room to the other and collapsing in exhaustion afterward. Pathetic was more like it. He was an

247

invalid. After so many years of striving to get away from the weakness his father had so hated in him, Guy found his current condition rather revolting.

"You are doing well, Guy. Considering the state I found you in, every shuffling step you take is a giant miracle."

Guy grunted, and rolled his eyes. "Miracle, indeed. It's pathetic."

"You are on your feet and moving, if only a few steps at a time. Three months ago you were executed in brutal fashion. You should not be alive, Guy. That shuffling walk you just accomplished is miraculous!"

Guy didn't respond, but he knew Walter was right. He simply wished he was healing faster. He desperately needed to find his family.

As soon as he was able to walk and move more efficiently, not just his legs but his arms as well, Guy was going to France. He had no other goal. Just get to France and find his wife and daughter.

Gilbert and Roger had informed him they were accompanying him, and Guy had welcomed the chance for traveling companions. He would be eternally in Gilbert's debt.

But first he had to learn to walk.

After he'd woken up that first time, Walter had started him on a strict routine of stretching and strengthening his muscles to get Guy back into shape. So far it had only resulted in Guy managing to shuffle across the room and collapse.

KING JOHN

John sank heavily into the chair in his room at the tavern.
He was staying in a little town many miles northwest of Paris,
located on a little island in the river Seine. Le Goulet.

He'd come here to finalize a treaty with Philip. An end, at
last, to the fighting.

John was tired and wanted to return home to comfort and
peace, and was glad at last to have a treaty signed. But even so, he
was not what one might call pleased with the outcome.

John grabbed the tankard of ale his servant had brought
and gulped it down. It wasn't enough to wash away the sting of
the treaty he'd chosen to sign.

The treaty was signed; it was done. The war for control of
Normandy was finished and its borders reassigned. Philip came
away from the treaty in far better shape than John; and if he
wasn't already exhausted from too much fighting he'd probably
start a war over it. Maybe he still would, but not today.

Several Counts were now vassals of France rather than
England, and John's lands had shrunk considerably. Those that
were left to him, were his only as a vassal to the King of France.
It wasn't exactly the outcome he'd been hoping for.

John refilled his mug and took a long swig of ale again.
He was in a terrible mood.

The only good thing to come of the treaty at all was that Philip finally recognized John as King of England and withdrew his support of Arthur's claim. It was a measly victory when placed beside all that he had lost.

John was miserable, but he couldn't change the outcome without another war and he was in no mood for more fighting. All that was left now was to deal with what remained of Arthur's support, and then return to peace and tranquility. Not that his life had ever truly contained either, but a man could always hope. Sir Hugh had sent word that he was now on the continent and in pursuit of Robin Hood once more. He seemed to believe that he would find them soon and that job, at least, would end how John had imagined it.

Chapter 15

GUY

Guy swung himself into the saddle of Saxon Rose, a horse that Gilbert had bought for his use. He subconsciously reached up to feel where most of his left ear was missing as he watched Gilbert and Roger mounting the horses they'd stolen from Sir Hugh's men all those months ago, which they had dubbed Pinch and Snatch.

In the month since he'd woken up, Walter had been putting Guy through his paces to get his body back to the health and strength it had once boasted. It had been a long month, full of frustration and failure. Even after a month of hard work, Guy could only shuffle about, rather than walk normally. But Guy was more than ready to find his wife and he wasn't going to wait until he was truly himself again. The road to recovery was yet long but it was going to have to wait.

Gilbert and Roger had found provisions, as well as the mare Saxon Rose, and the three of them had made their plans— much to Walter's chagrin. He would have preferred to keep Guy on bed rest and continue his slow re-training of his muscles.

"Be safe," Rachel called from the doorway.

Guy lifted a hand in farewell. He and his companions were headed for Dover, and Walter was going back to his home in Oxford.

"Farewell," Walter said, reaching over from where he was mounted on his own steed to shake Guy's hand.

"Thank you for everything," Guy said.

"You know I wish you would let me do more."

"I know."

"Take this with you." Walter pulled a small book from the bag slung over his shoulder. "I've filled it with notes on your injuries and healing process. Give it to your friend Dusty, if you ever find her."

It wasn't an emotional farewell. Though grateful for all that Walter had done for him, his continued presence had made Guy only too aware of how broken he was. Guy watched with impatience as he shook hands with Gilbert and Roger. He wanted to be free of Walter and on his way to his wife and the rest of his family.

"Are you sure you're ready for this?" Roger asked Guy as he and Gilbert brought their horses alongside his.

"Of course I am."

As they set out at a trot along the dusty road, the sun already up and shining down on them and the morning warm and filled with the promise of spring, Guy couldn't help but be filled with hope. He, by all accounts, should be dead. Yet he wasn't. By some miracle of God, he was still breathing. Guy wondered what

God could possibly have in store for him that He so desperately wanted to keep him alive. Perhaps the miracle of his life was enough reason. But whatever it was, Guy was looking forward to finding out. Faith was going to be ecstatic, not only that he was still alive but also at the prospect of discovering the purpose God had for his extended life. It was precisely the thing his little wife would find enjoyment in.

Thinking of Faith made Guy smile. The flowers dotting the fields they were passing reminded him of his wife, as she so often braided such blossoms into her hair. Little Lucy would love to frolic in those fields, too. Guy didn't know how long it might take for them to find his family or the rest of the gang, but he was confident that they would. He, after all, ought to be dead. If that obstacle could be overcome, what was a little distance or time?

He was alive.

ROBIN

Robin rested his head in his hand, elbow crooked on the table in front of him, watching his wife across the room. She was sitting on the floor under the window, Marian surprisingly and mercifully sitting still beside her. Lucy had a basket with cloth between them and appeared to be teaching Marian to sew.

They were happy here, building productive and fulfilling lives. Robin had thought many times in the last few months that Paris could easily be their home for the rest of their lives. He knew the rest of the gang felt the same way. Watching Marian quietly listening to instruction for possibly the first time in her life was practically proof that this was where their home would be till the day they died.

But Robin knew he couldn't stay, not now.

Marian took the needle and cloth Lucy handed her and concentrated on following the simple stitches that Lucy had marked out. Robin felt a strange mixture of pride and astonishment as he watched their daughter, and he could see from Lucy's expression that she was experiencing the same.

Lucy glanced up at him suddenly, eyes shining, and Robin's heart burst.

Robin attempted to return her smile but knew immediately he'd failed because hers faltered for a second. Lucy glanced at their daughter, dutifully working away, and then got up and moved toward the table.

"What's wrong?"

Robin sighed, gesturing toward a vacant chair at the table where he sat. "I received a letter today, from an old friend."

"An old friend?"

"Queen Eleanor."

Lucy grinned, tilting her head slightly, considering her husband. "And this is a bad thing, how?"

"She found us, Lucy." Robin studied his wife, wondering how her brilliant mind hadn't already awakened to the danger they were in.

Lucy was still watching him with curiosity and concern.

"With all her connections, she found us. And you think for a moment that King John and Sir Hugh couldn't do the same?"

"What did her letter say?"

"She wants us to come to Fontevraud Abbey. She said she wants to help, that she's going to speak to her son."

"That's good news."

"That's not all. She said she began looking for our whereabouts because Ida came to her and asked for her help."

"Ida! She's alive? Was anyone with her?"

"Eleanor said Ida came with Andrew, Faith, and little Lucy. And she said Ida brought news." Robin paused, unsure how to continue. He knew how much this next sentence was going to pain his wife, considering how fond she had always been of Guy.

"It appears Sir Hugh went after them instead of us when he escaped his grasp at Dover. He found them, and . . ."

"And what, Robin?"

"Eleanor said that according to Ida, Guy sacrificed himself so that they could escape."

"What do you mean sacrificed himself?"

"As far they know, Sir Hugh killed him, Lucy."

Lucy grimaced, her hands slowly curling into fists.

"We need to leave Paris," Robin said, reaching out to take one of her hands in his own. "If Eleanor could find us so easily, King John and Sir Hugh likely will too, given enough time. We can't stay."

"Is she certain? About Guy?"

"Lucy, that's not the point! I'm sorry that he's dead, but we have more pressing business to attend to."

"More pressing business than a member of our family dying?"

"Lucy!" Robin felt, not for the first time since he'd known her, like shaking his wife. "Sir Hugh is still trying to kill us. He chased us to Scotland and Dover for that purpose; he went to Gisbourne estate and killed Guy," Robin ignored his wife's sharp intake of breath and plunged on "for no other reason than to get at us, at *me*. Eleanor found out where we were, without trouble. How long before Sir Hugh does as well?"

"He hasn't found us yet."

"Only because he wasn't looking, he was still in England. And now that Ida and the others came to the continent as well, he'll be following. If we can be found so easily by one person searching for us, how difficult could it really be for another to do the same? Sir Hugh is undoubtedly coming for us. He's already proven that no distance is going to dissuade him. He will be coming. That is a fact."

"And you think when he does come, it will be easy to find us."

"That is my fear."

"So what do you want to do?"

"We have to relocate."

"Where?"

"Further into France? Or even deeper into Europe? I don't know. But we need to address this problem."

"So we call a group meeting, and you tell everyone your fears. Then we make our decision together, as always."

Robin nodded. "I want to visit Eleanor first, and reunite with Ida and the others."

"When did you hear from Eleanor? How long have you known about Ida, about Guy?"

"Only today, Lucy. I didn't want to say anything at first. I was clinging to the illusion that we could be at peace here. I'm tired of running, Lucy."

MARK

Mark listened quietly as Robin addressed them all. The entire gang was gathered in Robin and Lucy's chambers, listening to Robin tell them he was afraid of Sir Hugh catching them. Robin was convinced they needed to leave. To run. Again.

Mark leaned against the wall, arms crossed, anger coursing through him. The group was silent for the most part, though the children causing chaos in the next room were not exactly quiet. Robin simply watched them after he'd finished speaking, calmly waiting for their response.

"You're certain it's Ida," Allen asked, his voice wavering.

257

"Eleanor was clear," Robin replied. "She began looking for us at the behest of Ida, who came to her for aid after escaping Sir Hugh at Gisbourne estate."

Allen nodded, clearly choking back tears. Mark was glad for him, that he finally had news of his wife. And he was glad for himself at the news that Marian's murderer had finally gotten what he deserved.

"We don't know that Sir Hugh is even in France at all," Much finally spoke into the stillness, his arm wrapped protectively around Mary who sat beside him.

"I think we can all agree he'll eventually come though," Will responded from where he sat in the windowsill. "Robin's right; he won't give up until we're all dead."

"I don't think we should run," Mark said, trying not to talk through clenched teeth.

Robin studied him intently but didn't say anything.

"If he isn't going to give up, then maybe we should simply face him," Mark said. "Stop the running and hiding, and just take him on."

"What, the eleven of us?" Little John scoffed. "Or nineteen, if you expect the children to fight, too."

Mark shook his head. "We have friends here, we could get support."

"We couldn't raise an army," Allen said. "We don't have that many friends, and we certainly don't have the support of the French government. There's already too much tension between

England and France, despite the recent treaty of peace. Philip won't risk angering John so soon after their fight had ended."

"So we can't fight," Will said, looking around at all of them. "Which means the only other option is to move on, as Robin suggests. We find a new place to hide."

"Why is running the only option," Mark demanded. "Why not stay here? Even if we don't fight."

"Sir Hugh is coming, make no mistake," Robin said.

"Maybe he is. I'm not arguing that point." Mark sighed.

"We have to stay together," Lucy said firmly, though no one had spoken.

There was a pause, and then Little John shook his head. "Maybe it's the fact we've been sticking together that has made us so easy to follow."

"No." Robin stood up from where he'd been sitting at the front of the room. "We are not separating."

"You've always led us well, Robin, I know that," Little John said. "But I have a six-month-old little girl to care for. Forgive me for saying it, but my family comes first in my life."

"We are family," Lucy insisted. "All of us."

"I know," Little John smiled at her. "I know. Robin's right; Sir Hugh is coming. And if, as a group, we are so easy to find, then Robin is again right; we must scatter from Paris. But why, I ask you, must we scatter together? Aside from sentimental feelings, Lucy," he added as she started to interrupt. "Strategically. Why is it better if we're together? More numbers?

We don't have the numbers to ever beat an entire army like the one Sir Hugh has at his disposal. Tell me why it's better to be together; safer to be together."

Mark was impressed that Little John could string so many words together, as he rarely ever did. He was also furious with Lucy. The gang separating? All because she hadn't killed Sir Hugh back in Dover. And now she just sat there, sputtering, without any sort of argument or persuasion to keep them together.

"As much as I don't like the sound of it," Jane said. "Little John could be right; maybe we do need to go our separate ways, at least until it's safe."

Robin was still shaking his head. "We're not separating."

"Robin," Dusty spoke softly, but sharply. Everyone turned to look at her. "I don't want us to break apart any more than you do. Yet I think this time it isn't about the group. We all need to decide what is best for our own families. I suggest we take a few days to pray about all of this, and then gather again to discuss what we've decided to do."

Robin didn't seem too pleased with this decision. Mark knew he wasn't pleased either.

And it was still Lucy's fault.

Mark had known his bitterness was growing since their arrival in Paris, had half-heartedly tried to control it. But it was futile.

That was probably Lucy's fault somehow, too.

"Whatever the rest of you decide," Allen said, "I'm going to Fontevraud Abbey. I'm going to my wife."

MARIAN

Marian threw the last feather pillow off the bed and onto the floor and then leaped, spread-eagle, into the air. She crashed into the floor with a loud and painful crack, having missed her pile of pillows by a foot.

Marian sat up, rubbing her head where it ached, waiting for Mama to come running to scold her for being reckless and then kiss away all her problems.

She didn't come.

Marian stayed where she was a moment longer, and then she crept to the edge of the room, peering cautiously through the doorway.

They were still there. Mama and Papa, standing by the fireplace in the room where they ate. The room where everybody important in Marian's life had been sitting that morning. Her aunts and uncles had all gone away again, but Mama and Papa had stayed there talking for longer than Marian could count. Papa was pacing, pausing now and then to kick at the hearth. Mama was watching him, head shaking. Both were talking a lot, and loudly.

Marian sat in the doorway and watched. She knew something was wrong. Uncle Mark never smiled anymore. Uncle

Allen didn't even tussle her hair when he took the twins back to their home across the hallway. Mama hadn't come running when Marian had whacked her head into the floor.

Something was very wrong.

". . .after everything we've been through."

"I know, Robin. I don't think we can change this, or stop it from happening."

"I can't believe that. I can't."

"Robin, we've all been through so much—"

"Together!"

Marian curled into herself, watching with wide eyes. Mama and Papa didn't usually shout at each other.

"We've been through it all together, and *now* they want to separate?"

"They have to do what's best for their own families, Robin. I don't like it any more than you do, but I understand."

"I shouldn't have let them make that decision, I should have just said we were going to the abbey and that was that."

"That isn't how this family works."

Papa sank to the floor in front of the fireplace and Mama sat beside him, putting her arms around his shoulders. Marian darted forward, jumping into his lap.

"Hey, little one."

"Why are you sad, Papa?"

Papa smiled and kissed her cheek, and already Marian began to feel better. Mama reached her arm around Marian, hugging both her and Papa. She was safe here, with Mama and Papa.

"It's okay, Marian," Papa kissed her again. "We just have some big decisions to make."

GILBERT

Once again, Gilbert found himself at Dover in search of Robin Hood, but this time he had companions. They'd found themselves lodging for the night and then Roger was off to find a ship that would let them cross the channel. Gilbert sat in a chair in their room and watched as Guy sat down and worked through exercises that Walter had insisted he continue to do. The poor wretch was not the man he'd once been. Weak, in pain, and missing an ear.

He was pathetic.

Still, given time, he might return to his former glory. And then, with the scars, he'd be quite impressive. Gilbert could admire that.

"What are you staring at," Guy huffed, sinking into a chair and clutching his side, where not too long ago there'd been a giant hole exposing his innards.

"You."

"Obviously," Guy rolled his eyes.

"The fact that you are alive is a miracle."

Guy grinned. "Believe me, I know."

263

"Should you return to the man you once were, physically speaking, it will be even more of a miracle."

"Are you simply sitting there contemplating whether or not I'm going to be a weakling for the rest of my life? Don't you have better things to do with your time, Gilbert?"

"Roger is finding us berths on a ship. We have no other occupation at the moment to keep our attention."

Guy studied him, bemused.

"You were well known through England, you know. Years ago, the name of Sir Guy of Gisbourne could send the bravest men cowering. Robin Hood was great with a bow, which I can hardly compete with, but you—always, I wanted to meet you just so we could duel. I have wanted to know which of us was the better swordsman since I was a young man."

"And now that you finally got your wish to meet me, I'm a broken man."

"But living. There's hope yet for that duel."

Guy shook his head, chuckling.

Roger opened the door to their room, rather unceremoniously ending the conversation. "I found a boat. It leaves this evening."

"Perfect," Gilbert said. "Let's get on board now."

"Right now?" Guy asked, looking very much like he didn't have the strength to walk down to the docks.

"We could carry you," Roger suggested.

Guy sent him a scathing look and got to his feet. "Don't you dare."

Gilbert grinned. "Come on, both of you. We'll be in Calais by morning. Let's hope it isn't too difficult to find Robin Hood."

MARK

Mark threw a stone into the Seine, watching it fall slowly and then plop into the water, causing a small mountain of ripples that grew ever smaller as they neared the shore. He was standing on one of the many bridges that crossed the river within Paris, contemplating his life. If he wasn't with Dusty, he tended to wander aimlessly through the city or the countryside, remembering his beloved sister Marian. But that wasn't where his thoughts were today.

Sir Guy of Gisbourne was dead, presumably.

Everyone, save for a deceased Guy, was practically together once more. Mark had been glad, like the rest of them, to hear that Ida, Faith, and Andrew were safe. And though a part of him wanted to grieve for Guy, a part of him was quite glad he was dead. The latter part of him had been growing steadily ever since Dover. His anger towards Lucy, his ever-increasing bitterness over Marian's death, and now a dark satisfaction at her killer getting what he deserved.

Mark knew it wasn't fair. He'd forgiven Guy long ago; Guy had turned his life around and become a truly honorable man. He was as good as any of them. But Mark couldn't stop the hatred that was brewing once more within his soul.

He could still remember that day; it was burned in his mind.

The rescue of the king, and then the ambush . . .

He could feel Marian's arm in his fingertips as she and Guy argued.

Mark stared at his hands, rubbing his fingers together, trying not to think too much about it but it wouldn't stop. He could still feel the way her arm shuddered just before she fell to the ground, Guy's sword in her chest.

"Mark?"

Mark winced, his hands curling into fists. Will was walking toward him.

"The sun will be setting soon, and the streets of Paris aren't nearly as friendly as those of Nottingham. You should come home."

Mark didn't respond, turning to watch the river once more.

"Mark, are you okay?"

"Fine," Mark growled.

"I know you don't like that we are contemplating running again, but we may not have a choice."

"Lucy could have—"

"Don't start that again." Will shook his head. "Come on, Mark. You can't hate Lucy for valuing life."

Mark said nothing. Will meant well, but Mark couldn't talk to him. He couldn't tell him that the forgiveness he'd given Lucy and Guy all those years ago had only been skin deep, that he'd reverted to his anger and bitterness. It would disappoint him; it would disappoint all of them.

"Just come home for now, Mark. You don't have to talk to me yet, although you should probably consider talking to someone. I know there's a lot going on in your head these days. You're not happy."

"I'm happier now than I've been in months," Mark grunted. He couldn't finish that sentence. He was happier now because Marian's murderer was dead. It was true in many respects, and yet because Guy had proven himself worthy later in life, Will wouldn't understand. He would be shocked and disappointed.

Mark turned to follow his friend back to their tavern without saying another word, and Will chose not to disturb his silence.

Whatever decision everyone made about staying together or separating and scattering to the four winds, Mark was sure of one thing: none of it would have happened if Lucy had killed Sir Hugh in Dover all those months ago.

267

Chapter 16

GUY

Darkness was falling as Guy leaned against the rail on the deck of *Saint Thomas*, a small ship on which he and his companions had booked passage across the channel. In a short time, they would be in Calais, and from there they intended to head to the Fontevraud Abbey. Guy knew that Robin, Much, Dusty, and Allen had all known the Queen Mother while Richard the Lion-Heart was alive and that she was fond of them or at the very least fond of Robin. It made sense in Guy's mind that Robin would take his friends to her, in order for her to protect them. Gilbert had no information other than that the gang had fled Dover, so he was working off of common sense more than actual knowledge.

Guy's working theory of Robin taking everyone to Eleanor was a guess at best. Yet they were going to follow it, because where else could they go? They had no word from any of the gang, of course, and no gossip either in any quarter of England. No one knew what had become of Robin Hood and his friends. As for Ida, or his wife, there was no trace to be found of them either.

Guy hoped that they would, indeed, find the gang with the Queen Mother, but if they did not he would search the rest of the French and English lands on the continent until he found them.

Until he found his wife.

He knew Andrew would take care of her, assuming they were still together, but still, he wasn't going to rest easy until she was by his side again.

Roger came to stand beside him on deck, leaning against the railing.

"What are you thinking?"

"I need to find my wife, and the rest of the gang."

"I know that," Roger chuckled. "I thought that the brooding look was a bit more specific."

"It's not."

"Well, the first step is to get across the channel. Then to Eleanor of Aquitaine. We take this journey one step at a time, and we'll get where we are going."

Guy rolled his eyes. "Very helpful advice, Roger."

"You'll find your wife with the same determination and stubbornness with which you refused to die, and then forced yourself to not only live but heal completely."

"I'm not completely healed," Guy sighed. "Or haven't you noticed?"

"You are still gaining strength back every day. You haven't collapsed yet today, that's an improvement."

The lack of such a fainting episode was hardly encouraging to Guy. To be reduced to a state wherein not fainting at least once a day was seen as an improvement? Being an invalid did not suit him in the least, and certainly brought back every dark memory of his father beating him for being weak as a child. Oh, how his father would beat him now. . .

ROBIN

Robin watched his friends slowly entering the room in groups. Every few minutes another piece of the gang would arrive. The sinking feeling in his stomach grew with each person added to the room. Robin didn't want this meeting to begin.

Eventually, however, everyone was present and the children were left to their own devices for a few minutes in the adjoining room.

"Well, we all know why we're here," Lucy said from her place at Robin's side. "At Dusty's suggestion, we've all been praying and thinking over what is best for our own family units, rather than thinking as one family as we used to. I know we've all been making hard decisions, about whether we're staying together and where we go from here, so what have you all decided?"

"We're staying with you," Will said firmly. He was standing to Robin's left, Dusty beside him. "Dusty and I, and our children, are staying with you, Robin. Wherever you choose to go."

270

"I'm following you, too," Mark said from near the door. "Even though I think running isn't the best course of action. My sister wouldn't let me leave you if she were alive."

There was a pause after Mark's declaration. Robin's heart was pounding in his ears. He wasn't sure he was breathing. Lucy took his hand, and Robin was keenly aware of how sweaty his hand was.

"My family is staying here in Paris," Little John said. He was standing against the wall to Robin's right, his eyes fixed on Robin's. Elinor was curled into his side, Rachel in her arms, crying softly.

Robin couldn't reply for the lump in his throat.

"We have a life here, and if any of you leave it will be that much easier to remain hidden ourselves. Besides, little Rachel doesn't need any more running about the countryside. She's had far too much adventure in her young life already."

"I'm going with you, Robin, at least to the abbey," Jane said. "I have to get to Andrew."

"You already know my answer," Much said, his eyes flickering toward Little John for a moment. "I'm following you, Robin, to the very end."

Robin could feel a smile tugging at his mouth, despite the devastation he was feeling. He could still remember when they were fifteen years old and Much had sworn to follow him to death if need be.

Robin turned his eyes slowly toward Allen.

"And what about you?"

"You know I'm going to the abbey, with or without you. My wife is there."

Robin glanced around the room. It wasn't as bad as he had suspected it would be. Only Little John had chosen to stay in Paris and everyone else would remain together, at least for now. Mark's decision was the most surprising to Robin.

"All that remains is to make our plans," Dusty said. "There's much to be done in preparation of all our departures." It seemed like an end. Mark was the first to exit the room, and then slowly they all seemed to be walking away from him and there was nothing to be done about it.

Robin collapsed into a chair in defeat, his head in his hands. They were, except for Little John, staying together. And yet it didn't feel right; Sir Hugh was still trying to kill them and he was about to uproot his family from their new home.

He remained there for several minutes, his head in his hands. When he finally looked up, he jolted in surprise. Much was staring at him with wide-eyed concern, Mary looked sympathetic and Will and Dusty were clearly understanding.

Lucy wrapped her arms around his shoulders and kissed his cheek. "We'll be okay. And so will they. We still have the Creator of the universe watching over all of us."

"You aren't alone, Robin," Will said. "And neither will Little John and his family be. It isn't ideal, but we'll be fine."

MARK

Mark shoved another tunic into his satchel. He'd already packed most of the belongings that he would be taking with him. It wasn't much. Mark hadn't needed to be collecting toys the way most of the gang had for their children, he wasn't creating his own library of books as some of them had been, and he certainly didn't need a whole herbal garden as he was sure Dusty was trying to pack. He just needed a change of clothes and his weapons.

Mark grabbed his extra pair of boots from the floor by the door and strapped them onto his satchel. He wasn't going to miss Paris all that much. It wasn't his home the way that Nottingham was. He had a lifetime of memories in Sherwood Forest, in the little village of Wetherby where he was raised, in the city of Nottingham itself. But here? This place was nothing but a nightmare.

Mark ran a hand through his hair, glancing around the room to be sure he'd grabbed all of his belongings. He didn't know where Robin intended to take them after the trip to see Queen Eleanor and reunite with Ida and the others. Mark tried not to think once again that if only Lucy had killed Sir Hugh back in Dover they could all be going home now.

But they weren't headed home, were they? Because Lucy couldn't do what Marian would have done.

Thinking of Marian did not put Mark in a better mood. He stormed from his room, swinging the door shut behind him with a loud crash, and stomping outside to the stables to wait for the others.

He tossed his bag onto the floor by Jack's stall. As he stepped into the stall and began to saddle Jack, his mind slowly registering the pungent smell of manure and leather, Mark thought about Marian again.

She had died in his arms. He'd been standing right beside her during the fight to get King Richard out of Austria. His hand had been on her arm when Guy had plunged his sword into her. Mark shuddered and sank onto the floor, abandoning Jack's half cinched saddle.

Shoulders shaking, heart squeezing, lungs unable to draw breath, Mark sat there on the manure and hay strewn stable floor aching to see his sister again.

It wasn't Lucy's fault; not that time.

It was Mark's fault.

SIR HUGH

Sir Hugh bit into an apricot, wiping the sweet juice that dribbled down his chin away with the sleeve at his wrist. France was not a bad place to be hunting down outlaws. The sort of beautiful landscapes to make his daughter Isla's heart sing, fresh fruits, and exotic foods that would never be found in Scotland.

Spring was giving way to Summer and the days were warm and clear. All in all, it was pleasant to be searching for the outlaws under such conditions, and Sir Hugh was hopeful that he'd have a bag full of deceased knaves before the summer was over.

His first order of business after getting his army across the channel was to methodically search Normandy for any sign of Robin Hood. After roughly two months of exhausting that activity, and wearing out his welcome, he turned his army around and headed straight for Anjou.

"Any word from our scouts?" Sir Hugh asked Torin, who was riding beside him at the head of their long column of soldiers.

"None yet."

"Doesn't matter. We'll hear word of Robin Hood sooner or later, and then he'll be dead before he can slither out of my grasp again."

"No doubt," Torin responded, sounding nearly as frustrated as Sir Hugh felt himself. The failure at Gisbourne estate, when Torin's own friend had betrayed them and helped the outlaws escape, was still raw. Whether or not Lord Gisbourne was still alive was unlikely, but that didn't assuage the anger they both felt.

The two months of wandering Normandy with no word of Robin Hood hadn't improved their mood. Which is why they had mutually agreed to change tactics and go to the Queen Mother of England herself. Robin Hood was rumored to have known the Queen Mother personally, and had certainly been close with the late King Richard; therefore, if he'd gone anywhere for refuge, would it not be to a powerful friend? Robin Hood was wrong, however, if he believed anyone was strong enough to give him sanctuary against Sir Hugh. He was going to die, painfully and slowly, no matter where he was currently hiding.

Sir Hugh left a company of soldiers in Normandy to continue the search, in the event that Robin hadn't gone to the Queen Mother for refuge. And he and Torin were taking the rest of them to the little abbey where the Queen Mother had retired. If Robin Hood wasn't there, he would continue his search of the rest of the continent. No matter how long it took, he was going to find Robin Hood and that outlaw was going to die.

ROBIN

Robin was the first to enter the barn, as the rest of his group were wrangling children. As he entered the dark, aware of the unique smell of horse sweat and manure, his heart was heavy. He moved toward Hero's stall slowly, contemplating the unfortunate turn of events that had brought them to this place of separation. He had been worried about Sir Hugh finding them, but he had no desire to send the gang scattering in all directions. They had always stayed together, always. Even when they first discovered Sir Hugh was coming to Nottingham to kill them, everyone had insisted that they stay in one group. Yet now Little John was choosing to remain behind.

276

As Robin finished saddling Hero and adjusting their packs on her back, he became aware of a muffled sound, almost a whine. He thought perhaps one of the many dogs off the streets had wandered into the barn wounded.

Robin turned slowly, trying to decide where the sound was coming from.

It was human, that sound. Robin startled slightly as he realized the sound was issuing from Jack's stall.

"Mark?"

Robin moved around the stall door and saw Mark on the floor, sobbing.

"Mark!" Robin moved forward, dropping to his knees beside his friend. It was gut-wrenching to see Mark crying in such a manner, but the fact that he was actually letting his pent up emotions out was reassuring.

Mark leaned into Robin's hug, and they sat there for a minute. Robin heard the barn door open and the sounds of Will and Dusty chiding Daniyah for some unsavory behavior toward her brother, but he paid them no mind.

Mark, on the other hand, straightened, roughly wiping the tears from his face. "I'm fine."

"What is upsetting you?" From his peripheral, Robin saw Will pause near the door of the stall they were occupying, and then move on to saddle Fiddle.

Mark sighed, slowly getting to his feet. Robin followed suit. "I've been angry with your wife since leaving Dover."

"I noticed," Robin grinned wryly.

Mark rolled his eyes. "Yeah, well. I still think she should have killed Sir Hugh. It would have saved so much . . .but I've also been remembering Marian a lot since coming to Paris."

"Marian?"

"Is it such a surprise that I would think about my sister?" Mark snapped.

"No, not at all."

"It's my fault she's dead."

"Mark," Robin shook his head. "I thought you worked past this years ago."

"Yeah, well, so did I, but apparently not." Mark shrugged, but Robin could see how much pain he was still in. "I was right beside her, Robin . . ."

"I know. I was there, too. And I still grieve for Marian, of course, I do. But it wasn't your fault. It wasn't you who put a sword through Marian, it was Guy, and we've forgiven him for that."

"How could we possibly have come to that conclusion?"

"Jesus."

Mark smiled, if only a little. Then he set about finishing saddling Jack. Robin stepped back and watched him work, knowing there was still more conversation to be had, though perhaps now was not the time to do it. Mark's movements as he worked were rough; he was angry.

The barn door opened again and Lucy came in with Marian in tow.

"I miss my sister, Robin," Mark said softly, swinging in Jack's saddle.

"So do I," Robin replied. He left the stall, leading Jack out with him, and then moving toward Hero, whom Lucy was just beginning to lead out of her stall.

"Are we ready to go?" Lucy asked.

"I am. Are all the children accounted for?"

"Yes," Dusty replied. "Though if Mark is willing, it would be helpful if he carried either John or Daniyah so Will and I don't have to carry both."

"I'm perfectly willing," Mark said.

Children were shuffled between horses as Much and Mary made an appearance and set about saddling their ride, Dandy. Allen was close behind, preparing Outlaw for their journey and pulling Jane up to ride behind him. In what seemed to be no time at all, they were all ready.

"Let's go to see Eleanor," Robin said, leading his party out into the quiet streets of Paris. Before long the sun would rise and the streets would be loud and messy, but for now they were mostly empty.

"I've missed her," Much said. "Where is she these days?"

"Last I heard, she was retiring to Fontevraud Abbey, some four days ride from here."

"Four days? Is that far enough to be free of Sir Hugh following us?" Mark asked.

"Possibly not, but Eleanor will protect us," Lucy said. "She is still a powerful Queen, despite her age."

Robin hoped his wife was right; hoped he was making the right decision for what remained of his followers. At the very least, they would be reunited with the missing members of their family. After that, who knew what would become of them?

With a final worried glance at Mark, Robin set his mind on the task at hand and led his little family out of Paris.

IDA

Ida watched as Faith carefully twisted the stems of a few flowers together, creating a little crown for herself. Her hands were gentle and her movements calm. They were sitting outside under a tree behind the abbey, surrounded by small blossoms. Ida was getting bored with the sameness of every day, waiting anxiously for her family to arrive.

"What are you thinking?" Faith asked, looking up with a smile.

"I am wishing Robin and the others were here already."

"It may take time for them to hear from Queen Eleanor, or to respond to her letter," Faith said. "But the fact that she has found them out is reassuring, is it not? I told you God would bring your family to you."

"They aren't here yet, so don't get smug on me."

Faith laughed. "I'm not being smug. But I'm sure Robin will answer Queen Eleanor's summons, and then you'll be reunited with Allen and your boys. At which point, I fully expect you to admit that I am not crazy to trust my God."

"He didn't save your husband," Ida said softly. "How could you be so sure He'd save mine?"

Faith was quiet for a time, methodically twisting her flowers together. Ida began to worry that she'd offended her friend by mentioning Guy.

"I know He's good," Faith said at last. "Even if Allen doesn't make it here, after all, I will still rest in the knowledge of his goodness."

"How can you be so sure."

"Because He's never failed me."

"Your husband is dead!"

"Presumably," Faith said quietly. "And even so, I am alive, my daughter is alive. And if Guy did die to save all of us, then he died the hero I always knew he was. And I know he's in heaven, so why should I mourn?"

"I don't understand you, Faith."

"I know. But I have faith that you will someday."

"I want the sort of confidence that you have, Faith. I'm just not convinced it's true. You trust Him, but he didn't save Guy."

"I don't know what to tell you, Ida. We keep having this same discussion and we go around and around, but neither of us is changing our position. I trust Him and believe Him to be good in spite of what happened to my husband, and you refuse to trust Him in spite of how far He's gone to keep you safe. We won't reach an agreement, my friend, so I will simply continue to pray for you."

Ida didn't know what to say. Faith was right; every time they spoke on this subject it was the same.

Chapter 17

LUCY

Lucy slid off of Hero's back and took a moment to stretch her arms over her head to ease the tension in her back. It wasn't the most ladylike pose, but that couldn't be helped. Robin had already dismounted and pulled Marian off of Hero. He was carrying her on his shoulders now as he strode up to the front door of the tavern where they planned to spend the night.

The sun was sinking into the earth in the west. A light wind had picked up as the afternoon progressed, and Lucy knew her hair was likely as wayward and out of place as she could see Mary's was. Dusty, having never let her hair grow long again after chopping it off during the Crusades twelve years before, did not have the same problem.

A young boy came running up to assist with the horses, and Will and Much followed him to the nearby stable with their mounts.

Everyone began to follow Lucy inside, the children in tow. The room they entered was dark, lit by only a few candles scattered among the handful of tables that filled the otherwise empty space. There was a family seated at one table, and a lone traveler wrapped in a fur coat in the farthest corner. Robin was near a door, speaking to what Lucy assumed was the proprietor.

He was dressed in a simple brown tunic and tan trousers. His long blond hair was pulled back with a black ribbon. His sleeves were rolled past his elbows, revealing muscled arms which, along with his calloused hands, were covered in a light dusting of flour. He had a linen towel in his hand and was cleaning himself up as he spoke to Robin.

Lucy moved to stand beside her husband, circling his arm with her hands.

Robin half-turned toward her as he addressed the man standing before them. "Firmin, this is my wife," he said in French, "Lady Lucy."

Firmin gave a half bow, still wiping flour from his hands. "M'lady. You are all welcome. I will see to it that you have rooms prepared. How many will you need," Firmin glanced behind them at the rest of the group, all of whom had settled at one of the tables.

Lucy's eyes settled on Marian, who was sitting on the table, braiding Mark's dark hair and Lucy smiled at the sight. Mark was troubled and had been since their flight from England many months before, and Lucy was grateful to see that her daughter, at least, could bring him some measure of relief.

"Five rooms, if you can spare them," Robin replied.

"I'll let Henriette know." Firmin glanced behind him through the door to what Lucy assumed was the kitchen, given the smell of fresh bread wafting from it. "My sister will be delighted

284

to have more guests." Firmin bowed again and then walked through the door.

Robin led Lucy to the table where everyone was sitting. It was not long before a young servant girl came out of the kitchen, followed by Firmin, and Lucy and the rest of them enjoyed a satisfying meal of roasted lamb on a bed of peas, carrots, and onions. There was plenty of fresh bread, as well as blackberries, cherries, and raspberries.

Within minutes Marian's face was a canvas painted in vivid reds and darks hues as she shoved fistfuls of berries into her mouth.

"What will we do when we reach the abbey?" Much asked.

"We'll ask to see Eleanor," Robin replied, as if that was obvious. "And hopefully it won't be long before we see Ida, Andrew, and Faith."

"Seeing Ida is certainly my priority," Allen said.

When their meal was finished, Firmin returned to show them to their rooms.

Later that evening, as Lucy was brushing out Marian's hair before bed, waiting for Robin to return from the stables where he had gone to check on their horses for the night, Mark came creeping softly into her room.

Marian jumped up from her mother's lap where they had been sitting on the floor near the window. Lucy's hand was midstroke, and when her daughter leaped up the brush remained caught in Marian's tangled hair. For a brief moment, Lucy didn't think to let go but just as her daughter's head started to snap back from the pull she opened her fingers.

Marian ran gleefully to Mark, the brush still hanging from the back of her head. Mark scooped her up and kissed her cheek before dutifully walking across the room and plopping her back into Lucy's lap.

"Thanks," Lucy laughed.

"Uncle Mark!" Marian whined. "You were supposed to *sauver moi!*"

"If I had saved you, your mother would not be much pleased with me, I think," Mark replied.

Lucy set about finishing her task of ridding Marian's hair of its many tangles, wondering why Mark had chosen to seek them out. She had noticed how Marian seemed to bring back his light-heartedness over dinner, so perhaps he simply wished to be near her.

Mark sat in silence as Lucy brushed Marian's auburn mane. Marian, on the other hand, kept up a steady stream of conversation, directed sometimes at Mark and sometimes at her mother, in a mixture of both English and French.

When Robin appeared, Mark finally spoke. Before Robin had taken two steps into the room Mark said to him, "Could I ask a favor...?"

He didn't finish his sentence and Lucy stared at him, unsure what he wanted. Marian jumped up and ran toward her father as soon as she saw him. Robin swung her upward, kissed her, and then settled her onto his shoulders. He nodded at Mark in understanding, which left Lucy even more bewildered, and then announced, "I'm taking Marian for a walk. I'll show her some constellations."

And then they were both gone and Lucy was sitting alone on the floor beside Mark. When she looked at him, sitting quietly beside her, he was staring at his hands.

"Did you want to speak to me? You could have said as much."

"It wasn't anything Marian needed to hear."

Mark had winced, if only slightly, when he spoke her daughter's name and Lucy's curiosity and confusion heightened. While the tragedy of his sister's death was something every member of the gang who had known her would never truly move on from, they had all healed many years ago. Mark had never winced saying Marian's name in the past. In fact, he'd been overjoyed when Robin and Lucy had agreed to name her after Robin's first wife.

"Mark?"

"I need help."

"Help with what? Of course, I'm willing to help with anything you need."

Mark sighed heavily, still staring at his hands. "I'm sure you've noticed how angry I have been with you—with the world—since we fled England."

"I have noticed."

"I haven't really spoken to anyone about the reasons why. Dusty and Will have tried to pry it out of me now and again, but I couldn't talk to them, or anyone."

"You wanted me to kill Sir Hugh. That's where this started."

"It is how it started, but that hasn't been the main source of my bitterness recently." Mark leaned his head back against the wall, closing his eyes. Lucy watched as tears began to slowly slip beneath his eyelids and slide down his cheek.

"Mark?"

"I just can't stop thinking about my sister, about the day she died. And when we heard from Robin, from Queen Eleanor, that it was likely Guy was dead." Mark shook his head, his brow furrowing. "I wasn't upset, Lucy. I was glad he died."

"Mark!"

"I know, I know. It's terrible. I told you, I need help. I'm just so angry all of the time, and I don't know how to stop it. I don't want to feel this way, towards you, towards Guy. And I don't want to keep reliving Marian's death in my mind. I don't want to feel the guilt."

"It wasn't your fault."

Mark didn't respond. Lucy reached over to wipe a few tears off his cheek, letting him internally process his emotions until he finally spoke again.

"I need to apologize for so many things. The anger I have harbored for so many months because you refused to kill Sir Hugh, ignoring you, and yelling at you by turns in the days since Dover. I feel we haven't had anything but a poisonous relationship ever since that day on the ship, and that's my fault."

"I understand, Mark. We talked about this on our way to Paris, remember?"

"Yeah, we fought about it, and then once we were there I stopped talking to you, or anyone. I was just angry at you, at everyone. And I couldn't stop thinking about her, about Marian. I thought . . ." Mark sighed, and then continued, "I thought I had moved on. Forgiven Guy, forgiven myself, forgiven you for whatever part you chose not to play that day."

"But you haven't forgiven us? Is that it?"

"No. I don't know." Mark pushed a hand through his hair. "I had forgiven everyone, I had. And I had healed from that terrible day, but in Paris it all came back, as vicious and painful as if it had just happened, and my emotions were still raw and unchecked."

"What are you feeling now?"

Mark sighed, and Lucy let him reflect quietly. She didn't know what to say. That Mark had been in pain in Paris Lucy had known. That he was sullen and angry she had been well aware of. Yet the reason for the ache she had seen was not what she had imagined in any way.

His sister.

Marian.

Lucy hadn't known Marian personally. When Lucy had first arrived in Nottingham all those years ago, she had done so as a fugitive, an outlaw. Not that she had broken many laws and been branded an outlaw by the local authorities, but rather that she chose not to show herself to anyone and lived in obscurity. She'd stopped some of the Sheriff's hangings, and passed food to the poor when she could, doing it all without letting anyone in Nottingham become aware of her presence. And though the gang had known someone was in Nottingham working toward the same goals they were, they had never crossed paths because Lucy hadn't allowed it. She saw them, though. She watched them and grew to care for them from afar.

When the Sheriff had set out to kill the King while he was still imprisoned by the Duke of Austria, and Robin Hood and his followers had gone after him to stop the murder, Lucy had followed. All the way to Austria. She had been there to witness the ambush. Had tried to help Robin and the others without being seen. She had watched Marian die.

More than that, she had seen what Guy was about to do, and she had chosen not to put an arrow through his heart to stop it. And Marian had died.

As Lucy let the past come back to the forefront of her mind, she realized it was hardly a surprise that not killing Sir Hugh had forced Mark to relive the worst day of his life. Her decision to never take a life had arguably cost Marian hers.

290

"Mark, I'm sorry."

"I know, I know." Mark turned to her, tears in his eyes. "You weren't trying to get Marian killed, you were trying to live by what you believe in. I can't blame you for that. And you certainly weren't trying to make our lives difficult by not killing Sir Hugh."

Lucy could feel her throat beginning to tighten, the familiar prick in the back of her eyes as tears sprung up.

"I also know that despite how it ended, you would still make the same choice," Mark said. "And it makes me angry to think about that and yet I also feel that there is no shame in such a decision. You don't believe in killing people, that's not a bad thing. Or it shouldn't be. But Marian . . ."

"I wish I could say that I would not do things differently, Mark, but that isn't true."

Mark's eyebrows shot to his hairline.

"Mark, I was so self-righteous back then . . .nineteen years old, raised by a monk for much of my life. I was so sure of myself and what I knew to be true. The arrogance that pervaded my every action was inexcusable. I wouldn't kill Guy, if I could go back, I wouldn't kill him. That isn't different. But I wouldn't act like killing Guy or saving Marian were mutually exclusive decisions. That I had done what was right and your sister dying wasn't, in some way, my fault."

Mark began to protest but Lucy pushed on. "I do not believe that we should point fingers at each other, or that I should

291

live the rest of my life carrying the weight and shame of Marian's murder. I didn't kill her. But I do know that I could have done something, anything, to stop it. Mark...I had a clear view of Guy. I could have shot his sword hand, I could have shot his shoulder, his leg, I didn't have to kill him to stop him but I didn't do anything at all."

Lucy hesitated, unsure whether she wanted to be completely honest with her friend. Mark just stared at her so she pressed on again. "That's because the only shot I wanted to take that day was the one to his heart. When I panicked and saw what was happening, the first thought that came to mind was 'kill him' and I had my arrow to the string immediately. My eye was trained on his chest and while I did manage, by the grace of God, not to kill Guy, I didn't have the time to consider other options before she was dead. Because I thought to kill him first and then had to fight myself not to, Marian died. If my first thought had been simply stopping him, somehow, I could have. I should have."

Lucy was crying, tears working their warm way down her cheeks and dripping on to her collarbone. Mark was staring at her, wide-eyed and horrified.

"Lucy . . ."

Lucy wiped the tears from her cheeks and fought to gain her composure.

"I can't blame you for my sister's death," Mark said. "I have, and I some part of me desperately wants to, but I can't. I forgave you before, and I forgive you again for any part of it that I have blamed you for in the past or that you blame yourself for."

Mark turned so that he was facing her completely, "Lucy, I was standing right next to her, my hand was on her arm. I could have done so many things in that moment, but I froze. I *froze*." Mark shook his head. "I just stood there and watched it happen."

"It wasn't your fault—"

"It wasn't yours either."

Lucy nodded. "I know. I know, and yet somehow I did have some small part in her death. And that truth will stay with me till the day I die."

"It haunts me," Mark whispered, tears falling from his eyes in a cascade.

"Not as much as it haunts Guy."

"I forgave him, too, years ago," Mark said. "But somehow, it all came back. The anger, the hatred. And now I have to forgive him all over again and I don't know how."

"I think that's okay. Our God forgives us every time we sin, even when it's the same thing over and over. He has gotten pretty good, I imagine, at forgiving the same crime. Therefore, in my humble opinion, when you ask Him for help forgiving Guy over and over, however many times you need until you are with Him in heaven, He will have more than enough of that forgiveness to spare."

Mark sighed. "I know. But it's hard. And some part of me doesn't want to forgive him, or you even."

"But enough of you wants to that you are here, talking to me."

"I suppose."

"We have a lot of work to do here, Mark, but we'll get there. Can I pray with you?"

Mark agreed and Lucy began to pray.

GILBERT

They had made as good a time to the Fontevraud Abbey in Anjou as could be tolerably expected, considering the invalid in their midst. The road from Calais had been relatively uneventful and Gilbert, had they not been in search of Robin Hood and likely to meet with Sir Hugh once more, might have otherwise been bored out of his mind. They rode their horses by day, slept at various taverns by night, and the sameness was beginning to be irksome by the time they stopped in the city of Chinon. The castle of Chinon had been King Henry's court not too many years ago, or so Guy told Gilbert. Gilbert cared very little for such details. All that interested him was that the abbey in question, where they were intent on finding the Queen Mother and Robin Hood together, was only one more days' travel from their current location.

The night spent in Chinon was a restless one for two, at least, of the traveling companions. After securing rooms at an inn, and feasting on a meal most amply and eagerly provided by the proprietor, they had removed themselves to their room. Gilbert had seen no necessity on their journeys to pay for multiple rooms where one would suffice, and had therefore resigned himself and Roger to sleeping on the floor, or at the most a straw mattress, and leaving the bed to their invalid friend for the entirety of their travels.

When they had retired to their room, Roger lounged in a chair and seemed content to do nothing at all with his evening. Guy had situated himself on the bed, though sitting up against a few pillows, and Gilbert threw himself onto the floor under the window. But staying there was impossible. He was up again only a few minutes later, pacing about in no particular fashion.

They had only one more day to go. He would transfer the care of Guy to Robin Hood tomorrow, and then would be free to take his revenge on Sir Hugh.

It was clear that Guy was equally restless. He had not the strength to pace as he might have wanted to, but he could not remain still upon the bed. Gilbert was aware of his constant moving and fretting, first running his hand through his hair, then finding a loose thread in the blanket upon the bed and picking at it until he'd unraveled half of it. Gilbert assumed this restlessness was born of being so close to reuniting with his wife, not to mention the rest of his friends. Being so close, and yet still not there, was irksome to Gilbert as well, though for rather different reasons, and he could sympathize with Guy.

Eventually, however, the night did pass. Roger may have been the only one to sleep that night, but morning came nonetheless, and the three companions set off for the last leg of their journey.

Gilbert was on high alert, taking in their surroundings, and ascertaining where potential threats might lie. They followed the river Vienne for some time, before striking out westward in search of the abbey. The terrain was mainly forest, but the roads through them were wide and decently well-kept. The forest could provide ample cover for any number of ambushes, and Gilbert kept a well-trained eye on the trees, assessing first one side of the road and then the other continually as they rode along. When they passed out of the trees and the abbey itself came into view, Gilbert felt a great deal of relief. Robin, it was to be hoped, had brought his friends here for refuge, which meant Gilbert could leave his companions in good hands and go kill Sir Hugh.

As they rode closer to the low wall surrounding the courtyard, Gilbert could see through the open archway that the courtyard was broken into small plots, all filled with different plants. There were several monks moving about the strange herbal garden, and beyond them the church towering over everything else. As they rode under the archway several other buildings came into view on the right and left.

The monks noticed them immediately and moved towards them, smiling cheerfully.

"Welcome! How may we assist you, gentlemen?" a monk greeted them in French.

Gilbert studied the five monks who were now all gathering around them. All were dressed in simple black tunics and seemed harmless enough. None of them appeared armed.

"We are seeking Eleanor of Aquitaine," Guy said, also speaking French. He dismounted slowly. In the past, Gilbert would have thought Guy did so to lessen his imposing nature, and in the past, it would not have changed his impressive stature at all; but now, he looked broken from the back of his horse and he looked broken standing there, stiff and in pain, before the monks.

"Benjamin, will you send for Eleanor?" one of the monks said, turning to his friend who quickly scurried off to one of the buildings that wasn't the church. Gilbert watched him go, remaining on his horse as Roger dismounted.

"Wait!" the monk called out, and his friend stopped, and turned back. The monk doing all the talking turned to Guy. "Who shall we say is asking for the Queen Mother?"

"A friend of Robin of Locksley," Guy replied.

The little monk named Benjamin hurried off again, unimpeded by any other remarks from his friend.

"I'm Alexis," the spokesman said. "These are Pierre, and Norbert," gesturing to the two remaining monks.

"I am Sir Guy of Gisbourne, these are my companions, Roger and Gilbert. We are looking for Robin, and have come to Eleanor because she is a mutual friend."

297

Gilbert watched the faces of the monks carefully, searching for any sign that might suggest Robin was, in fact, here at the abbey.

"Robin Hood?" Pierre asked. "He has not yet been seen in this abbey. Whether the Queen has discovered his whereabouts or not, I do not know. She hasn't discussed the search with me. But there are others who came here looking for him as well. Perhaps you wish to see them?"

"What others?" Guy asked eagerly.

Before Pierre could respond, the little monk, Benjamin, was returning. Gilbert watched as he approached, scurrying along beside an elegant lady well advanced in years, moving towards them with an air of grace and urgency.

The lady's eyes flicked over the whole scene, seeming to take in every face. "I have not had the pleasure of being introduced to any of you fine gentlemen before. You are friends of Robin?"

"Sir Guy of Gisbourne, my lady," Guy bowed. "Roger Sparr, and Gilbert."

"Two of these names I know," the Queen Mother said thoughtfully, eyeing Guy with curiosity before flicking her gaze to Gilbert. "What brings you to my door?"

"We are looking for Robin. We had hoped we would find him here."

For a moment, the lady said nothing. And then she sighed. "I have had no word from Robin. I know my son is trying to kill him; I had heard rumors he fled England, but he hasn't come to me."

"He has fled England," Roger said. "But we can't find him."

"Why don't you join me in my quarters," Eleanor said. "You are welcome to rest here at the abbey for as many days as you need. I have friends of yours already staying as guests of mine. Once you are reunited and rested a bit, we can discuss what we know of dear Robin and his whereabouts."

"I'll stable your horses," Norbert offered.

Gilbert finally dismounted, relinquishing his horse to Norbert and following the Queen Mother as she led Guy, Roger, and himself back to the building housing her apartments. She sent a nun scurrying off to fetch her other guests, and Gilbert hoped for Guy's sake that that included his little wife.

Once they had situated themselves in a small apartment, furnished with a small table, a dozen simple wooden chairs, and several candelabras, and been given refreshment at the Queen Mother's direction, Gilbert got to the point.

"If Robin didn't come here, we are unlikely to ever discover him. The world is vast and he is trying *not* to be found."

"Start at the beginning," Eleanor said. Though Gilbert had spoken in French, she'd responded in English. She'd arranged their chairs so that the three of them were seated facing her. The small table between them to one side, filled with refreshments.

"When you say 'the beginning'" Roger responded, following her lead and speaking English, "What do you mean? Robin's birth? The adventures in Sherwood, which I was not a part of? Or some part of the tale thereafter?"

"The last communication I had from Robin was after Richard's death," Eleanor said, her eyes darkening somewhat as she spoke her son's name. "So that is where I would like your tale to begin if it can. I have my own tale to tell from the more recent history regarding Robin and his whereabouts, but I'd like to hear your tale first."

Guy sat forward, resting his elbows on his thighs and clasping his scarred hands together. "Robin sent for all of us, the members of his gang from the Sherwood days, as soon as Richard died. We gathered in Nottingham to see what King John would do. Unsurprisingly, Robin was removed from his office as Sheriff of Nottingham and another man given the title. Then King John sent a mercenary to kill us. We fled, first to Sherwood, until that was compromised, and then we scattered."

"I was not a member of Robin's band of men," Gilbert put in. "My lord and I happened upon a small part of that band fleeing the attack on Sherwood and we gave them refuge, later joining them on their journey. We set off for Scotland, and met up with almost everyone else belonging to Robin Hood, save for Sir Guy, his wife, his friend Andrew, and a woman named Ida."

"I took my family back to my own estate," Guy said. "Sir Hugh, the mercenary your son has hired to kill us, eventually

300

found us there and I narrowly escaped with my life. Gilbert here made sure I was looked after. Whatever became of my wife, my daughter, Ida, or Andrew, we don't know. I pray they safely escaped. Are they here?"

"I was only present on Gisbourne estate because Sir Hugh had followed us to Scotland." Gilbert took up the tale before the Queen could answer Guy's eager question. "He killed my lord, and nearly fatally wounded me. Robin and the rest escaped. Once I was well enough to travel—"

"Or even sooner, in truth," Roger put in.

"I tracked Robin Hood to Dover, where I learned he crossed the channel to Calais. I also learned Sir Hugh was still in England, so I made it my mission to follow him and find Robin later. I tracked Sir Hugh to Gisbourne estate in time to witness the siege; get in long enough to get Sir Guy's family out."

"Guy had been caught," Roger spoke up again. "I was there, fighting with Sir Hugh's men, only because he hired a friend of mine to fill his army and I happened to be under his employment as well . . .at any rate, I helped Gilbert get Faith, Guy's wife that is, and their daughter and Andrew out of the estate. Guy himself was executed."

Guy winced. "I was. But thanks to Gilbert's timely rescue, and his tireless efforts to ensure I had a physician and proper care, I survived."

"Barely," Roger said, eyeing Guy with awe.

"Once Sir Guy was well enough for travel—" Gilbert began.

"If you can call it that," Roger interrupted.

Gilbert paused, glared at Roger, and then when he cowered somewhat, continued, "We set out for Dover, knowing that Robin had crossed the channel. We came here directly, thinking that this would be the first place Robin would have gone."

"Unfortunately, Robin did not come to me," Eleanor said. "I wish that he had. How long ago did he cross the channel?"

"Six months ago," Gilbert replied.

"He's had six months to burrow somewhere in the known world?" Eleanor laughed. "He couldn't be found, for years, when everyone knew precisely the forest he was hiding in. And now you haven't the faintest idea of a place to look, but you think you'll find him?"

"No," Gilbert said. "As he isn't here, I have nowhere else to look. He's lost until he chooses to resurface again."

"On the contrary," Eleanor grinned rather smugly. "I have many powerful friends in every city in the known world. My reach is long; I have found our missing friend and sent word to him to come to me immediately. I haven't heard back; he may not agree to come. But if he does, we should see him soon. As for my other guests, they are indeed your missing family. Ida and her companions turned up on my doorstep some days ago, also

302

presuming Robin would seek me for refuge. It appears his companions are wiser than he."

"Although since everyone assumed he would come here, maybe it was wiser after all that he didn't," Roger suggested.

"Where is my wife?" Guy interrupted before the Queen could offer Roger a clever comment.

At that moment there was a knock on the door and the nun the Queen had sent off came striding in, holding the door wide. And there was the fiery young woman Gilbert had met briefly at Gisbourne estate. Behind her were the others.

IDA

Ida and Faith were walking arm in arm with Andrew behind them carrying little Lucy. When Sister Nicole pushed open the door to Queen Eleanor's apartments they had walked in confidently. Sister Nicole had only said that the Queen Mother wished to see them urgently, not why. Though the why was immediately obvious upon entering the room. Ida caught sight of Gilbert and the soldier Roger that she'd met so briefly at Gisbourne estate before Faith suddenly stopped walking, jerking Ida's arm backward and causing her to stop as well.

Faith had gone ashen. She had also stopped breathing.

"Faith!" Ida grabbed Faith by both shoulders. "It's just our friends, Faith. Don't faint on me."

"G. . .a . . .eee…"

303

"What?" Ida shook her friend. "Faith?"

"Papa!" Little Lucy cried out from her perch in Andrew's arms.

"Guy!" Faith shrieked, loud enough for Ida to wince and take half a step back.

Faith shoved past her, sprinting forward. Ida spun around to watch her and then saw him. He eased himself out of his chair and hobbled across the room.

They collided and clung to each other, both crying.

Ida stared wide-eyed for a moment, and then she could no longer watch them. She couldn't see anything for the tears in her eyes.

Guy was alive? How was that possible?

She stood for a moment, frozen. Then, when her tears cleared enough for her to see, she bolted for the embracing couple.

Ida reached them as they pulled back, Guy placing his hands on either side of Faith's face.

"Guy!"

Guy glanced up and grinned through his own tears. "Ida."

Ida paused, not wanting to take more of his attention from Faith, but feeling the need to do or say something. This man she had hated for so long and then slowly, grudgingly, come to respect had died. She'd watched over his wife for months and grown more fond of her than she'd thought possible considering her years of disgust. And now he was alive, standing in front of her.

Guy chuckled and opened his arms. Ida was still unsure, but with one arm around his wife, Guy embraced her with his free arm. Ida's arm snaked around Faith, too, and the three of them stood holding each other for several minutes.

"Okay, that's more affection than I can handle in a day," Ida said, pushing away. "I'll leave you two to it."
Ida moved toward the rest of the group shaking hands with Gilbert.

"How did you make it out? How did you get him out?"

"I am glad to see you got your friends to safety," Gilbert said. "As for how Guy survived his execution I will never understand. He was practically dead when I freed him from Sir Hugh. I nearly killed Sir Hugh in a duel, yet somehow he, too, survived. It is rather irksome, all this living when one ought to be dead."

"We spent a few months just waiting for Guy to live or die, and then healing," Roger said. "And then he insisted we begin our search for you and Robin Hood. And here we are."

"I still don't believe it," Ida said, turning to face Guy and Faith again. Andrew had joined their little embrace and the three of them were talking animatedly.

"I cannot explain how this happened, though I witnessed the entire thing," Gilbert said.

"Someone had better explain everything. This is not possible," Ida said. Little Lucy was now wrapped around Guy's legs. After a moment he pulled back from Faith and scooped her up, letting her join the hug.

"How is this even real?" Ida asked no one in particular.

FAITH

Guy was alive.

It was more than Faith could have ever dreamed of. Guy was alive!

The first day after the arrival of the three men was spent in catching up—everyone relating the events that had occurred since the last time they parted. Faith hardly paid any attention to the accounts. She just sat by her husband and gazed into his scarred face and marveled that her God was so merciful. Her husband had survived, against all odds. Faith couldn't stop stroking his dark hair, or tracing her finger along the scars on his face. She kissed his wrists where the ropes had made their lasting mark on his skin more times than she could count. She kissed him, too, far more than was appropriate in most settings. But she didn't care about being ladylike; she had her husband back.

In the days that followed her wonder at her husband's life did not abate, but she was able to pay more attention to the other people around her. Providing Guy was beside her, holding her hand. She never left his side, never let him out of her sight. Little

Lucy also clung to him, always wanting to be sitting in his lap or held in his arms. Guy was more than willing to oblige both of them.

About four days after the appearance of the three men on their doorstep, Faith was sitting with Guy by the hearth in the rooms they'd been put up in at the abbey, once more tracing her finger along his scarred face, when Ida came into the room. She glanced at them and then paused, staring with deep questions in her eyes.

"Ida?"

Ida met her eyes and smiled. "Faith. Sorry, I don't mean to interrupt."

"You aren't," Guy said. "Come and sit with us."

Ida seated herself on a low stool across from Guy and Faith. Ida watched Guy, her face betraying a wealth of emotions, but she said nothing.

Faith eyed her friend for a while in silence, but she couldn't stay quiet for long. "Ida, what's bothering you?"

"Nothing is bothering me."

"Are you sure? You can't keep your eyes off my husband any more than I can."

Ida wrinkled her nose. "I have a perfectly good husband of my own, thank you. One I expect to see any day now, if Robin chose to follow Queen Eleanor's advice and bring everyone here."

Faith laughed. "That's not what I meant."

307

"I know," Ida said. "And you're right, I can't stop staring."

"Am I so hideous?" Guy asked, mostly in jest.

"No. You're alive."

Faith smiled, kissing Guy's cheek. "Yes, you are alive. How marvelous is that?"

"Only by the grace of God," Guy replied.

"Precisely!" Ida said. "That's why I can't stop staring! I thought you were, well, crazy. All of you. With your perfect assurance and trust in your God. Believing you could actually have a relationship with God."

"You can," Faith said.

"I know. I didn't understand it, and the forgiveness thing," Ida shook her head. "That drove me crazy."

Ida glanced at Guy, and Faith couldn't help but think of the past—how spiteful Ida had been toward her husband for so many years. But that had changed while they lived at Gisbourne estate.

"Your peace, Faith," Ida continued, "at Gisbourne estate, I desperately needed that. I didn't have my husband and my sons and I was broken. I needed what you had but I didn't have it. And then when Guy died, I thought . . ."

"What did you think?" Guy asked quietly when it became apparent that Ida wasn't going to continue.

"I thought," Ida sighed. "I thought you were wrong, Faith. Completely wrong. If God loved you so much, and knew you personally as you claimed He did, why would He kill your husband? You were always praying for His protection, and obviously He hadn't given it."

Ida paused, staring at the wall in silence for a moment. "But then Guy came back, seemingly from the dead. You weren't wrong."

Faith smiled, reaching out to take Ida's hand in her own. "Do you believe me now? Do you trust Him yourself?"

"I'm certainly starting to."

Faith squealed and jumped up to hug Ida. When she resumed her seat, Guy spoke. "You have to understand, though, that even if I had died that doesn't change who God is. He would still be the loving Father that he is."

"But you didn't die," Ida responded. "And that's the point."

"I've been thinking these past few days that God has been so good to me," Faith said, "bringing me back my husband. But maybe He didn't do it for me at all, maybe He did it for your benefit, Ida."

Chapter 18

DUSTY

Their progress to the abbey had been swift and without
hindrance; yet within the last two days of their travel they could
easily make out the cloud of dust floating just above the horizon.
There was an army to their right headed in the same general
direction. Whether this was a French lord on some business of his
own, or Philip's army attending to Crown business, could not be
ascertained without approaching the army, and Robin had
forbidden such action. The terrible idea that it was somehow Sir
Hugh had entered his mind, and everyone else now latched onto
the idea, with varying degrees of strength. Dusty wouldn't make
any predictions as to who that army belonged to, but the simple
fact that they were clearly headed in the same direction was
unsettling enough. After the first day of the distant cloud of dust
following along parallel to their position, Robin had insisted they
travel more inconspicuously, keeping to any trees or villages that
they could and avoiding the chance of meeting the army—
whoever they were—in an open field.

All the anxiety of the unknown army was now coming to a
close, at least for the present. The abbey was in view, they were in
fact riding under the very archway that led them into the first
courtyard and garden in front of the church.

Robin rode nearly to the church steps before dismounting. Dusty followed his lead. After sliding off of Fiddle's back she pulled John down so that Will could dismount as well. Daniyah was riding with Mark, who kept her in his arms when he came to stand by Robin. Lucy stayed on Hero trying to contain Marian's ceaseless energy, while Allen, Jane, Much, and Mary joined those with Robin on the stone steps, their children in tow.

"Well," Robin said. "We made it to the abbey at least."

The door to the church opened and a monk came striding down the stairs. "Welcome!" he called in French. "How may I assist you?"

"We are here to see Eleanor of Aquitaine," Robin replied.

"As is everyone these days," the monk chuckled. "I am Alexis. Whom should I say is asking for the Queen Mother?"

"Robin of Locksley."

"Robin Hood!" The monk stared for a moment and then began laughing. "Your friends arrived only too early, it seems."

At the mention of friends, Dusty straightened. Were Ida, Faith, and Andrew truly here, as Eleanor's letter to Robin had suggested? Allen and Jane would be overjoyed to see them again.

Before Dusty could imagine anything further, the monk was explaining. "Three friends of yours arrived only a week ago trying to find you. They had hoped you came to the Queen Mother for refuge, but you had not. And before that three other visitors came in search of you as well. Since then they have been

311

working with the Queen Mother to discover your whereabouts. She did not tell me she had found you already."

"Two sets of three friends?" Much asked. "I assume Ida, Andrew, and Faith are one, considering Eleanor said as much. But who are the others?"

"Their names are Gilbert, Guy, and Roger," the monk said. "If you'll follow me I'll take you to the Queen and she can show you to the others, I'm sure."

"Guy!" Lucy cried from atop Hero's back, Marian finally breaking free from her grasp at the same moment and tumbling to the ground, unharmed.

Several other voices uttered both Guy and Gilbert's names with incredulity.

"Who is Roger?" Dusty asked quietly.

"Their traveling companion, apparently," Robin replied.

"Where are they now, Father?"

"Your friends are likely sequestered in our lady's room, as they spent much time with her. I will take you there if you'd like."

"Please do!" Lucy said, leaving Hero's back and scooping up Marian, who was trying to pull the poor mare's tale.

"One moment, while I fetch someone to care for your horses," Alexis said, disappearing into the church for a moment.

He returned shortly with several monks behind him, and then motioned for Robin and the rest to follow him, walking off to the right of the church toward a low building a stone's throw away.

"Eleanor's rooms are this way."

Dusty, like the rest, immediately followed the monk.

"You are certain that one of them is Guy?" Will asked. "We had reason to believe he was dead."

"He is not dead, or was not at breakfast this morning," Alexis replied.

"Sir Guy of Gisbourne," Lucy questioned. "Are you certain?"

"I am certain, madame. Here we are," opening the door to the building, "just down this hall."

"Tall, imposing man? Dark hair?" Lucy continued to question the monk.

"You'll see in a moment," he chuckled. "Dark hair, yes. Tall, yes. Imposing, perhaps not. He's a broken man, still healing from very serious wounds."

Dusty's interest, already keen, was now even more so. Wounds were, after all, her specialty.

The monk finally stopped before a door and knocked. "My lady?"

"Do come in, Alexis," called a female voice from within.

The door was open, and in a moment they were all inside. The Queen Mother was seated at a table spread with maps, and had one in her hands as she turned to see who entered. Gilbert was standing behind the table, leaning on it with his hands flat against the surface. Ida stood beside him. A young man that Dusty did not recognize was off to the left, standing with a book open in

313

his hand, and in a chair next to him sat Guy. Faith was behind her husband, her hands on his shoulders.

For a moment, they all stared at one another.

Then everyone moved at once. Lucy ran to Guy's chair as he slowly rose to his feet and threw herself into his arms. Eleanor leaped from her chair and rushed to pull Robin into an embrace.

Will had moved to greet Guy as well, though Lucy beat him to it and he was forced to simply watch an embrace he had no part of. Mark and Gilbert shook hands eagerly, Much stood by Robin and was soon encompassed in the embrace with Eleanor. Andrew and Jane were caught up in an embrace, kissing each other passionately. Ida and Allen were no less enthused to see each other, though their embrace was interrupted by William and Edward shrieking "mama!" and leaping toward Ida.

Dusty watched the various greetings with pleasure. Allen finally with his wife again, and Jane with her husband. Everyone was there, apart from Little John and his family, and it gave her heart joy. The fact that Guy was alive and standing before them gave the greatest pleasure of all.

As none of the hugging seemed likely to stop soon, Dusty greeted Gilbert and then moved toward the unknown young man.

"This is Roger," Gilbert said. "He helped me get Guy and his family out of Gisbourne estate, and has helped me watch over Guy ever since." Gilbert glanced back at Guy, still being crushed in Lucy's embrace. "He should be dead."

"I am glad to meet you, Roger. And thank you for all you've done for our family."

"I would do more for Robin Hood, and all of you, if I could. I'd do anything to help."

When Lucy finally let Guy go, tears in her eyes, everyone else took a turn shaking his hand or giving him an embrace.

"I am glad you are not dead after all," Dusty said, kissing his cheek. The scar covering his left cheek caught her attention first, followed by the observation that his left ear was missing its top half. "I will want a full description of your wounds and how they were treated before long," Dusty added cheerfully.

"I'd expect nothing less," Guy replied. "But you'll have to get that information from Gilbert and Roger. I'm afraid I was unconscious for several weeks and missed a great deal of my initial recovery."

"You do still have the book don't you?" Roger asked.

"Book?" Dusty questioned.

"The physician who healed me gave me a book detailing my recovery," Guy said. "It's for you if it'll help."

"I'm sure it will."

"Why did you not come to me immediately," Dusty heard Eleanor chiding Robin as the various hugs and greetings drew to a close.

"I took my family to Paris," Robin said. "I had no desire to draw attention to myself, and seeking out old friends seemed likely to do so."

"You've been in Paris?" Guy asked, sinking back into his chair heavily, his head falling into his hands. Faith wrapped her arms around his shoulders.

"For some time," Robin replied. "We have reason to believe Sir Hugh is in France looking for us now. Indeed, there is an army not too far from here that traveled the same way we did, only a few miles distant, that might be him."

"Sir Hugh is coming here?" Gilbert took an eager step toward Robin. "He's close?"

"We don't know if it's Sir Hugh," Will replied. "That is only a guess. It could be any army. We didn't get close enough to ask."

Before Gilbert could ask another question, which he clearly wanted to do, Guy removed his hands from his face and spoke again, his voice steadier though his cheeks were wet with tears, "And what of Little John?"

"Little John stayed in Paris with his family," Dusty said. "We lived peacefully there for some time and had begun to have lives of our own; jobs, friends, and the like. Little John was unwilling to leave and Elinor, I think, tired of travel."

"Now that we know everyone is alive and well," Gilbert interjected, "Can we get back to this business of Sir Hugh's army? How distant from the abbey is the army you saw?"

"They might arrive," Mark answered, "assuming this is even remotely their destination, within the day, or tomorrow at the latest."

"Sir Hugh will be here tomorrow?" Roger asked, looking rather panicked.

"We don't know that it was Sir Hugh," Lucy said. "That is only conjecture."

"It is likely," Will said. "We don't know, but who else would be traveling with an army in the same way as us? Philip's armies have been much further north and east dealing with King John for some time, even with their treaty."

"Would this Sir Hugh be of the sort of character to attack an abbey?" Eleanor asked, concerned.

"I am not sure," Robin said. "I wouldn't put it past him."

"Then we must prepare for such an event," Eleanor said calmly. "I will speak to the monks and nuns here and ascertain what they would like to do in preparation of Sir Hugh's arrival— if indeed it turns out to be his army following you. You will be tired from your travels from Paris, I am sure. I'll see to it you have food to eat, baths to clean yourselves, and beds to sleep in and then I will be on my way to speak to Alexis and the others."

"Thank you, Eleanor," Robin said. "Whatever we can do to assist you, let us know. It is our fault, after all, if Sir Hugh is going to attack the abbey. He's only after us."

IDA

Ida brushed a lock of Allen's unruly blonde hair out of his eyes, marveling that he was alive and near her once more.

317

The planning for the arrival of the army, presumably Sir Hugh's, hadn't taken long. The nuns and monks who lived in the abbey were to stay within the outer walls for their own safety, and everyone else was to be on alert. They had only to wait and see what Sir Hugh—if it was indeed Sir Hugh—might do once he arrived.

Once the meeting had broken up, Ida had led Allen and her sons back to the room she had been living in since her arrival at the abbey. They'd curled up on the bed together, all four of them, and Allen and Ida had commenced regaling each other with the tales of their time apart. The boys, rowdy as ever, had clambered over the two of them and caused many distractions in the conversation until eventually they had fallen asleep.

Now Ida was curled up on her side, facing Allen whose eyes were closed, both boys snuggled between them—half on top of Allen's chest, half tucked between their parents.

They were alive, they were safe.

Guy was alive.

Maybe there was something to Faith's assurance in the Creator after all.

Sir Hugh was coming with an army, or so they thought, and yet for the first time Ida wasn't concerned. Whatever happened, God would take care of them. It's what Faith would say, and for once Ida could believe it.

ROBIN

They had arrived at the abbey, and what was more had found friends waiting for them—more than simply Eleanor. Guy was scarred and weak, unlike his old self; Gilbert was as bloodthirsty and incorrigible as ever; and Eleanor was precisely as Robin remembered her. Andrew was much as he had ever been, but Ida seemed different. Gentler, somehow.

After taking a meal the nuns had graciously provided, many of Robin's traveling companions had gone to their new quarters to rest. Robin couldn't sleep with the possibility of Sir Hugh so near, and had instead gone in search of Eleanor. He found her within the chapel. She sat calmly on a pew bench, staring kindly up toward the altar.

Robin took a seat beside her. "What are you thinking?"

"I am thinking it has been far too long since you and I spoke in person. And, indeed, you have been very remiss in your letters. All news I ever had of you was from Richard's correspondence."

"I am no great letter-writer; you should have applied to my wife."

Eleanor smiled. "I will do so in the future, for however long I may remain on this earth. Now, Robin, I have had an idea."

"Queen Eleanor using her brain, a dangerous proposition."

Eleanor chuckled. "Hush, Robin. Now listen...John listens to me. I should have done this before you were sent fleeing across

319

the continent, but I was unaware how bad the situation truly was. I knew John wasn't pleased with your role in his rebellion while Richard lived, and I knew he would likely want you out of the way when he took the throne, but for all that, I still didn't think he'd go so far, especially with his war with France and his nephew and everything else he had to deal with."

"He has quite a lot of turmoil as a new king," Robin said. "But he did not forget his old foes."

"I can see that now," Eleanor said. "The arrival of Ida and the others gave me an explanation of how bad things had truly become, and also gave me an idea of something I should have done the minute my son became king."

"And what is that?"

"I wrote to him when I began to look for you, Robin dear, and tried to persuade him to forgive you for your wrongs against him—however right you may have been to oppose him is not the question at hand. We have had much communication between us in the last couple weeks, though I haven't heard yet what his decision is. I told him to give up on killing you, trying to convince him that you could be useful to him as an alley, beloved as you are by the people, expert military man that you are, and so forth. He will listen to me, he nearly always does, and therefore will call off Sir Hugh."

"Assuming you are able to convince him, which seems unlikely, even so Sir Hugh will be here tomorrow, if that is his army we saw, you won't be able to reach King John before Sir Hugh kills us all."

Eleanor shook her head. "It may not be Sir Hugh, you know. And if it is, he may have the good sense not to attack an abbey. Does he want the Vatican at his throat? I think not."

"Wait for the King's response, by all means, my lady. If you succeed, then we can all return home. That is worth more than I could ever repay you."

"Nonsense. All you ever did for Richard is more than reason enough to help you in this way. And our own friendship is even more reason."

SIR HUGH

Sir Hugh studied the abbey with interest as he and Torin rode towards it. The army they had stationed, arrayed to intimidate, some yards from the abbey itself. As they approached, they could see several monks tending the garden within the walls. Their approach was noted, and a monk moved forward to greet them at the gate. "Welcome!" he called in French. "How may I be of service to you?"

"We come as friends," Sir Hugh said. "As long as you cooperate. Is there a man by the name of Robin of Locksley within these walls?"

The monk eyed him carefully. "Robin Hood is indeed here. Yet I would caution you against a massacre within the abbey; the church will not look kindly on such an event. The Pope would retaliate, Sir Hugh, of that you may be assured."

"I have no inclination to fight with the church," Sir Hugh said impatiently. His heart was racing; Robin was here! And was expecting him, considering the monk knew exactly who he was. "Let Robin face me as a man, and I will not have to find him wherever he cowers. I may have no wish to kill monks and nuns or desecrate your abbey, but my army will not be leaving until I have Robin Hood. I do hope you have enough provisions to sustain a siege, Father."

Sir Hugh wheeled his horse around and galloped back toward his army, Torin following. Sir Hugh was eager for another fight. Robin Hood was nearly within his grasp; he had only to wait for the monk to relay his message and then the outlaw would likely come to him to avoid any bloodshed within the abbey.

Chapter 19

MARK

Mark stood with his back pressed against the outer wall of the courtyard near the gate, peering through it carefully. The army had encircled the abbey that first day and then simply remained. They were too well walled-in to escape the abbey, but something would have to be done. In the days since his arrival, Sir Hugh could often be seen trotting around on his horse, his red hair flying about, laughing in the direction of the abbey. He knew as well as they knew that despite the fact he refused to attack the monks and nuns within the walls, Robin and his gang would not survive. They would slowly starve to death due to the siege, or they would try to escape and be killed.

Mark sighed, watching Sir Hugh from his vantage point. He was near enough to see every haughty expression of his face, but too far away to kill. Mark had taken Robin's bow on more than one occasion over the last few days to try and shoot him down, but he was clever enough to remain just out of reach. Robin had finally forbidden the unnecessary waste of arrows. Lucy and Dusty spent a great deal of time in the church praying. Others would join them at times, and everyone spent more than a few hours a day sneaking to get a glimpse of Sir Hugh and the army surrounding them. They had to be subtle with such endeavors, because not killing the monks and nuns was a grace that did not extend to Robin's gang. On the few occasions they were visible to anyone in that army outside the abbey walls, arrows would fly. Will had been grazed by an arrow on the second day, though it wasn't a serious wound.

Gilbert was the only person who refused to cower. When he wanted a view of Sir Hugh he would simply walk out to the gate and look at him. Arrows still flew, and Gilbert would duck and pirouette like a dancer on a stage to avoid them when he had to. Though, more often than not, he simply stood still and dared them to kill him. The army, like Sir Hugh, generally stayed out of range so as not to be killed by those inside the abbey and therefore could not always easily reach their target. Somehow Gilbert always seemed to know precisely when no archer was within range, and he'd march out of the gate and cross his arms, challenging someone to approach him.

Mark might have done the same, but Will wasn't the only one who'd been hit, or nearly so, by the onslaught of arrows from Sir Hugh's men. Mark was beginning to think Gilbert was the only person immune to such attacks.

Mark's eyes followed Sir Hugh's progress as he rode along the line of archers. He tried not to consider how very obvious it was that they would all die in this abbey. More than once the flicker of 'if Lucy had only killed him' came and went through his mind, but he ignored it.

Whatever happened now, Lucy was not to blame. Sir Hugh had made his own decisions.

SIR HUGH

Sir Hugh stroked Night's dappled grey neck, enjoying the feel of his horse's muscles rippling under his palm. Night was a powerful horse and had always served Sir Hugh well.

He was standing almost directly in line with the gate of the monastery where he could watch nuns and outlaws scurry across the courtyard from time to time in a panic. That they tried to be inconspicuous and stealthy only made the watching of their antics that much more amusing. Sir Hugh was, of course, just outside of range of any arrows that might fly, though they hadn't been flying for several days. The outlaws had apparently given up on that futile activity.

He had expected Robin Hood to come out of the abbey to face him, but instead he'd been sent a messenger that first day. The Queen Mother herself had strode out of the abbey, regal and unafraid—nothing at all like her son—and had told him to stand down and leave the outlaws alone. She'd told him to leave, and then had returned to her abbey. No one else had come out, except that duel-wielding Gilbert who was somehow still around. He'd come out and stand at the gate, daring Sir Hugh to come to him. And oh how Sir Hugh wanted to do just that. That knave had

325

nearly killed him once; he deserved as much of a painful death as Robin Hood himself did.

The sound of another horse galloping nearby caught Sir Hugh's attention and he turned from his own steed to watch another approach. He was accompanied by several of Sir Hugh's men, and as they approached Torin came striding over to stand beside Sir Hugh.

The rider pulled his horse to a rough stop a few yards from Sir Hugh. "Your men would not let me ride to the abbey, where I am bound. Perhaps you will convince them to let me through."

The rider was a young man, not at all handsome though clearly fit. One hand was resting on his sword hilt as he studied Sir Hugh, the other held captive a parchment. Sir Hugh could not make out the seal on it, as the youth's hand covered partially.

"What is your business in the abbey?" Torin asked.

"I have a message from King John himself to deliver to the Queen Mother."

"Let me see the message," Sir Hugh said.

The youth hesitated.

"I am in the service of the King," Sir Hugh said. "He will not mind."

"The message is for Eleanor of Aquitaine, not Sir Hugh," the rider said. "King John did not think you would need to see it; he expressly told me not to show you until after I'd given the message to the Queen Mother."

Torin easily snatched the parchment from the young man's hand as he was speaking to Sir Hugh.

"What are you doing?" The young man was clearly angry, and made to draw his sword, but Sir Hugh's men closed in and pinned his arms to his sides.

Torin studied the seal. "It is from King John."

"Open it," Sir Hugh snarled. Whatever the King was telling his mother, he'd made a point to tell his messenger not to show Sir Hugh. Sir Hugh did not like secrets.

Torin broke the seal and opened the parcel; there were two separate parchments which he now held in each hand.

"Well?"

"One is a letter to his mother, a reply to a message she apparently sent him, the usual 'love' and greetings, a great deal of gratitude for her advice . . ."

Torin's eyes widened and he went silent.

"What?" Sir Hugh growled. "What does he say?"

"'I have taken everything you said into consideration and deliberated long with my counselors,'" Torin read aloud. "'It seems good to me to do as you have asked. A King needs more allies than enemies. Therefore, you will find enclosed a copy of the pardon I have issued for Robin Hood and company.'" Torin stopped reading and glanced at his friend. "Sir Hugh, Robin is no longer an outlaw."

Sir Hugh snatched the letter out of Torin's hands as Torin held up the other parchment, the pardon.

"It is signed by several witnesses, it has the King's seal, it can't be a fake," Torin said.

Sir Hugh threw the letter to the ground and grabbed the pardon, tearing it in half. "This changes nothing."

"I'm sorry, Sir Hugh, but it does change things. I am no friend of Robin Hood, as you well know. I have followed you on this quest to kill the outlaws far longer than I originally agreed to because I believed the end goal was worth it, but I will not risk the ire of the King of England."

"I have no fear of John," Sir Hugh spat.

"Perhaps not, but I do respect the Crown. I will not openly fight Robin Hood now that he is pardoned, I cannot. I will take my army back to England. You have only a few men at your own disposal, old friend. What you choose to do with them, and the outlaws, is your decision. I would advise against killing Robin Hood now, however."

"I will not let him go."

"I know." Torin shrugged. "So ambush him on his way back to England, or something of that nature. Or have him poisoned after he's returned to Nottingham. Anything rather than openly oppose the order of the King."

ROBIN

Robin was sitting on the steps of the church, watching Sir Hugh. He'd been nonchalantly pacing around for several hours, nearly straight in front of Robin, but far too distant to be a threat. His vibrant red hair getting wilder all the time as he raked his hands through it every now and again. And then a messenger had come. Robin could by no means hear the conversation that ensued, but it was clear that Sir Hugh was not happy with whatever the message said. He'd thrown one parchment to the ground and ripped the other one and at the moment was toe to toe with his commander, yelling. Robin could hear his voice quite clearly, though the words were indistinct.

"What's happening?" Much asked, plopping onto the step beside him.

"Sir Hugh has heard from someone, and whatever the contents of that message, he is now very angry."

"Angry is rather his natural state, isn't it?" Much asked, chuckling.

"Perhaps, but he's angrier than usual. Look at him."

Much looked, seemingly amused by the violence of Sir Hugh's emotions. "What do you think he heard that would rile him up so much? The last time we saw him this angry was when you—when he wanted his daughter back."

"You mean when I kidnapped her? He had every right to be angry then; I was truly a criminal, for perhaps the first time in my life."

"Well, we all make mistakes," Much said.

Robin shook his head. "Perhaps, but that was a low one, even for me."

As Robin and Much sat and watched, Sir Hugh's commander soon walked away from the mercenary and his yelling. Within the next hour, a great deal of the army had clearly begun packing themselves up to move on. Tents were being torn down, and less and less archers were paying any attention to the abbey.

"Are they leaving? Just like that?" Much asked.

"I don't know." Robin stared, unsure of what to think.

Was it possible Eleanor had gotten through to King John and that was the message that Sir Hugh had received. Or was this some kind of trap to draw them out of the abbey?

Chapter 20

GILBERT

They were gone.

Not all of them, of course, but most of the army had packed up and left. Sir Hugh, thankfully, was still there with what remained of his loyal men. Night was falling, and Gilbert stood under the archway of the outer wall, watching the small campfires spring up. Henry would be avenged this night.

There would likely be more threats in the future, and his goal in life after avenging Henry would be to protect Robin Hood's family until the day he died. His desire to follow Robin Hood had begun as simply following Henry's orders but then it had evolved; the events in Nottingham had piqued his interest. Sir Hugh was a worthy adversary, the likes of which Gilbert rarely met anymore. And then Henry had been killed and it was his death that fueled Gilbert's motives. That was still his deepest desire, but somewhere in the middle of all his vengeance, Gilbert had begun to care for them. Sir Guy, in particular, was a soft spot. A childhood hero broken by war that he could take under his wing. And the others.

He had a family, such as he had never had in his life before. He wasn't going to let them go.

But he had to kill Sir Hugh.

They had all joined Robin and Much watching the army pack up and leave. When it became clear as the day wore on that only Sir Hugh and his most loyal followers remained, Queen Eleanor had retreated to her own apartment. She and Robin agreed that it was likely King John had listened to her and pardoned all of them which was why the army had left. Sir Hugh, of course, would not so easily give up his quest to kill them. That Gilbert could easily understand.

Gilbert began to pace in the gateway, weighing the options. If he managed to kill Sir Hugh that night then what remained of the army might disperse and leave the outlaws alone.

As Gilbert stood watching, the darkness deepened. Gilbert watched, curious and concerned. He could still make out the outline of Sir Hugh, marching angrily here and there among what remained of the soldiers. The sun was dipping below the horizon; whatever Sir Hugh was planning, it would likely happen under the cover of darkness.

Someone was approaching from the camp of soldiers. Gilbert leaned nonchalantly against the gate, hands resting on the swords at his hips. One soldier, even if was Sir Hugh, was not a fight to be worried about.

As the man drew nearer, Gilbert could see that he wasn't a soldier at all. He had no chainmail or armor, no leather jerkin. He did have a sword though.

"Hello." The young man paused. "I'm not an enemy. My name is James. King John sent me, but I was detained by Sir Hugh for most of the day."

"You're the messenger? I heard about the altercation; Robin watched the ordeal. We didn't know you were from the King."

"I am. And I had a letter and a pardon to show Robin Hood and the Queen Mother, as well as Sir Hugh, but Sir Hugh took them and ripped them up."

"What did your letter and pardon say?"

"That Robin Hood is no longer wanted as an outlaw. The King has pardoned all his past crimes and asks that he will visit him at the manor where he currently resides with his wife Isabella, that they may discuss how to proceed. Sir Hugh is no longer being paid to kill the outlaws . . .I mean, the individuals in question."

"No wonder he was angry. So the army is going home to England."

"That is their objective. Sir Hugh's men alone remain, Torin is taking his men home."

"Sir Hugh still wishes to kill Robin Hood."

"Undoubtedly."

"Let him try, then."

"I wouldn't advise it. Defying the King would not be wise."

"I doubt Sir Hugh cares what the King has to say; he doesn't strike me as a man to fear royalty."

"He doesn't."

"Is he planning on attacking the abbey?"

"Yes, I believe he is. He won't hurt those who make the monastery their home if he can help it, but he is going to search for the out—Robin Hood and the others."

"Well you'd better warn the monks," Gilbert waved his hand toward the abbey. "You'll find them at prayer, I believe."

"You'll warn Robin Hood?"

"You tell the Queen Mother your news as soon as you've told the nuns, they'll point you in the right direction."

"And what will you be doing?"

"Waiting right here for Sir Hugh."

SIR HUGH

Completely against Sir Hugh's judgment, Torin had left. Why he'd left at such a late hour when he could have had his army spend one more night at the abbey, Sir Hugh didn't understand. The pardon and letter from the King had altered Torin's perception. He suddenly had no desire to kill outlaws, which was absurd.

The same could not be said for Sir Hugh. His anger was only fueled by the King's surprising change of heart. Robin Hood would die, and that was the end of it.

334

The messenger had escaped from their grasp by twilight. Sir Hugh had the two soldiers who had been watching him brought to him.

They were dragged over by four of his other incompetent imbeciles.

Without a word, Sir Hugh motioned for them to be forced to their knees. Once they were on the ground he walked slowly toward them, his sword held loosely in his hand. "Back off." His growl at the others had them scooting backward rather quickly. The two soldiers who'd let the messenger escape glanced up.

"Sir Hugh, listen—"

The soldier never finished his explanation for the simple reason that his head was no longer attached to his body. Though Sir Hugh had been holding his sword at his side as he approached the soldiers, a quick flick of the wrist had left the blade slicing through both their necks. The four other soldiers waited, faces white.

"You're dismissed."

Sir Hugh ignored the bodies at his feet and glared at the abbey. Within the next 15 minutes he would be there, and he would find Robin Hood.

And Robin Hood would die.

IDA

Ida drew her dagger slowly across the whetstone in her hand wishing, not for the first time, that she hadn't been forced to leave the rest of her weapons on Gisbourne estate. She needed her bow right about now, and a sword certainly wouldn't be amiss. The likelihood of the monks or nuns having an armory for her disposal was slim, but she'd asked anyway. Of course the answer was no.

Much of the army that had been laying siege to the abbey had packed up and left. If the sun had still been up Ida was sure they would have been visible in the distance, kicking up dust as they left Sir Hugh behind. And therein lay the reason she wanted more weapons; Sir Hugh still had enough men to outnumber the gang and he was still there, intent on killing them. Robin had relayed what he and Much had witnessed to everyone, and Gilbert had taken up his post at the gate to watch the proceedings for the rest of the day. As for Ida, she had set about preparing for a fight. She was sitting outside a few yards from the sprawling building that housed the nuns chambers, the same one that Queen Eleanor resided in. It was also where the gang had spent the last few nights. The last light of the sun as it sank beyond the horizon made the world grey, and the rising moon was lighting the abbey courtyard in an eerie manner. The monks had set up and lit a number of torches for their use as soon as Robin made it clear they would be fighting that night. Robin and Lucy were not too far away from Ida now, huddled with Will and Mark, discussing battle plans. Everyone was convinced Sir Hugh would make his desperate attempt tonight. And he was going to be desperate. The King's messenger had finally been able to deliver his message, albeit without the actual parchments in hand. They were all pardoned. Sir Hugh was working outside of the King's blessing now.

As Ida continued to sharpen her remaining daggers, she listened to the sound of her husband Allen walking Jane through a few different strikes. Much and Roger were also preparing for the fight to come, and Ida knew Dusty was working with the monks and nuns to prepare herbs and potions to heal any injuries that might arise.

Whether Sir Hugh or the gang won tonight, Ida was sure this would be the end. The end of living as fugitives, the end of fighting for their lives. This was the last stand.

Faith settled into the grass beside her, helping her husband ease to the ground as well.

"I assume you'll be staying somewhere safe," Ida spoke to Faith.

"Of course."

"Good."

"And you?" Ida eyed Guy, wondering just how much use he could possibly be. He was alive, and that was a miracle worth celebrating, but he was rather pathetic these days. Still, he had a sword in his hand so perhaps he would try and help after all.

"I can barely walk across a room," Guy sighed. "I would be a hindrance, not a help."

"I thought as much."

"But you'll need more than your daggers in the fight to come, Ida. This isn't the most well-crafted sword I've ever used, but it'll do." Guy held the sword out to her. "I purchased it on our travels here to the abbey, clinging to the illusion that I could wield a sword still. But I can't. And you need it."

Ida took the sword and stood, stepping away from her friends so that she could swing the sword around, testing the weight and the feel of it in her hand. It wasn't like her own blade, but it would do.

"Thank you."

GILBERT

The soldiers, now numbering roughly fifty or so by Gilbert's calculation, were now moving stealthily toward the abbey. They were hardly visible in the darkness, the moon partially obscured by clouds. Gilbert watched their progression eagerly. Every glint of the moon off of a helmet quickened his heartbeat.

Sir Hugh was coming to die.

Gilbert wasn't sure what the messenger was doing, or the monks and nuns for that matter. He hadn't paid any attention to the goings-on inside the abbey that night and no one had approached. He stayed in the gate and simply watched. Slowly as the evening gave way to night Robin Hood and his motley crew had been gathering near the gate as well, but Gilbert paid them no mind.

The sight of Sir Hugh executing two soldiers had been the only interesting moment while watching Sir Hugh throughout the afternoon until the group of soldiers had started to crawl slowly toward the abbey after nightfall.

Fifty soldiers. Sir Hugh.

Gilbert hoped Sir Hugh would be so eager to kill Robin that he would lead the search and assault on the abbey. If he had to wade through fifty soldiers to reach Sir Hugh at the rear of the line, he'd be tired from exertion and he wanted no disadvantage on his side. Sir Hugh had to die tonight. There would be no interruptions and no escapes, and definitely no resurrection this time.

SIR HUGH

The abbey seemed quiet. The courtyard was dark, the church behind it a looming shadow just a shade darker. The moon was covered, but that was to Sir Hugh's liking. He didn't want Robin to be watching and therefore warned of his impending doom.

Of course, the King's messenger that had escaped due to the carelessness of the idiots Sir Hugh employed may have already put Robin Hood on his guard, assuming the messenger had figured out what was going on before he departed for the safety of the abbey.

The abbey would not be safe tonight, however. Sir Hugh had ordered his men not to kill any monks or nuns that they could spare, but if anyone got in their way in their search for the outlaws, they would die. He didn't need the might of Rome bearing down on him for slaughtering an abbey, but he wasn't going to let anyone stop him from killing the outlaws. Sir Hugh intended to head to the right of the church as his men fanned out and searched every building. Watching the outlaws over the last few days had given him limited information—the walls surrounding the abbey hindered much of their observations, but the outlaws seemed more often than not to come from and return to a place to the right of the church, so that was where Sir Hugh would go.

The idea of falling on them while they slept was delightful, though Sir Hugh did hope Robin would wake up with the presence of mind to at least put up a decent fight before he died.

As they approached the gate, Sir Hugh motioned for his men to slow.

All remained quiet within the abbey. There wasn't anyone within sight, though the darkness of the night prevented Sir Hugh seeing much farther than a foot or two in front of him. Anyone could be lurking in the darkness beyond his reach.

The grass crunched softly beneath his feet. Sir Hugh curled his fingers tightly around the hilt of his sword, relishing the mental image of skewering Robin within the hour.

Sir Hugh felt a breath of wind to his left and ignored it. A little wind was hardly going to stop the justice that would be delivered this night.

The soft thud that followed distracted Sir Hugh, but he continued to creep forward, under the archway, through the gate. He was nearly within the abbey courtyard.

Another thump, a groan, and shout of "hey!" and then the clash of metal.

Sir Hugh swung to his left. He could hardly make out more than the outline of bodies beside and behind him.

As he watched, one of those outlines fell to the ground, and two more dove for a spot just behind him. A spinning shadow seemed to flitter out of their grasp and both men fell. Sir Hugh could hear the blood splattering from sliced necks, the coughing of the men who had not yet passed beyond life and were choking on their last breath of air and blood.

The shadow was still dancing among his men, and there were more of them now. Sir Hugh could hardly tell one from the other until the shadows fell to the ground. Then he knew which were his men.

Robin Hood had prepared an ambush. Clever.

Sir Hugh drew his sword and watched the shadows moving in the darkness, trying to make out individuals, without much success. But then he did notice one particular shadow. More of his men fell at this shadow's hand than any other, and as he danced through the skirmish, he appeared to have both arms swinging.

Gilbert.

It was the only explanation Sir Hugh could think of.

The dual-wielding swordsman was the only person he knew who could single-handedly cause such havoc in a company of soldiers. Sir Hugh cursed the darkness that made it nearly impossible for him to see Gilbert, the outlaws, or his own men.

"Find Robin Hood!" he shouted.

His men who weren't already in combat with the outlaws began to sprint into the courtyard and toward the buildings where candlelight could be seen in windows. How many had fallen during the silent and deadly assault by the assassin that plagued Sir Hugh's dreams nearly as much as Robin Hood himself, he didn't take the time to count. It was too dark to count anyway. Sir Hugh was sure, though, that of the men who had fallen most had been at Gilbert's hand. What could a small band of outlaws do compared to that man?

For a moment the moonlight glinted off of the two swords, still twirling lazily through the air, although they had no targets at the moment, and then the moon was gone again.

Sir Hugh settled back on his heels, gripping his sword with both hands. Darkness or not, he'd deal with Gilbert, and then he would kill Robin Hood.

MARK

They had lain in wait with Gilbert, and when Sir Hugh and his men had come creeping through the gate they had ambushed them. It was difficult to see in the dark, especially when the moon only made the briefest appearances. As Sir Hugh and his men had come creeping forward they were barely visible, but as they were the only moving objects in that darkness Mark could just make them out.

Mark set upon the first soldier easily enough, but after the gang and Gilbert were intermixed with Sir Hugh's men, Mark was hesitant to strike anything for fear of harming the wrong person. Sight was not a sense that was in use during the fight, and his ears could not easily judge if the footsteps behind him were Robin or Sir Hugh. Judging by the agile shadow that flitted about followed by cries of pain, Gilbert had no such qualms.

When Sir Hugh had shouted for his men to find Robin, they'd raced for the abbey. Mark settled his gaze onto one particular shadow of a soldier running for the church and took chase. A brief visit from the moon and it was clear he was indeed following a soldier and not one of his friends. He ignored every other shadow, whether friend or foe, he couldn't tell, and kept his eyes trained on the one soldier. He caught up to him just as he entered the chapel and plunged his sword through the soldier's chest.

He could almost hear Lucy in his mind telling him not to kill people like that, but he ignored it.

Mark exited the church and glanced around, searching for another quarry. When he sighted another soldier who didn't belong in the abbey, he took chase again.

GILBERT

It had been impossible to distinguish the soldiers from one another in the darkness. The moon only coming out for a second or two every few minutes when the clouds would part long enough to assure Gilbert that, yes, they were still creeping toward the abbey.

Unable to make a guess as to which shadow was Sir Hugh, he'd merely chosen to kill every outline of a man that he saw. As soon as they entered the deep darkness under the gate's archway, he'd fallen on them. The first two had dropped before the others were aware of their companions' demise. Three more had been easy work, as they swung about in the dark blindly.

Gilbert couldn't see much better than they, but he at least knew what he was looking for. They, on the other hand, only knew that a nameless shadow of death had fallen on them from somewhere and was now in their midst—unseen and untouchable. Gilbert grinned as he danced around them with ease; what he couldn't see, he could feel and hear. He felt the presence of a man behind him and spun around him, putting a sword in his heart on

344

the way around. The crunch of feet to his right and he danced backward, pulling his sword from the other chest and keeping it low to the ground—that soldier was merely creeping forward and unaware of Gilbert at all. Breathing to his left, and his sword was up again, slicing through the back of a man.

After a moment of fun, though, it became harder to simply swing his sword at every sound; Robin Hood and the others were among the soldiers now, too, and it would be rather unfortunate to put an end to the legend of Robin Hood while trying to protect him.

Then Sir Hugh's voice had rung out. "Find Robin Hood!"

The archway had cleared quickly as the soldiers bolted into the courtyard, as much to get away from Gilbert and the others as to follow Sir Hugh's orders.

Gilbert grinned again. His blood was boiling, his excitement building. This was what he lived for. He watched what he assumed was Robin and the rest of the gang bolt into the courtyard, chasing after Sir Hugh's men.

When the moon made another brief appearance, Gilbert could see that the soldiers were disappearing into the various corners of the abbey and the gang was hard on their heels. He could also see the unmistakable outline of Sir Hugh, waiting for him. He was just inside the courtyard, barely past the gate.

Gilbert felt his pulse quicken and tried to temper his excitement.

Sir Hugh was going to truly die this time.

Henry would be avenged.

And then the moon was gone.

Gilbert moved cautiously forward, keeping his eyes on where he'd seen Sir Hugh. The darkness added just enough unknown to make the fight even more exciting to Gilbert. He wouldn't kill Sir Hugh quickly in this darkness the way he might in daylight. He'd have to work for it, using every one of his senses and all of the expertise he'd gained over his many years wielding a sword. Gilbert was glad of it. If there was one thing Gilbert hated, it was an easy kill.

Sir Hugh was breathing heavily; probably due to his own excitement. He was so close to catching Robin Hood. Gilbert could comprehend perfectly what was going through Sir Hugh's mind, for it was precisely what was going through his own. He was so close to his goal.

"For Henry," Gilbert thought silently, moving swiftly toward the sound of Sir Hugh's breathing.

SIR HUGH

The soft thud of boots in the dirt alerted him to Gilbert's approach. Sir Hugh tried to gauge where precisely those boots were coming from—to the right, the left, or straight in front of him?

Unable to tell, he guessed.

Sir Hugh sliced his sword through the air in a long, swift arc as he leaped to his left. He thought perhaps it had met with some resistance toward the end of his swing, but not enough to be sure of what he may have struck.

Spinning to ensure Gilbert was still in front of him—as far as he could judge—Sir Hugh pulled his sword back in and dropped into a defensive stance. He stayed still, trying to quiet his breathing. His heart was pounding in his ears and he couldn't hear through the sound. He needed to be able to hear to know where Gilbert was.

Sir Hugh rocked on his heels, trying to steady his heart so that he could focus. He needed clarity, not ringing in his ears.

GILBERT

Gilbert had felt Sir Hugh's dive to his right and had only just avoided the sweep of his sword. The tip of the blade had cut through his tunic just below his shoulder, but had not pierced his skin.

Gilbert spun around and faced the archway. Sir Hugh, judging by his heavy breathing, was somewhere near the wall to Gilbert's left. If only the moon would give him enough light to see for only a moment. His left wrist was screaming at him from the exertion of the evening's activities, and his lower back was reminding him that he'd only recently healed from nasty wounds.

347

Gilbert paused to listen to Sir Hugh's breathing, and to let his eyes do their best to decide how much of that darkness and shadow might be the outline of a man.

His eyes failed him, but his ears did not.

Gilbert darted forward, his swords swinging in opposite arcs to cut Sir Hugh's escape on either side, should he choose to dance away.

There was little else for Sir Hugh to do, after all, Gilbert concluded. Sir Hugh couldn't see him, so an offensive wouldn't do him much good.

The sword in his right hand caught on flesh, but only for a moment. Gilbert distinctly heard the thunk of a body slamming into the stone wall as Sir Hugh shoved backward out of the reach of Gilbert's blades.

While he had the advantage, Gilbert dove forward again, swinging both swords.

SIR HUGH

His left arm now sported a deep cut, but it was still attached to his body, so Sir Hugh wasn't too concerned. Sir Hugh's back ached from the abrupt run-in with the wall. He had thought it was further behind him. Apparently it was not. It didn't matter. He knew Gilbert was coming forward again, so he dropped, staying on his feet but letting his knees nearly touch the ground. He felt the wind of both of Gilbert's blades move his

348

hair as they passed over his head. As he knelt, he struck out with his own sword and felt the satisfying resistance as it connected with Gilbert's leg.

A moment later Gilbert's presence had disappeared and Sir Hugh stayed crouched low to the ground, waiting. He couldn't hear Gilbert, but he was sure he'd be back in a moment.

His palm was sweaty against the hilt of his sword, his left arm stung and he could feel the blood trickling down his arm. This distraction from his aim—Robin Hood—was getting tiresome.

GILBERT

Sir Hugh's sword had gone straight through his left thigh and come out again as Gilbert jerked backward and out of reach. It was the same leg that had sustained a similar wound back in Scotland; Gilbert could feel the sharp pain of the new cut and the deeper ache of his old wound mingling. Standing was now excruciatingly painful and walking seemed impossible.

Gilbert stayed on his feet, but leaned heavily against the wall opposite where he'd met Sir Hugh's blade, feeling the flow of blood that soaked his leg. This was not going to be easy.

He was still listening to Sir Hugh's breathing. How was it possible for one man to make so much noise with a single pair of lungs?

Gilbert steadied himself against the wall opposite where Sir Hugh was still breathing hard. Was he still crouched low? Or had he stood?

Gilbert considered his options.

Darting forward would be painful with his useless leg, but it had to be done swiftly. If Sir Hugh was low to the ground, he would likely cut Gilbert's legs out from under him if he approached again, but Gilbert could easily cut off his head at the same time.

Gilbert rather liked his legs, however, so this option did not appeal.

He could move to the right, sneak up on Sir Hugh from one side and try to get at him that way. If Sir Hugh didn't notice his maneuvering then he might be able to get a cut in before Sir Hugh could turn to face him to get a swing of his own.

He could pull a dagger from his boot and simply throw it at the sound of breathing on the opposite side of the gateway and hope to hit one of those obnoxiously loud lungs.

SIR HUGH

The clouds around the moon were not parting, but they were thinning. The deepest blackness of the night was turning into a lighter darkness. Sir Hugh thought that he might be able to make out the outline of Gilbert in a moment more, if only the clouds would thin faster. Preferably before the swordsman came back for another chance to kill him.

He knew he'd struck his leg the last time, but how deeply he wasn't sure. Was it enough to keep Gilbert off his feet? He hadn't heard him fall.

He hadn't heard anything at all.

It was as though Gilbert was a ghost. A ghost of flesh that Sir Hugh could prick, but never see and never kill. It was annoying.

And then the sound of a pebble bouncing off the stone wall to his left drew his attention. It must have bounced off a boot in that direction—this thought darted through his mind as he swung on his feet, still in a crouched position, toward the sound and sliced his sword forward in the hope of cutting off the legs of the knave who was delaying his killing of Robin Hood.

GILBERT

Gilbert heard the pebble he'd accidentally kicked—no thanks to the cursed darkness—and swung both his swords parallel with each other, starting the swing to his left and aiming down and to the right. With any luck, he'd miss the wall to his right but hit Sir Hugh.

At the same moment he jumped.

His left leg spasmed, refusing to give him the spring that his right did, and his leap was likely the least graceful thing he'd ever done. His only intention was to get out of the reach of Sir Hugh's sword, assuming Sir Hugh was still crouching low to the ground.

Both of his swords connected with what he assumed was Sir Hugh's left shoulder and caught. Sir Hugh let out a cry at the same moment that Gilbert's foot felt the cold slice of metal and Gilbert heard it smack into the wall to his right.

When he hit the ground, he crumbled.

His left leg gave out—the hole from the first wound was leaking more blood than seemed healthy, and without a foot it was difficult to stand on. He dropped to his knees, wincing from the pain.

For a moment, his vision wavered. The blackness of the night, starting to lighten from the slowly reappearing moon, vanished to be replaced with a blinding whiteness as his mind went numb from the searing pain.

Gilbert shook himself back to reality, biting back a groan as he did so.

He yanked his swords from Sir Hugh's shoulder and stabbed them forward again, unsure where Sir Hugh was exactly but knowing he was very close—close enough to be stabbed again.

SIR HUGH

Sir Hugh heard Gilbert grunt and fall after his own sword had cut an appendage off. Had it been a foot? A portion of his leg? Whatever it was, it had smacked into the wall and there would likely be a messy bloodstain for the monks to clean off of their otherwise pristine abbey. Gilbert had fallen to the ground, but Sir Hugh had not had the presence of mind to enjoy it, as he now had a gash in his right shoulder gushing blood. The splatter had soaked his cheek and his chest and the pain had caused Sir Hugh to slump into the wall.

He refused to die.

He still had to kill Robin Hood.

He swung his sword with all his remaining strength—which, granted, was not much.

He thought perhaps it had connected with Gilbert again, though he wasn't sure, when white-hot iron had rammed through his stomach and he lost consciousness.

Chapter 21

DUSTY

As she stitched up the cut on Mark's forearm, Dusty glanced over to where Lucy was similarly occupied with a wound of Allen's. The skirmish with the soldiers hadn't lasted too long; the gang, though mostly Gilbert, had managed to kill most of them before they entered the abbey and after that it was a simple matter of chasing the rest down one by one as they spread through the abbey. Much to the horror of the abbey's occupants, at least two of the soldiers had been killed inside the church itself. But that was over now.

As the sun rose and morning dawned, Robin and Will gathered the dead soldiers to bury outside the abbey while Much, with help from the monks and nuns, brought the wounded to Dusty and Lucy. They had set up outside the church, near the herbal gardens where they would have a ready supply should they run out of the ointments and remedies Dusty had prepared before the fight began.

"Any other wounds I should know about?" Dusty asked, turning back to Mark.

"Nope," he shook his head. "I'm fine."

"And emotionally speaking?" Dusty glanced at Lucy again.

"Better, though not perfect by any means."

"I'll keep praying."

"I'm sure you never stopped."

"Obviously not."

"I'm working my way back toward forgiveness and peace, Dusty, but it isn't easy."

"I know. I watched my entire family be murdered by Saladin; forgiveness of evil men is difficult. At least Guy turned his life around."

"I think that makes it harder," Mark sighed. "I could hate an evil man, but now I feel guilty for what otherwise would be justifiable emotions. I'm not as strong as you; I couldn't forgive someone the way you forgave Saladin."

As Mark moved off to help Robin and Will with cleaning up the abbey, Dusty turned back to the one patient she hadn't been able to help. Gilbert lay sprawled on the blanket Robin and Guy had used to drag his body to the healers. But heal him they had not. Lucy and Dusty had both worked furiously on his numerous wounds, but it was no use.

As everyone else appeared to have been patched up, Dusty set about cleaning Gilbert's bloodied body so he could be buried.

His body had been found in the gateway, tangled up with Sir Hugh's. They were both mangled pretty badly, sporting many wounds, and Gilbert was missing a foot. Sir Hugh had been dead already, but Gilbert had had just enough breath in his lungs for

Dusty and Lucy to make a desperate attempt to revive him. They had failed.

MARK

By the end of the day, all the soldiers had been buried and most of the blood and gore had been washed off of the walls and floors within the abbey. The church had a bloodstain on the aisle leading to the altar but it was possible it would fade in time. They had gathered to bury Gilbert within the walls of the abbey; Queen Eleanor had suggested he be buried near where the late King Richard was laid to rest. It hadn't been much of a service; just a simple burial and a few simple words of gratitude for his help and sacrifice.

As they dispersed from the small gathering, Eleanor spoke to Robin. "Where will you go now?"

"With the pardon, I believe it is time to go home," Robin said.

"You won't stay to keep an old lady company?" Eleanor laughed.

"No," Robin grinned. "But we will always be grateful for your role in securing our pardon." Robin gave her a swift kiss on the forehead and the Queen Mother patted his cheek in a familiar, motherly way.

"How did you persuade your son to leave us alone?" Mark asked.

"I am a very persuasive mother," Eleanor replied archly, her eyes twinkling merrily.

"According to James, the King expects us in the home of his new wife Isabella," Will said.

"That's true," James jumped into the conversation. "I hope we can set off today, if you will accompany me, and return to the King."

Robin agreed. "We will gladly do that. And then we will return to Paris to collect the rest of our family from there."

"For now you should all rest," Eleanor said. "You've had an eventful few days. Take a break before you head for Isabella's home. And then you can prepare for your journey."

KING JOHN

John watched Robin Hood enter the room and couldn't decide on his strongest emotion. Was it anger, at finally meeting the man who had nearly single-handedly ruined his chances of rebellion against his brother Richard by providing the people with hope? Was it a relief that Robin did not himself appear to be harboring any hard feelings? Was it anticipation, for what the future might hold with such a man as an ally instead of an enemy? John didn't know, but his many and varied emotions were kept buried as he waited at the end of the room for Robin to approach and bow. The rest of the outlaws, or, rather, Robin's companions, followed him and knelt as well.

John enjoyed the sight for a moment before motioning for them to stand.

"Robin of Locksley, I am pleased to finally meet you. Your fame, I assure you, is well-known. I have heard much indeed of the famous Robin Hood."

Robin inclined his head with a barely visible smile. "Your Majesty."

"We have much to discuss."

Most of his companions seemed placid enough, though a few glared openly at him. Sir Guy of Gisbourne, a man John had known previously—a man who had served him well for many years during the rebellion—gave him a slight nod of acknowledgment when their eyes met.

John tilted his head to one side, eyeing Guy. "You look well, all things considered. I had heard you were executed."

"I was, but I survived it."

"You do have that uncanny ability; I recall it well. The untouchable Sir Guy of Gisbourne."

Refreshments were called for and everyone sat down at the long table that filled the majority of the room. John intended to have everything dealt with within one interview and then never have to think of it again. Peace with Robin Hood and the rest of them, the assurance that they would not oppose him in the future. There must not be any animosity between them by the time Robin and his friends left for England.

They would not, perhaps, ever be friends. But they could at least be civil enough to not warrant watching them too closely in the future. And to have the knowledge that he could call upon Robin Hood for aid when he required it would be useful.

ROBIN

After the meeting with King John, Robin had brought his family to Paris once more. The parting with King John wasn't entirely friendly, but at least they could be sure that for the present at least the King wasn't going to try and kill them.

When they arrived in Paris, Little John was gone; he'd taken a job protecting traveling merchants as they moved from one city to the next and was often gone for weeks at a time. Elinor had been overjoyed to see everyone again, and shocked to see Guy among them. Baby Rachel took a few minutes of convincing to remember that she knew and loved all of these people now invading her home. But within a few days they were all back to enjoying each other's company as they had always done. It was a bit cramped staying in Little John's quarters, so Robin and Will paid for rooms of their own for their families. The innkeeper let Much keep a room for free, having been so fond of him during their previous stay. He was hopeful, indeed, that they would all be staying for good. He wanted Much in his kitchen once more, and he had grown rather used to telling people that the great Robin Hood lived in his tavern. That, however, was not the case.

359

They were only waiting for Little John's return. Once he arrived, they would set off for England. Everyone was eager to be home again. It had only been a year of chaos, far less time than they had spent in Sherwood during the rebellion, but Robin was equally ready to return to Nottingham. He wanted to raise Marian in a home, not always live on the run. Paris had been good for all of them, but now that he had the freedom to choose his home, he wasn't going to choose Paris.

MARK

Nearly three weeks had passed since their arrival in Paris. Three weeks of bliss, reunited with everyone. Three weeks of having no other purpose than enjoying one another's company, telling the stories of the past year with a relish, remembering the adventures in Sherwood fondly. They all told stories sitting around Elinor's table or fireplace in the evenings, but Lucy had a true knack for it. As soon as she opened her mouth the children gathered around eagerly, and the adults quieted to listen as well. She would spin tales of heroics from the days of Sherwood and leave the children begging for more.

One night as they all sat around Lucy, several of the children in her lap and everyone else gathered as close as they dared, Little John burst in on them.

He came into the room calmly, shaking off his cloak that was dirt-caked and smelled worse than the streets outside. Then he'd caught sight of them all and came to a stand-still.

"Hello, Little John," Robin grinned.

"We're back," Mark said wryly.

"And pardoned, too," Will added. "Did you hear about that?"

Little John surveyed the group quietly, and then his eyes came to rest on Guy. His eyebrows shot to his hairline. "You're alive."

"Only by the grace of God," Guy replied.

"And you say we're pardoned?"

"We are, indeed," Robin said. "I meant to come for you before we went to see King John but James, the King's messenger, was far too impatient for that. We are free. Though King John does expect us to refrain from defying him in the future."

"That will depend on his behavior, of course," Little John replied. He pulled off his mud-caked boots and then found himself a chair, eyeing the gathered group. "Well? Tell me everything."

The rest of the evening was spent in catching Little John up on all that had happened.

Mark was enjoying the peace that they were now experiencing. There was still some measure of anguish over Marian's death and his role in it, as well as that of Lucy and Guy,

361

but it was a distant ache and not an ever-present one. They were all alive, and all safe, by some miracle. Pardoned, even! They were truly free; there was no room for resentment in this place of joy.

ALLEN

Allen watched as his old friend William caught little William in his arms and tossed him toward the sky, releasing a long squeal of laughter from the boy. Allen was sitting on a bench he'd carved and put in front of his house—the house William had rebuilt for him not far outside of Edinburgh. He was carving some wooden toys for the boys. The boys were chasing William everywhere, and he gladly chased them back. The laughter of all three filled the air.

They'd been living in Scotland for two months. After the joyful weeks spent in Paris with everyone, they had finally gotten around to the business of deciding what to do with their lives. After returning to England, to Nottingham, with the rest of the gang Allen had chosen to return his family to the place of his birth. His sons being raised where he had been raised; it gave Allen more joy than he thought it would. It was just a place, just a house. But it was home.

He'd forgotten just how much he had missed this place. He'd buried it after the fire—after he'd lost his wife and his parents and his infant child. He'd buried it all and he'd set off on

362

the Crusades with the hope of dying. And then he'd met Robin, and had returned with Robin to Nottingham and buried any thought of Scotland or the memories of his past life and years had passed—years filled with many varied adventures. But now, now he was ready to face all that he'd buried.

All the memories resurfaced now that he was home. He and Ida would often talk of his childhood and she seemed delighted with all he told her.

Guy and Faith had chosen to live with them; Guy relinquishing Gisbourne estate to Andrew and Jane. It had surprised Allen at first, but Ida and Guy seemed to have come to an understanding, and at any rate Ida was loathe to let Faith out of her sight ever again. Faith had become, somehow, her dearest friend in the time that Allen had been separated from his wife.

Little Lucy was currently sitting at Allen's feet, watching him carving. She seemed fascinated with the way his hands moved over the wood, his knife delicately removing first this piece and then that, an animal slowly taking shape.

Faith and Ida were currently in the market. Their blossoming friendship was one of the more shocking developments over the past year. That, and her forgiveness for Guy himself. Apart of speaking of Allen's childhood, Allen and Ida frequently discussed her change of heart in regard to the Gisbournes.

The laughter of the twins filled the air again and Allen glanced up from his carving and his reveries. William was on the ground now, with both boys crawling over him—wrestling, if it could be called that. William was getting quite ancient these days, but somehow he managed to find the energy to keep up with the twins.

Marcus and Lillian lived in Edinburgh still, having never returned home after their escape with the gang all those months ago. Marcus had set up a blacksmith shop in Edinburgh and was slowly building up a reputation. He was, after all, the blacksmith who had served the great Robin Hood during the rebellion all those years ago and even in Scotland that meant something.

Marcus and Lillian would visit at least once a week for dinner or a walk through the field or just about any excuse to see their friends. Their lives here in Scotland were peaceful and Allen hoped it would stay that way. He'd had more adventure than anyone needed in a single lifetime.

ROBIN

Robin leaned against the windowsill, staring down at the village of Locksley; it was a familiar sight. He had grown up in this very house when his father was the Earl of Locksley. He knew every inch of that village and every person who lived there.

Despite the pardon, King John had not given Robin the distinction of Sheriff once more; though King John had left Sir Ralf as Sheriff of Nottingham, Robin was still the Earl of Locksley as his father had been before him. So instead of returning to the castle in Nottingham upon his return to England, Robin had brought his family to his home in the village of Locksley.

The gang had scattered again, but this time it didn't sting the way it had in Paris. They weren't running in different directions this time. They were going home, and they visited often enough that it wasn't a travesty.

"Are you just going to stare out of that window all day?" Much asked, leaning casually against the doorframe. "Your wife expects you downstairs to greet your guests."

Much, with his wife and daughter, had come to live in Locksley at Robin's request.

"Who has arrived? I've been watching from here and haven't seen anyone."

"Mark came the back way," Much grinned.

Together, Robin and Much headed downstairs to greet Mark. Mark had chosen to live nearby in Wetherby, where he had grown up with Marian, and was easily within walking distance. They saw him almost daily.

When Robin and Much entered the front room of the manor, Mark and Lucy were sitting near the hearth talking and Mary was on the floor keeping her daughter and little Marian entertained.

"Nottingham is in a frenzy," Mark laughed. "All those merchants and tourists."

"Well, the Nottingham Fair always brings merchants and tourists from all across the world, and it's only a week away. Many people from outside of Nottingham have already made the journey to the city."

"I forget every year though," Mark said. "I forget how insanely full the city gets. The city itself is overrun, I saw many merchants and tourists setting up small camps outside the city walls today."

"I well believe that," Robin said, coming to lean against his wife's chair.

"Do we know if Allen and Guy are bringing their families from Scotland?" Mary asked.

"I haven't heard," Robin said. "But I know Andrew and Jane will be coming from Gisbourne estate."

"Are they going to rename that estate at some point?" Much laughed. "It seems odd to keep calling it the Gisbourne estate when no Gisbournes live there anymore."

"Dusty and Will should be coming from Middlesborough with Little John, Elinor, and baby Rachel," Lucy said. Will and Little John had taken their families back home where they had all lived before the adventure with Sir Hugh began.

"Shall we move to the dining room?" Robin asked.

"How much do you think you'll eat today?" Lucy laughed. Mark gave her a questioning look, so she explained, "The people of Nottingham are busy preparing for the Fair, of course, but they have also been so overjoyed that their favorite resident has returned with his family. Every day another family comes to ask if Robin will attend a small gathering—which usually turns out to be a feast with half of Nottingham in attendance—just to celebrate our return."

"I've taken to eating very little at every meal because I know I'll have to eat so many times in a day," Robin laughed.

The pardon was now old gossip, and everyone in Nottingham was hopeful that the future would hold no more events to send Robin Hood into hiding. Robin could not help but agree with them. Their lives were once again peaceful and nearly perfect; he had no desire to run off to another war or be a fugitive on the run yet again. And for the present, at least, it appeared he would not have to.

GLOSSARY

Ca alors = good grief/my goodness

C'est tellement merveilleux = it is so wonderful.

De rien = you're welcome

Merci = thank you

N'importe quoi = nonsense

Oui = yes

Parfait = perfect

Sauvor moi = save me

Vous etes stupide = you are stupid

Quel malheur = what a disgrace (Literally: what misfortune)

Acknowledgments:

As always, I have a number of people deserving of gratitude for their assistance in bringing this story to life.

Rebekah—you are my sounding board, my biggest fan (well, really, Gilbert's biggest fan), and my greatest encouragement always. I could never fully put into words how much you mean to me and how much you bring to my writing process.

Benjamin—your advocacy for Mark over the years is a large part of what led to this story being what it is, so thank you for that.

Jonathan—your feedback on my stories is always greatly appreciated, as well as your ability to uncover my pesky mistakes.

Noelle—thanks for your help on the book blurb and other more nuts-and-bolts aspects of my book. It's my least favorite part of being an author and I love all the help!

Elizabeth Hutchinson—thank you for taking the time to find all my mistakes and make my book better.

Mandi Lynn—my AMAZING cover artist. I thought I would never be more in love with a cover than I was with *Return to Sherwood,* but you managed to change my mind. Thank you for bringing my vision to life!

Jesus—you will always remain the inspiration for my stories and my purpose for writing and sharing said stories.

And finally, a note to my readers:

If you made it to the end of the book, thank you! I hope you enjoyed it. This may be the end of my Robin Hood saga for now, but if you need more Robin Hood in your life and you haven't read my original Robin Hood series you can find it at my website mandigrace.org

If you have any questions, comments, etc, feel free to email me at mandi@mandigrace.org

If you want to read even more books by me you can find them at my website mandigrace.org, and you can find me on Facebook, Instagram, and YouTube.